D1563525

FRACKED!

By Mark A. Dobbs

Mark Dobbs

FRACKED!

To my wife... she makes patience look easy.

Mark Dobbs

Table of Contents

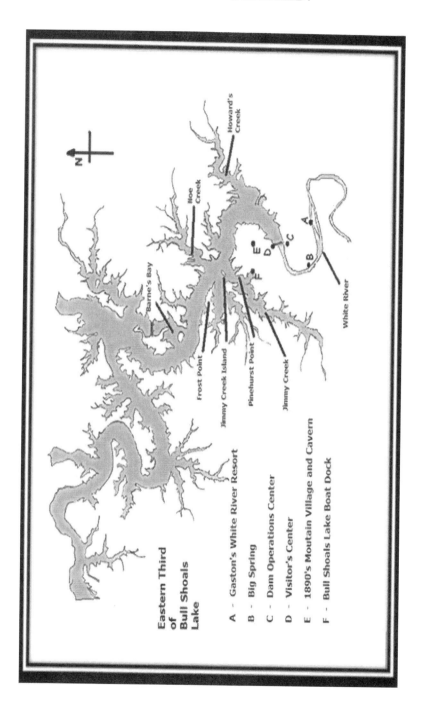

Eastern Third
of
Bull Shoals
Lake

A - Gaston's White River Resort

B - Big Spring

C - Dam Operations Center

D - Visitor's Center

E - 1890's Moutain Village and Cavern

F - Bull Shoals Lake Boat Dock

Prologue

Greenbrier Times, August 30 –

A recent and sudden cluster of earthquakes, including the largest quake to hit the state in nearly thirty-five years, is very possibly an after effect of natural-gas drilling according to some experts who declined to be named.

At issue, the practice called hydraulic fracturing, or "fracking," in which water is injected into the ground at high pressure to literally fracture rock thereby releasing the valuable natural gas that might be trapped within it. Geologists argue that the fracking itself is a problem.

Professor Shelby Eaton, an earthquake specialist at the University of Memphis Center for Earthquake Research and Information (CERI), has expressed some worry that there may be a correlation between the Arkansas earthquakes frequency and the disposal of wastewater from the fracking processes which is pumped back into the injection wells at high pressure.

FRACKED!

"Over ninety percent of these earthquakes have happened over the last two years and they have been clustered within seven or eight miles of the waste water disposal wells," he recently told the paper. Eaton believes the timing is just too coincidental to ignore. He also believes that the toxic waste water created by fracking and then pumped back into the injection wells can actually lubricate the surrounding rock, possibly leading to quakes.

"They started doing these injection wells in the area that we're talking about just before the earthquake cluster was detected. Since that time, there has been a dramatic increase in the occurrence of seismic phenomena," stated Eaton. Eaton also noted that a seismologist, Dr. Dorothy Guinnon from the University of Arkansas in Fayetteville also indicated, in a recent TV interview with a northwest Arkansas station, that there could be two kinds of seismic activity in the area -- one natural, the other apparently caused by the fracking processes. Dr. Guinnon indicated that more research concerning fracking was needed, particularly as it related to the unique shale and limestone formations found in the northern half of Arkansas.

Scientists haven't drawn any specific conclusions on the subject of fracking, and despite years of speculation within the geological community, there is still little consensus about whether the practice is contributing to the quakes. Also within the last two years, the town of Cleburne, Texas, experienced the first recorded earthquake in their town's one hundred forty plus years of recorded history, followed by four more shortly afterwards. Was natural gas drilling causing the quakes?

Drilling began in 2001 and brought great prosperity to Cleburne and other towns in North Texas. "I think the average guy on the street thinks there is a connection between the drilling and quakes," Cleburne's Mayor Bob Redmond said. "We haven't had a quake in our recorded history. Now, all of a sudden you drill and there are earthquakes." Eaton also noted that quakes in West Virginia had the same pattern of unusual seismic activity after fracking where previously there had been none.

"This part of Arkansas isn't a place where you usually have earthquakes," Professor Eaton added and then went on to say: "When the West Virginia Oil and Gas Commission forced the disposal companies to cut back on their injection rate and pressures the earthquakes in West Virginia seemed to have gone away giving a great indication of scientific cause and effect."

While the debate continues, the members of the Arkansas Oil & Gas Commission have imposed an emergency moratorium on the drilling of new injection wells in the area. However, wells that were active before the moratorium, which was passed in December, will remain in operation. According to the list published on the commission's website, there are currently over four hundred companies connected to the oil and gas industry in the state and there are only three companies currently drilling for gas using six active disposal wells in the restricted area.

Some scientists remain unconvinced that there is a relative connection between the wells and the seismic activity, such as Berkeley Professor Chen Wang whose research includes the interaction of water and earthquakes. "I believe we need more detailed study before one can clearly assess if fracking waste water injection is even partly responsible for the earthquakes," he explained during the phone interview.

Some facts are very clear: Seismic activity in Arkansas has been increasing lately, lending support to the theory that drilling is having a destabilizing effect on the shale shelf. Sunday's record quake was at the "max end" of what scientists expect can happen based on the data from the recent swarm of activity. The central Arkansas town of Greenbrier has been plagued for months by hundreds of small earthquakes. The largest quake to hit the state in thirty five years happened during fracking activity and residents said Monday they were "unsettled" by the increasing severity and lack of warning. The U.S. Geological Survey recorded the four point seven magnitude quake at 11 p.m. on Sunday and noted that it was centered just northeast of Greenbrier, about 40 miles north of Little Rock. It was the largest of more than eight hundred quakes to strike the area since September in what is now being called the Greenbrier Earthquake Swarm.

During this same period, nearly two dozen small quakes had been recorded in Arkansas on a single day.

Those are the facts.

Chapter 1

Night time fishing always had an allure for Jim and Bill, and surely many other serious fishermen. There was something particularly special about a calm late September night. These nights tended to be amazingly beautiful, especially on their favorite place to fish, Bull Shoals Lake in the Ozark Mountains of northern Arkansas. Cloudless, starlit skies frequently blanket the lake and surrounding hills and there are virtually no bright man-made lights to prevent a person from seeing every star in the night sky or from watching with wonder as the occasional meteor shower would streak across the brilliant starry palette...

Bill's rod bent, the drag on the reel whined, and the trophy fish on the end of his line went under the boat one more time and then held before gliding back out. She silently gave in to exhaustion and surfaced lazily on her side ready to surrender after a short but fierce fight. The dim moonlight fluoresced on her green and white silhouette...

"Jim - Get the net!" Bill was obviously excited about what he had on the end of his fishing line. He was hoping for a personal record.

"Have you got another one?" Jim was getting pissed. Bill seemed to be catching all the fish this night.

"Hey, come on, this is a good fish… get the net!" Bill didn't want to chance losing this fish. He was sure now that it was probably a trophy.

Jim fumbled in the darkness as he grabbed the dip net from the deck of the boat and then slipped it quietly into the blackened moonlit water.

"Wow, nice fish. Get her closer so I can get the net under her." Jim was quietly embarrassed when he realized how jealous he really was at Bill's success.

"There she is! What a hog, must be at least eight and a half pounds!" Now Jim was excited holding the fish up in that net. "Do you want a picture before you let her go?"

"Absolutely! None of the guys at the breakfast table will believe this without pictures. Those guys don't believe anything they can't see, touch and smell themselves." Bill knew the picture was required. He was almost as giddy as a four year old child wanting to show off a new toy.

FRACKED!

Jim pulled out is cell phone for a quick picture. "Crap, this thing doesn't have a flash."

"That's okay. Let's put her in the livewell and run to the marina. The office and store area are pretty well lit. We can get a picture and weigh her on their scales while we're there. Who knows, maybe the dock owner Jerry will put the picture on the Bull Shoals Lake Boat Dock web-site." Bill was genuinely hopeful that his picture would make it to the web-site.

"Sounds good, fire up the motor and let's go." Jim was ready to get this done and get back to fishing.

The silhouettes of the surrounding hills framed the water making an eerily beautiful backdrop for fishing and typically these late summer nights were virtually windless where the water could become mirror flat. Running a boat on this kind of water, particularly at night, gave the driver and passenger the sense of flying. Any lights above the water were clearly duplicated in the mirror-like surface of the massive lake. The glassy slick water made the ride so smooth it was like flying in calm air. It was almost disorienting.

The two fishermen strapped down the loose rods on deck, put on their life jackets and eased their big Bass Boat out of the small inlet from Barne's Bay just off the main channel of Bull Shoals Lake where they had been fishing for the past hour. As soon as they cleared the eastern point of the bay they got the boat up on step to make the short run to the Boat Dock. No reason to turn on the GPS. They had a little moon light. A beautiful orange late September half-moon rising in the east. They were only about two miles from the outer buoys of Bull Shoals Lake Boat Dock and had driven this stretch during the day and at night hundreds of times. Push the throttle down, trim the boat up, watch the speed and RPMs, wait for the speed to hit 64 miles per hour and let her fly across the silky smooth, undisturbed surface of the main lake channel. The night air seemed to freshen when the boat was moving and had enough coolness to give a small chill to the riders and hint that autumn would soon be on them.

The moon's reflection would help guide the fishermen past their two biggest landmarks in the dark. Once they cleared the first one, Frost Point, they would aim the boat at the lights in the distance coming from the huge Boat Dock and watch out for other boats that might be on the water. Next, the boat would have to clear the gap at Jimmy Creek Island before that last part of the run across the mouth of Jimmy Creek to the Dock. Nothing better on this planet for a diehard Bass fisherman than running wide open on a slick lake with a big Bass in the livewell.

Bill imagined the guys at Tuesday morning breakfast would certainly be envious of this one. They would want to know where he caught it and what kind of lure he used. Everything a person needed to know about the town, local politics, hunting and fishing could be discovered on Tuesday mornings at the self proclaimed "Table of Knowledge". This buzzardly group would meet for breakfast at the Village Wheel Restaurant in downtown Bull Shoals.

FRACKED!

It was a love – hate relationship for the Restaurant owner, Bill's wife Margaret. She loved the business but hated to hear some of the ripe language that frequently wafted above the smell of bacon cooking. That group could flit from presidential politics and wars on foreign continents to the finer points of shooting Sporting Clays. Hedonism was at the true core of that group's unpublished bylaw. One thing remained true, however, if you told a fish story to this group you had better bring proof! Lies wouldn't work, especially with fish stories.

Of course there would be the usual jibes about how much the fish cost per pound after adding up the expenses of boats, motors, tackle, gas, and the like. Right now, Bill really didn't care. His first priority was to get that fish to the Boat Dock for a picture and posterity. Push the throttle down and just follow the moon –

"What the hell is that?" Jim couldn't believe what he saw. Something was out of place.

"I see it. Hold on!" Bill shouted.

"Stop the boat! Turn, TURN, TURN…." That was all Jim had time to holler before the impact.

They didn't realize that Frost Point was now completely in their path until it was too late. The moon light had always clearly shone on the outline of that point. What could have happened this time?

The twenty foot boat laid partly scattered across the narrow part of the rocky outcropping with its sharp bow now pointing down in the water on the opposite side of Frost Point from where they hit. The large outboard motor was screaming out its last revolutions sitting high out of the water behind the boat where it landed after ripping off the transom.

Lying on the rocks, Bill could still see what appeared to be moon light visible in front of the rocky ledge of Frost Point. Was he hallucinating? Was the light really on the water? It seemed to be coming from below the water, not above. With blood dripping heavily across his eyes he fell unconscious for just a moment. He awoke seconds later and looked again. The light was gone. "What could it have been?"

All he could think about when he was conscious was his wife's constant reminder before he would leave to go fishing at night. He seemed to hear her now as if she were there; "Be careful you big dummy, I want you back in one piece." He slipped into unconsciousness again.

The engine's final scream had signaled the attention of fishermen in another boat not far from them up the Gunnel Fork branch of the lake.

"What was that?" Keith asked when he heard the distant motor suddenly roar.

"I don't know Keith. It kinda sounded like a boat just hit something; maybe we should check it out."   Chris had heard this sound before and knew it was a boat wrecking on the rocks.

"Must have been something up at the point. Hold on, I'm going to fire up the motor and run over there." Keith already had his rod put away and was in his life jacket to get underway.

Within a minute's drive and using a flood light, they could see two men on the shore near a now broken boat.   It appeared the two men were close to unconsciousness and they could see that both were badly scraped and cut. One had what appeared to be a broken leg and was dragging himself back toward the destroyed boat. The other was beginning to struggle to sit up and had a blood covered face.

"Keith, use your cell and call nine-one-one, these guys look bad. I'll call Jerry at the Boat Dock. It's the closest place for the rescue team to launch. It's only about eleven p.m., I'm sure he's probably still at the dock office. He'll need to know what's coming." Chris had seen something like this once before and knew the routine.

Chapter 2

Jerry Burns grew up on Bull Shoals Lake. His Dad, Old Man Don as he liked to be called, bought the Bull Shoals Lake Boat Dock in the early 70's. If it had to do with this lake Jerry had seen it, heard it, or personally invented it. No telling how many times him or one of his crew had gone out in the middle of the night to haul some yahoo off a beach or point. Most of the time these unscheduled landings happened to folks new to the lake or people that had been drinking or in some cases a little of both.

As soon as he got the call about this most recent boat wreck he hollered at Jason, one of his crew members, and had him start the Fire Department's Rescue Boat and stand by for the EMTs. Then he called the duty Ranger from the Game and Fish Commission and placed a call to Thayer Davis, the resident Officer-in-Charge at the U.S. Army Corps of Engineers local office in Mountain Home.

One thing Jerry knew about "his" lake was that "his" lake really belonged to American tax payers and was under the close control of the U.S. Army Corps of Engineers. Like many other manmade impoundments, this lake was created for hydro-electric power generation and flood control.

Thayer Davis was asleep when his cell phone rang. He really didn't mind late night calls. It reminded him that he was the head man and he liked the fact that he was now the Officer-in-Charge. He had worked twenty years as a resident engineer at numerous jobs throughout the country and finally got recognized for being a leader and not just another geek behind an engineer's drafting desk. So you can bet, when something was happening on Bull Shoals Lake, or its sister, Lake Norfork, he wanted to know.

Thayer's wife was happy about this latest position. It gave her a little clout socially and she didn't mind the attention. Thayer's two daughters were grown. The youngest one recently married and living near Little Rock, the other studying engineering at the University of Arkansas in Fayetteville. Late night calls were barely even noticed by his soundly sleeping wife.

Being the Officer-in-Charge of the last and largest manmade impoundment making up the White River chain of lakes in northern Arkansas and southern Missouri had some challenges. There was plenty to learn. Driving a boat from the Bull Shoals Lake Dam up river to the next Dam meant driving approximately seventy-five miles to reach the tail waters of Lake TaneyCoMo. Taney-Co-Mo, which was short for Taney-County-Missouri, borders the city of Branson,

Missouri which was home to many semi-retired Las Vegas and Nashville artists and entertainers. Going down river south from the Bull Shoals Lake Dam a boat would follow the trout filled cold flowing waters of the White River and about four hundred miles later arrive at a muddy delta flowing into the Mississippi River. It ended in the middle of miles and miles of farm land somewhere just west of Gunnison, Mississippi.

Thayer was challenged daily to keep Bull Shoals Lake absolutely pristine to say the least. This huge lake was closely monitored by the Corps of Engineers and various government and private environmental groups. The water was so deep, clean and clear that it was used as a principle source of drinking water for many communities. In fact, Thayer was in frequent contact with the Marion County Water District which was located on the bluffs of the main Lake on the southern shore in the city limits of the town of Bull Shoals. An intake and treatment station serving thousands of customers throughout the county was operated there. Thayer's first line of good information helping him to ensure the purity of the water was the technician sampling water every day at that plant.

His biggest budget nightmares were maintaining and staffing the two huge hydroelectric Dams which were built to form both lakes. The newest and most complex to maintain was at Bull Shoals. In fact, he knew that if it hadn't been for the Dam, the little town of Bull Shoals wouldn't even exist.

FRACKED!

One of his first office visits after taking his current job came from the self appointed town historian of Bull Shoals, Robert Hudson. Mr. Hudson wasted no time before he launched into his much practiced monologue.

"You need to know that Bull Shoals is a young city. It was incorporated shortly after the Dam was constructed. Bull Shoals city is the largest town on the lake. You already know it is bordered on three sides by water. The lake borders the North and West, while the Dam and White River border the East. It is predominantly a bedroom community of retirees of all ages. Almost everyone is from somewhere else. Very few folks can claim to be life time residents of Bull Shoals. It is a melting pot of people from Wisconsin, Illinois, California, Missouri and Florida.

Bull Shoals was formed from several tracts of what was once the community of Newton Flats. Prior to the Dam's construction, Newton Flats was a large, though scattered, farming community. At that time the White River was a commercial river where goods could be ferried to markets to the East in Mountain Home or to the south in Cotter. The River was a world class fishery even then. It was renowned for its Walleye, Smallmouth Bass and giant Catfish. When the Dam was completed and the new Lake was filling, many homes, farms, churches, old roads, businesses, and cemeteries were flooded over and soon forgotten. We like to believe it's unique and we want you to know how important the Dam is to the town for more than just the hydroelectric resource and flood control ability." Mr. Hudson was finished. His message had been clear. Keep the Dam in good shape, it was the mother and the city was its offspring.

Thayer knew from experience that most of the people in town had a story to tell and many were worth hearing. Although the best stories to listen to were usually lies.

Thayer really liked that the fact that Bull Shoals wasn't on a main highway. It didn't have a McDonald's, Starbucks, or Holiday Inn. It seemed to still honor a bygone era. Thayer often thought that maybe the little town just couldn't escape from the past. Either way, there had been very few changes over the years. Even the old original resorts were still operating. Fast food meant a visit to D's Beacon Point, for a burger and fries, though some of the old timers still call it by its original name, the Big Wheel. A nice sit down dinner could be found at the Village Wheel or the 178 Club Restaurant and Bowling Alley. Pizza to eat-in or take-out came from Bush's Pizza where everything was still made from scratch. There is one gas station in town and it usually closed by ten p.m.

The local liquor store stayed busy six days a week, the VFW Post was busy every day.

It was a little town stuck in the mid-twentieth century. Amazingly bright folks moved here from all over the country because the town was not a hustling, busy tourist trap. They liked the fact that it wasn't on a main road and that people didn't just stop in town on their way to somewhere else. They had to be going to Bull Shoals or they would never know they missed it.

"What's not to like?" Thayer thought. Lake, river and wilderness recreation areas beyond compare and the residents had this to themselves almost nine months of the year. Even the so-called tourist season wasn't as busy as one hotel on South Padre Island during spring break. Perhaps this was part of the secret long range plan concocted over the years by residents who weren't quite ready to share this little paradise. They liked having the place to themselves. Maybe they were just selfish, bigoted and hardened. They put their time in to hard jobs in big, crime ridden, dirty cities. They found this little jewel in the Ozarks through secret handshakes and whispers akin to popularized lore surrounding the Knights Templar and the Free Masons.

Thayer knew all too well that these folks really didn't want their little secret paradise shared with just anyone.

Chapter 3

Jerry was quietly wrapping up a few loose ends in the store while he waited for the rescue crews. He knew that boating accidents usually got the attention of locals. Most accidents involved tourists and usually because they were trying to do too much in too short a time and trying to get every ounce of fun out of the toys they had rented for the weekend. But Jerry knew that not all accidents involved tourists. A couple of accidents had quite a bit of added attention.

About two years ago, two tourists were killed when their ski boats collided with each other at around eleven-thirty at night somewhere near point eighteen on Bull Shoals Lake. It took several days and lots of resources to recover one of the victims from this traumatic crash. Riley Dirkson was eventually found in one hundred twenty eight feet of water by divers assisted by sonar and underwater cameras. One of the boats involved in the open water collision was reportedly operating without lights. Although a couple of the witnesses injured in the wreck said the lights on both boats were out at the time of the accident.

FRACKED!

Every fisherman in the area took notice on this. First, what were ski boats doing on their favorite fishing lake that late at night? Second, if these tourists weren't using lights then that put local fishermen's lives at risk every time they cranked up the big motor to make a run to the next hot fishing spot. Fishermen knew to flash their lights when they heard or saw another boat, it was courtesy and tradition. You did it for the other guy and he did it for you. That way everyone stayed alive.

Jerry recalled that late last winter, local high school teacher Dick Jeffries died when the boat he was riding in was hit from behind by another boat. This was very unusual. Two bass boats and four local fishermen were involved. Lots of folks took notice on this.

Poor Dick didn't know what hit him. His fishing partner, who was driving the boat, made a sharp left turn and as he did he was hit from behind by a boat following them a bit too closely. The boat behind them was just to the rear and preparing to pass the slightly slower boat that Dick was in. The passing boat didn't see the front boat making a turn until it was too late and ran right over the top of the unsuspecting school teacher.

Dick Jeffries was a father, husband and part-time preacher at a small country church. His death reverberated throughout the county and emotionally touched many people. He was a well respected man and everyone loved him. His wife and kids eventually had to move and lost their home since Dick was the only income producer in the family. Jerry knew Dick personally. This was a horrible, horrible catastrophe that should never have happened.

But tonight's accident was different…

This involved two seasoned local fishermen after all. They weren't hit from behind or by another boat because of lights being out. These guys knew the lake better than many other people just because of the number of days and hours spent pursuing their one and only pastime.   Word spreads quickly when something like this happens. This is way out of the norm. Local bass fishermen don't wreck like this.   Fifty-thousand dollar bass boats owned by local guys don't usually get scratched on this lake. Wrecking one on a point was beyond belief.

Jerry was still at the Boat Dock office after midnight when the rescue boat finally came back in. He had quit smoking seven months, two weeks and three days ago. Standing and waiting in the shadows of his docks for the crew to come back he wondered if giving up smoking was really the right thing to do. His nerves were on edge and he thought a good smoke would calm him. Jerry really couldn't put a finger on what was making him edgy.

Something about this call was just too strange. He knew Bill, he knew him really well. He and Bill had been roommates in college. They learned to water ski together and later learned bass fishing from one of the local pros. They spent a lot of time together growing up.

Bill's father, Roger started the Village Wheel restaurant and the Big Wheel drive-in and had moved to Bull Shoals at about the same time as Jerry's Dad. Old Man Don and Roger were great friends and had moved to the area from different parts up north at around the same time. They were both active in the local Chamber of Commerce, Lions Club and Rotary and were well known throughout the region. They frequently traveled to Boat Shows and Outdoor Sporting Conventions all over the country to brag about Bull Shoals and the great opportunities available for fun on Bull Shoals Lake and the White River.

Bill and Jim were going to be fine, or so it seemed. They looked like hell and didn't say much. The last time Bill looked like that he had gone through the open windshield of his dirt track race car. Come to think of it, Jerry was there for that one too and gave Bill no end of ridicule for his shit kicking attitude on the dirt track and his lack of ability to match it with his driving skill.

Jerry knew better than to ask any questions while the two fishermen were being treated and had nosey attendants hovering. He would hear everything later, no censor, no reprisal, and no lies. Bill would tell him the truth, he always did. For now, Jerry would wait.

"Jason, take care of putting the rescue boat to bed for the night and then get out of here. Go home. Good work out there by the way. I'm going to lock up and kill the main office lights." Jerry was exhausted and ready to head home. He strolled back to the fuel dock and made one quick tour around to double check the gear and peek into the unrented house boats sitting in slips next the dock. All seemed quiet and fine as usual.

It had been a very slow year for houseboat rentals. The unusually high water in the lake was to blame. They were still fighting high water from record rains this past spring. The lake was at record levels, forty-one feet over normal pool. Technically speaking, normal pool was measured as six hundred fifty four feet above mean sea level and the current flood stage was six hundred ninety five feet. It had only been this high once before, and that was planned by the Corps of Engineers to test the Dam's flood gates. This situation was unique to say the least. Extremely heavy rains fell across the entire region in the spring, setting new records for the amount of rain that had fallen in this area in one hour and in one day. And, this happened numerous times during the weeks of rain.

Every creek, ditch and valley for thousands of square miles flows into the White River chain of Lakes. Bull Shoals Lake alone has over six thousand square miles of drainage area. Each of the lakes were already at flood capacity and Bull Shoals was the last line of defense on the White River before flooding could devastate homes and farms all the way to the Mississippi River. High water pouring into the White River from tributaries had already wiped out numerous homes and boat docks from the confluence of the Buffalo River south to Newport, Arkansas. Especially hard hit had been some of the old mining towns along the Buffalo River and the little town of Norfork at the mouth of the North Fork River where it flows into and meets the White River. Houses would literally float by and then crush against the pilings of the Highway 5 Bridge on the south side of town. There was debris scattered for miles downstream.

If the Corps released water from Bull Shoals, it could double the destruction further to the south. So they made the decision to hold the water and let it spill over the top of the flood gates if needed, but they would not release massive amounts of water until the Rivers receded. As if cursed by the decision, more rains came during the summer. Now there was no choice, the Corps would continue to hold water as much as the Dam and Lake could stand.

This decision saved lives and farms to the South, but really hurt the businesses around the Lake that depended on the summer flurry of tourism. By now, most of the usual returning tourists had heard that it was very hard to find boat launch facilities and that parking was non-existent in any of the normal parks and launch sites. So, except for the "diehard" visitors and the folks that just didn't know what was happening – it was really a slow tourist season.

So there they sat. Six beautiful, nearly new, sixty foot Destination Yacht houseboats, waiting to be rented. It was bad enough that he had to ferry most of his private boat slip renters back and forth to their docks and that he provided the service free. Everything was slow. Gas sales, bait and tackle sales, snack and soda sales were all suffering. This high water was hurting everyone.

He headed into the store, walked through the service counter to his office and killed the lights to the store and gas dock. He sat down at his desk to check his email one more time before calling it a night. Nothing there but the usual spam and porn promotions. As he got up from his desk and looked across the store his attention was suddenly captured by what seemed to be moon light reflecting near the gas dock. "Wrong direction", he thought. As soon as he moved, the light disappeared and he could see a small isolated island of fog. "Must have been reflections off the fog," he was positive.

"Dad if you're listening, I'm tired, its late, my best friend just got hurt and now I'm seeing things. Forgive me, but I'm going home and to bed. Watch the store like you always do."

Chapter 4

Jerry had been asleep for only an hour or so when his cell phone rang. He was used to sleeping in late since he always closed the Boat Dock in the middle of the night. Unexpected calls at 3:30 in the morning were traumatic for him. He still had memories of being on the town Volunteer Fire Team and getting bizarre wake up calls to respond to a myriad of mostly stupid things. Still, starting the adrenalin flowing after being fast asleep isn't great for your heart and can wear on a guy. "Who the hell could be calling", he wondered as he grabbed for the phone.

"Jerry, this is Greg at Pontiac Cove Marina. Sorry to wake you but I need to let you know what's going on up here." Greg's voice was urgent.

"What's up Greg?" Jerry nearly yawned as he asked.

"We just towed one of your houseboats to the bank near our launch. They started to take on water so we beached it to keep it from sinking."

"Everybody okay?" Jerry was fully awake at this point.

"Yeah, they seem fine. They say the engines wouldn't start and the generator died after they were supposedly bumped or hit by something. And, for what it's worth, it doesn't make any sense to me but the batteries are fried on that boat. I think the boat flexed and shorted out the battery leads. We towed them from one of the permanent mooring buoys up in Spring Creek. So we know they didn't run the houseboat up on the rocks. I have no idea what happened." Greg had been around boats of all sorts most of his life and this was truly confusing, even for him.

"What did the people on the boat tell you?" Jerry was used to drunks banging up his boats and wondered if these people might have been partying a little too hard.

"They went on about being woken up by a huge bump. Like the boat had been lifted up and let go. One of the kids said something about fog coming in the boat from the water and they all complained about something smelling like a sewer. Seems like a nice family, I don't think anyone would make something up like this."

"We'll check with them again in the morning. Were you able to get them some rooms?" Jerry felt obligated to check since they were still really his customers.

"They're at Cactus Ridge Resort.   Marge will call you tomorrow about the bill I'm sure. You know it's tight right now and they're all strapped for cash." Greg was starting to sound exhausted, his long night was coming to an end.

"Tell me about it. I don't even want to think about having to fix the houseboat, and now I'm losing rent and paying rent at the same time. Damn." Jerry's voice was strained at the thought of spending money he didn't want to spend.

"Well don't worry about the houseboat for now; it will be fine until tomorrow. Try to get some sleep." Greg was right, the customers were fine and the boat would wait.

"Thanks for the call Greg. I'll drive over late in the morning with a couple of guys from my crew." Jerry was yawning again and ready to get some sleep.

Jerry hung up the phone and wondered for a while about what could have happened to that houseboat. "What a night", he whispered to himself. He thought for a minute about calling Thayer Davis of the Corps of Engineers to let him know what had happened and then decided it would wait. No sense bothering Thayer in the middle of the night. It had already been bad enough to have bothered him once. The Bull Shoals Lake Boat Dock was licensed to operate inside the Corps of Engineers property boundaries on terms that no one wanted to challenge. Keep the Corps happy was the rule. Do what was needed; keep them informed, and treat them with courtesy had always worked.

The U.S. Army Corps of Engineers is made up of active duty military engineers and civilian engineers. They have a unique mission covering thousands of projects in the United States and abroad. The Bull Shoals Lake area is supported by a field office in Mountain Home, Arkansas and is a part of the Little Rock district which serves southern Missouri and most of Arkansas. They predominantly monitor, manage and maintain navigable waters, locks and dams throughout the area. They've been doing this mission for this region since 1881. The Corps of Engineers also coordinates emergency response and disaster recovery. They are specifically required to ensure river and dam safety and flood control.

The Corps has been very busy this year with floods. They already have recovery estimates and budgets worked up to repair or restore many state parks, public facilities near the shoreline and launch ramps that will be damaged or destroyed by the high water. Engineers have been traveling every mile of river and lake surveying damage and making educated guesses about what will be needed.

They've always been on the front lines for natural disasters and floods. They were helping with tornado recovery in late winter before the floods started in the spring of this year. In 1999 and 1997 they were there to help with recovery after devastating tornadoes ravaged many parts of Arkansas and then again with recovery efforts after the floods along the White River, Arkansas River and Red Rivers in 1998.

One of the Corps' biggest projects, the Bull Shoals Dam, is a huge monolithic concrete structure of over two thousand feet in length and nearly five-hundred feet in height housing eight generators capable of producing one hundred ninety megawatts of power at peak production. When operating with all eight generators the dam pours out approximately ten million gallons of lake water per minute. At that rate the lake level may only change by about seven or eight inches over a twenty four hour period. That's over one billion cubic feet of water! With the lake swollen from forty-five thousand surface acres to over seventy thousand it will still take weeks to get the lake level close to normal.

With the extremely high flood water, Bull Shoals Dam has been under intense scrutiny daily by the Corps' finest engineers. Technicians working the power generation plant have doubled their daily inspections of the Dam's internal components and stress observation equipment. The penstocks, or water intakes, have been fully open for quite some time now. Even when they aren't generating power, the water passes through a wicket gate at the base of the generator's disengaged turbine and goes directly to the River basin. The penstock openings at Bull Shoals are very deep on the dam face and have nothing more than grates as a means to filter the water prior to entering the power house. The forces that press against the Dam's deep water side must be unimaginable.

Any small leak or crack in this structure would quickly expand to an unmanageable level if not monitored and corrected every day. Leaks are not unusual and a series of sump pumps in the very deepest parts of the base of the Dam keep the leaks from becoming problems. Still, monitoring the structure is critical.

The smallest change in pressures, any vibrations, or any unauthorized visits are now closely inspected as part of the anti-terrorism movement by the federal government. Dams are considered strategic targets and, by consequence, get much closer attention than ever before. If the sensors spike, even a hair's width, somebody in Washington D.C. knows within minutes. After the September 11th, 2001 terrorist attacks on the U.S., the Corps of Engineers has improved its internal security at all Dams, bridges and locks under their control.

Chapter 5

Sheriff Neal Johnson got to his office early and did what he normally did every day of the week. He would say "Good Morning" to the desk clerk, stop at the nine-one-one desk and pick up the night log, grab a cup of coffee from the break room and head to his office to check his emails and review the night log.

Sheriff Johnson's popularity was at an all time high. He was on his third term as Baxter County Sheriff. He made huge improvements in the emergency services nine-one-one network; developed cooperative agreements with the Marion County Sheriff's office; improved tracking and reporting on sex offenders; and his intense efforts to rid the county of methamphetamine production were stellar. His county is bordered by two major lakes and rivers. Bull Shoals Lake is on the west and Lake Norfork is on the east. Marion County lays to the west of the Bull Shoals Lake Dam and west of the White River. His territory is over six hundred square miles of hilly, sometimes very rough country. Many county roads are barely rock trails and reaching some parts of the county can be almost impossible even by four wheel drive. The Baxter County Sheriff's Office has a relatively new helicopter and they are proud to use it whenever the time is right. Search and rescue operations for many counties in north central Arkansas rely on this helicopter when lives are on the line.

The night log from the nine-one-one desk was reading like normal until about ten twenty-five that evening. There were seven entries from different residences in Edgewood Bay and Forrest Shores along the Howard's Creek arm of Bull Shoals Lake. There was one Deputy available who was sent to the area to investigate.

Seems that all the reports had something to do with seeing strange fog and some with seeing lights and smelling what seemed to be an open sewer or rotten eggs. The Deputy reported that he had taken statements and looked around. He drove by the Lakeview Marina and then down by some of the private docks in Edgewood Bay but he never saw anything suspicious. He stopped and walked out on one of the private docks to double check. The Deputy also found it to be a good excuse to get out of the patrol car to stretch his legs and smoke a cigarette. There was nothing unusual to report according to the Deputy's log entry.

Sheriff Johnson called the desk clerk and had her bring him the statements that the Deputy had collected. He was amused more than concerned at first. Seems the statements were similar by each witness, so the credibility was high. Several of the witnesses said the light looked more like something on the fog rather than something in the water. "Moonlight reflections probably," he thought. He had seen this before. Now he wondered if that might be similar to what the residents had seen. It was certainly odd, but not worth getting too alarmed over.

He decided to call Sheriff Carl Wilson over in Marion County just to check in and share his strange reports. Sheriff Johnson figured it would be good for an early morning laugh if nothing else.

"Carl? Hey, Neal here. I hope I haven't disturbed anything important."

"Nothing going on here Neal. What have you got?" Sheriff Wilson was always happy to talk to Neal Johnson and enjoyed a very good working relationship with his office.

"This is going to sound a little strange, but we've got several reports of strange lights and fog on Bull Shoals. I thought I would let you know before the press gets wind of it and stirs up the public." Sheriff Johnson always wanted to be ahead of the press.

"Actually, that doesn't sound that strange. I was talking to Jerry Burns at the Bull Shoals Lake Boat Dock this morning about a houseboat he has beached with damage near Pontiac. He says the renters reported seeing fog right after the boat was hit by something. He also said they smelled...." Sheriff Wilson was interrupted.

"Don't tell me, let me guess. They smelled rotten eggs."

"That's right Neal. I'm thinking we need to call Thayer Davis at the Corps office and share this one. What about you?" Sheriff Wilson was almost always in favor of collaboration.

"I agree. I'll give him a call. I owe him breakfast and a cup of coffee anyway. Thanks Carl, call me if you hear anything new."

"Neal, by the way, Thayer may be a little busy this morning already. Jerry said he called Thayer last night about an earlier Bass boat accident. Quite the night on the Lake it seems. A couple of local guys were hurt pretty bad and wrecked their boat on one of the points. Jerry said they ran right over Frost Point trying to avoid some kind of lights that popped up right in front of them while they were driving back toward the boat dock. Thayer's folks will have to investigate the accident." Sheriff Wilson was surprised that Neal hadn't already heard this.

"Thanks for the head's up Carl. See you soon."

Sheriff Johnson called the Corps of Engineers Project Office. Thayer wasn't available at that time to take any calls according to the receptionist. He decided it was worth calling Thayer's cell phone. He wouldn't normally call the cell number for a non-emergency just out of professional courtesy. For some reason, he made the call this time.

Thayer Davis was already at Bull Shoals Lake helping with the investigation concerning the boat wreck. When his phone rang he

40

checked the caller I.D. and answered it right away. It was Sheriff Johnson. Neal never called unless it was an emergency.

"Good morning Neal, did I forget to pay a ticket?"

"Hey Thayer, how are you? I hate to call you with this. But I think it's worth it. Where are you? I'll come tell you all about it."

"I'm at the Bull Shoals Lake Boat Dock. I should be here another hour before I head to the Power Plant Operations Center."

"Thayer, let me meet you at the Dam. We can talk there."

"Alright Neal, see you in about an hour."

Sheriff Johnson knew how to play the press. He wanted to get ahead of all these little stories before they became something else. He also knew how to play smart politics. He called Guy Fredricks at the Arkansas Department of Environmental Quality in Little Rock and filled him in on the reports just like he had read them earlier, nothing more, and nothing less. Mr. Fredricks was obligingly thankful, but figured it was just kids goofing around during their last remaining nights of summer. Strange lights and funky smells weren't likely to endanger fish in the White River or hurt the area's drinking water. As long as the unofficial environmentalist groups weren't quacking like a stirred up flock of angry ducks and weren't engaging the press, then he was happy.

The next call he made was to Jack Sims, the CEO of ALS Technologies. This company made all types of what they liked to call less than lethal weapons. Jack's outfit had its international headquarters in the town of Bull Shoals and a manufacturing facility a few miles out of town. The Sheriff knew that one of Jack's best selling items was stink grenades. These things wouldn't hurt people, but they would wish they were dead if they couldn't get out of their smoke. They were made from a concentrated hydrogen sulfide compound that had been modified to disperse widely so that the gas was not lethal but the smell of rotten eggs was tremendously horrid and the smoke would burn eyes and throats just enough that the intended victims would have to run for clear air to escape the effect. This product turned out to be more effective and less expensive to manufacture than traditional tear gas. Maybe some of the guys at Jack's manufacturing facility were having a little too much fun and sharing some of the products. Jack had a fairly wild group of young people working out there. The only saving grace was the facility supervisor, Jenny.

Jenny Simpson was tough, an ex-Navy Underwater Demolition Team (UDT) saturation diver, very organized, and very beautiful. She was physically fit and could probably kick everyone's ass out at the bomb factory. She liked to call it a bomb factory because of all the gun powder and other explosives they stored and used every day. Jenny had been UDT and worked some unpublicized incursions near Basra and then was assigned to augment Army Special Forces when

Baghdad was taken. She had seen combat, survived uninjured and was glad as hell to get out of the chaos.

Her first three years in the Navy found her following around a commander in the medical corps who was the service's only forensic pathologist. She had taken two years of criminal forensics training in junior college before enlisting and the recruiters took advantage of the special training to fill a tough position that no one else had been qualified to take. She traveled nearly full time, mostly to the war torn mid-east where she and her boss would catalog human remains and begin the slow process of determining cause of death and identifying victims from nothing more than a DNA sample and the Combined DNA Index System, or CODIS as most folks have heard it called on popular TV crime shows.

After three years of handling dead people, or parts anyway, she decided she needed a change of pace. Somehow she thought it was a bit ironic that she went on to learn how to blow stuff up after having dealt with the after effects of blowing stuff up. Jenny had learned an enormous amount about forensics and even thought about becoming a crime scene investigator after her time in the Navy until she realized the pay was better in the private sector for an explosives expert vice what most city cops were paid.

Jenny was in her mid thirties but didn't look to be twenty-five yet. She was blonde, tanned and loved the water. These days, her passions were wake boards and spear fishing. Family life could wait.

She led a modest enough life. She had a small fixer upper house in the McDonald Meadows subdivision of Bull Shoals. She liked living in this neighborhood. It was quiet. She could walk or jog the neighborhood twice and get five miles in without any major roads in the way. There were also four short access roads leading to the water and she could run right to the water's edge and back during her outings. If she wanted, she could flip off her shoes and jump in the water for a quick swim or just to cool down.

Jenny had always loved dogs as a child and now that she was settled in her own house she owned a big stupid yellow lab named Buck. Her big yellow dog was clumsy, but loved to run and swim, which was about the extent of his worth. He wouldn't bark at strangers and was a little afraid of lightning. Jenny didn't care. Buck was great company and loved everyone. He went almost everywhere she went; always riding shotgun in her worn out Rubicon Jeep. Jenny wouldn't admit it, but her secret hero had always been E. Johnson, the female tracker and heroin in the cult fiction novel *Cherry 2000* written by Lloyd Fonvielle. Once you've seen Jenny, the puzzle pieces weren't hard to place.

Chapter 6

Thayer Davis was strangely concerned this morning. Something smelled, and it wasn't just the mysterious fogs. When he checked in with the Power Plant Operations Center the duty supervisor was busy re-analyzing pressure gradient print outs from the Dam facings near the eight penstock inlet pipes.

The supervisor was at a loss to explain the pressures. They weren't off by much so perhaps it was a calibration issue. He would get the head of maintenance to pull the gauges and check their calibration before getting too concerned.

Thayer listened to the techno-babble concerning pressure gradients and digital gauges versus the old tried and true analog mercury gauges. He had to endure the story because he knew this was literally the meat of what these guys did for a living. If you didn't listen it was a sure way to get the technicians pissed off. Technicians believed engineers were good at drawing up stuff that was improbable to build or nearly impossible to maintain. No reason to make them think any less. Being a good Project Office Manager meant being a great listener. The more they know you listen, the more they respect you when you talk.

Thayer shared a little of the story concerning the appearance of fog from the night before with the supervisor. Interestingly, the pressure gradients seemed to show the anomalous, nearly imperceptible, spikes at around the same general time. "Curious," he thought, and then he decided to ask the supervisor to have a technician pull an effluent sample on at least two penstocks. He wanted to see if there was anything in the water that might account for the smells reported last night. He knew it was long shot, but he figured it would be better to have it, even if it was just a baseline for comparison later.

Sheriff Johnson was escorted through the Power Plant visitor's gate and taken directly to the Operations Center. He had been there many times, mostly for dignitary tours. Every new Senator or Governor would make the tour and wave the proverbial flags of unfailing support for projects like the Dam to raise money for the State and make new jobs.

As the Sheriff entered the Operations Center he could see that Thayer was very interested in something. He was sure by now that Thayer was taking all of last night's occurrences seriously. Thayer could get drop dead serious when there was anything remotely impacting his mission to keep the Dam safe and secure.

"Hey Neal, come on over, take at look at this."

"Mornin' Thayer. What am I looking at?"

"Last night around the time people were reporting lights, we were recording a small pressure spike at the inlets. I'm not saying it's anything to worry about, but I'm probably going to report it to the District office in Little Rock just to make sure they aren't blind-sided."

"What could cause the spike?"

"Theoretically, any number of things can cause a spike. We don't have any evidence to tell us what may have caused this. I'm having the guys pull the gauges for calibration as a precaution and I've ordered some effluent samples from the intakes just to see if there's anything weird in the water which may be responsible for the smells. Broken sewer lines, leaking septic tanks and a few other things will give off hydrogen sulfide gases which smell much like rotten eggs. The chance of us seeing any traceable levels at the inlets is remote, but, at least we'll have a baseline for reference. I made a call to Guy Fredricks at the Arkansas Department of Environmental Quality just before you walked in to ask for some assistance with water sampling."

"Great minds... I called Guy earlier. I wanted him to know that something was up before he was surprised by anything getting into the press. Guy likes to vacation on Bull Shoals Lake and the White River. He keeps his eye on this area pretty close." Sheriff

Johnson had worked with Guy many times responding to reports of illegal dumping in or near the river.

Chapter 7

Guy Fredricks was appointed by the Governor to head up the Arkansas Department of Environmental Quality or ADEQ for short. It was a great job for an environmental engineer. He was the youngest Director in the Department's history. He had been a non-tenured professor at Arkansas State University for several years after getting his doctorate in environmental geology. While he was at the University he was used by the ADEQ frequently as a consultant. Now he was able put his knowledge to use in the real world nearly every day. Arkansas was so far behind the leading edge of environmental protection technology that Guy would be a hero if he was able to get the State into the twenty-first century even if it was ten years late.

The ADEQ was unofficially augmented in the field by many well meaning groups. Citizen groups formed around everything lately. The most recent irrational development was the group working to protect the environment around an extinct woodpecker. There was an unverified report that the Ivory Billed Woodpecker was flying around in wooded swampy low lying river oxbow lakes and bayous. That was enough to start the movement. No proof, but lots of energy to protect the habitat anyway. The Governor decided to take the whole project seriously and encourage the ADEQ to keep an open mind and help out if possible. Guy was smart, he stayed out of the argument concerning whether the bird was real or not. He was able to help make the Governor look good by getting the Secretary of the Finance Administration to have her Motor Vehicle Division to approve a new vehicle license plate with the extinct bird's picture on it. The extra money from sales of the license plates would go directly to his agency for supporting any programs related to the environment of the endangered species; assuming it came up from extinct status. It was a win-win. His Department gets money, the Governor looks good, and the environmental friends of the extinct bird are very satisfied with the attention and their new license plates.

Guy didn't hesitate to tell Thayer he would personally come up for the investigation. He needed time away from the State Capital and this was a great excuse. He had a fairly light calendar and no scheduled appearances in the State Capital for at least a week. The news media was quiet, no big issues bubbling. Even if there were, sometimes he was happier being hard to reach.

Two years ago, a land developer started a subdivision development project just above the North Fork River. The developer failed to take all the expected precautions to prevent any perceived harm to the River. His bull dozers had cleared several acres of pristine river front hill side property without putting up the required silt fences at the base of the property. As luck would have it, they had a heavy rain the first night and tons of freshly exposed top soil was washed into the River. The River muddied up for miles downstream. Members of the Trout Fishing Unlimited group were on the phone to the ADEQ the same day. Of course the group also called every newspaper in both southern Missouri and Arkansas and the TV stations in Springfield, Missouri and Little Rock. Guy had his political hands tied at that point. He had to take firm and immediate action to protect the River. There were several sparring sessions in court with lawyers on both sides dancing for the cameras. In the end, ADEQ prevailed and the developer was heavily fined. The subdivision project died after the developer fixed the hill side. Guy wondered some days if there was really a way to balance good economic development with protecting the environment. He hated the confrontation parts of his job.

Guy's secretary could read his mind before he opened his mouth. She knew he was headed to Bull Shoals and the White River. He stood there holding a water sampling kit in one hand and a fly rod in the other. "Two and a half hours in the car and Mr. Fredricks would be sampling water alright, by floating a woolly bug down the White River below the Bull Shoals Dam I'll bet", she thought.

Guy Fredricks loved the White River. His passion to fish for trophy Brown Trout was visible on almost every inch of his office walls. He had pictures of numerous fishing outings, including several with the current Governor and one with former President Clinton. He had several of his most treasured fish mounted for posterity and displayed next to the pictures as well. His fish mounts were synthetic of course, no sense in actually sacrificing the fish. Bob the taxidermist in Bull Shoals did all his work. He was an artist with both real fish and the synthetic duplicates. He could take a photo and measurements and create a mount that looked real enough to pull from the River. At the State Capital, Guy was considered the resident dignitary fishing guide. He sometimes thought that was a bigger accomplishment than heading up the ADEQ.

Guy had been married once. He fell in love as an undergrad and married in grad school. He was been married for just fifteen months when his young wife was killed by a drunk driver. She had been coming home from a routine grocery shopping trip when she was hit by a drunk who had crossed the center line. It was a clear, sunny day and it had happened for no possible reason. It could never be explained. She and the drunken driver both died in the collision. Guy was a zombie for weeks after the wreck. He barely finished his thesis that year.

After that, he found that he could forget most of the pain when he was fishing. Now he had a Bass boat, a River boat, and the best waders money could buy. Guy figured he had more money in fishing rods, reels, and tackle than most men had in their cars.

His second love was geology. He had inherited a love for rocks from his grandfather. A poor, but passionate old man, Guy's Grandpa loved to take the young boy with him out on the family farm years ago and walk around to explore every inch of the earth that he worked on so hard. Guy can remember being seven or eight years old when he was with his Grandpa walking through a freshly plowed field and stumbling upon his first real arrowhead. "Indian Rocks," was what Grandpa always called them.

Grandpa inspected the old Indian Rock and told Guy, "That's a real valuable piece of history there in your hand. That rock was probably millions of years old before it met an Indian who could skillfully change its character and shape it into a prized tool. When the arrow head was lost by the Indian, probably because it was shot at an animal and missed its mark, this old rock laid in the dirt for hundreds of years just waiting to be discovered by you so that its story could live on."

Guy was intensely caught up in that whole thought about a rock telling a story. He never looked at rocks the same way again.

By the time he was ten years old he could identify and name just about every type of rock on earth. Most other kids were learning about dinosaurs. Not Guy; he loved rocks. He would spend hours hiking the hills around his childhood home near Jasper, Arkansas collecting all kinds of rocks. By thirteen he had explored most of the small caves and deserted mines in the county. For him, the history of the world could be summarized with rocks.

It was nearly supper time before Guy could get to Bull Shoals. He was able to get a room at Gaston's White River Resort. Jim Gaston, the owner, liked the ADEQ and would always make room for the Director anytime. As soon as Guy put his gear away he called Thayer Davis.

"Thayer, this is Guy. I just got in."

"Glad to hear you made it. We've been checking stories all day and keep coming up with the same basic conclusions. People saw something and smelled something, but we can't prove anything yet."

"Listen, I'll run down to the Lake and get a couple of water samples. I'll probably go to Howard's Creek first and then I'll get some from the River. I brought a portable lab with me. I've got a mass spectrometer, liquid chromatograph, and some basic kits to check pH and dissolved gasses. We'll see if there's anything out there."

"We can compare notes first thing in the morning. I've had a long day already and I still need to finish some reports and emails. The District office in Little Rock wants an update. I really don't know what to tell them yet. Our pressure differentials at the Dam penstocks were still within so-called normal limits. All the gauges were recalibrated this afternoon and reinstalled without a problem. The Sheriff said there was nothing he could pin down as out of the ordinary, but he was still waiting to hear about some smoke bombs that might have caused the commotion."

"Sounds good, give me a call when you get started in the morning. I should have the chemistries done by morning."

"You need to know that I promised the local press an interview tomorrow. I would like for you to be there. So far they have only run a short report about the boat accident and the multiple calls to the nine-one-one operator last night. But since the nine-one-one logs seem to present more questions than answers, they want me to provide answers. I told them there wasn't a story, but they are insisting on follow up since they know we're still investigating."

"No problem Thayer. When and where?"

"Meet me at the Powerhouse at nine in the morning. That's where the press will be. Thanks for coming up Guy, we'll see you in the morning."

Guy collected some empty sample bottles, a marker, and some pH test strips. He really figured this would be a waste of time, but he would do it meticulously just the same.

It took less than ten minutes to get the Howard's Creek Resort lake access. He parked then walked to the water and collected three samples of water. He marked them each with a location code, HC for Howard's Creek, then a date and time, 09/20, 1742. He dipped the pH strip in the lake. He was a little surprised that the pH was about six point one. Seemed very acidic to him. It could be that the extra acidity was from surface water runoffs. The basic clarity was as expected this time of year. A little observable algae bloom, but otherwise clear.

Ten minutes later he was back at the Powerhouse river access ramp. He grabbed three samples the same way as before and headed back to his room at Gaston's. One sample from each location was set aside as a control in case there was ever a question concerning his testing technique, the second was packed for testing at the Little Rock lab, the third was for immediate use. He dipped a pH strip in the third sample and was a little surprised that it was several points higher than the lake sample. It was about eight point seven, a little alkaline. Then he remembered that the lake would normally be lower, particularly on the surface due to the lake's late summer algae bloom. He knew he would have to confirm his data with some deeper samples.

After setting the samples down by the portable lab he had set up on the counter in the small kitchen of the cabin where he was staying, he decided dinner would be a nice treat. Guy grabbed his fishing hat and walked out in the direction of Gaston's restaurant. He stopped by the main office to chat with Ron, the guest facilities manager. Ron was able to summarize just about every fishing tactic used in the last three weeks and how good or bad the fishing had been. Ron assured Guy that he had set a river boat aside for his use any time he needed it. He felt really spoiled by this place. After listening to about ten minutes of how to, where to and with what lure, he grabbed a few new locally hand tied flies of varying sorts and then headed for dinner.

Guy loved sitting inside Gaston's restaurant and watching the River flow by while he ate. The restaurant was built about forty feet up the river bank from the water and was buttressed to hang out over the edge of the River bed. When the Dam was releasing water through all eight generators the River was nearly as high as it could be short of catastrophe. When it was high like this, the water seemed to be under the edge of the restaurant making the views even better.

Guy could see a lone Blue Heron working up and down the bank. He watched the long necked, skinny legged bird swiftly stab the water. The bird raised its head and with a quick flip slid a fat fish from its beak down its long throat. "Amazing, how simple," he thought. Just then, he saw a long green river boat gliding up against the rushing current. Two fishermen were coming back up stream for another late afternoon drift back down stream to fish their favorite places for a possible trophy Brown Trout. The boat seemed to glide easily against the rushing water. The man controlling the motor eased off the throttle and allowed the boat speed to match the river flow, and then he put the motor in neutral.

Local fishermen never killed the motor on a drift with the water this high and fast. If the current started taking the boat into overhanging trees or some other obstacle you might not have time to restart the motor and maneuver away from the threat. Plus, if the fish started biting good, you might want to use the motor to hold position while fishing the area thoroughly.

River boats were great to fish from, but Guy preferred wading when the water was low and slow. It was the best way to get close to the action and pit your skills against a potential trophy. The fish were more cautious in low water. The larger, deeper pools were crystal clear and very hard to fish without spooking the already skittish fish. Your best hope was to stay low, use shadows to hide your silhouette and then make long casts up stream. If the cast was on target, the lure would float across the distant pool without the fish suspecting you were close. Just stay very still while the lure was in the prime target area and watch the strike indicator or your line for movement. Then repeat until you caught a fish or were convinced there was no fish to catch and move to the next potential spot.

The high water was beautiful to watch. It made the River look like a wild high mountain glacial river. Even now during the end of the hottest period of the summer, the river was clear, fast, deep and extremely cold. The water temperature was almost always constant between forty-nine and fifty-two degrees. The perfect temperature range for trophy German Brown Trout. The River had been high for nearly three months now and taking forever it seemed to get the Lake back to normal levels and ready for what was considered winter pool.

Chapter 8

Guy finished dinner and went back to his cabin. Within minutes, he had expertly run the lake side water samples through a battery of tests and was beginning the analysis of the river water samples. So far, nothing out of the expected. Dissolved oxygen was within normal limits for surface water in the lake during September. The water samples showed traces of nitrogen and phosphates higher than the baseline data taken from the mid-lake area south of Music Creek that had been provided by the Fish and Game Commission. These baselines were chosen because that area of the lake had the lowest likely points of direct contamination from homes, farms, or manufacturing facilities.

Samples from Howard's Creek were always a bit higher than other areas for nitrogen and phosphate. He assumed that the area also had a slightly elevated eColi bacterial level. Of course he wouldn't know how much eColi for sure for about a day since it would take about that long to grow the bacteria sample. But it was a good educated guess.

Several subdivisions in or near the little town of Lakeview bordered the banks of Howard's Creek. It was more populated than most other water front areas around Bull Shoals Lake and every home along that area was on private septic systems. Since this area was more populated, the septic drainage fields were closer together and the ground was more likely to saturate quickly. Leaks and overflows from septic tanks and drainage fields were more frequent as the homes along the water got older. Although it was late for the normal tourist season, there were multiple private homes with extra guests and the resorts were still being used. All of this added to the saturation of the surrounding land and its inability to control contamination into the lake. Technically, if you swam in Howard's Creek in September you were taking a small chance of getting sick if you accidentally ingested some of the water.

The mass spectrometer was showing a few small spikes for sulfates, sodium and calcium with traces of fluorine, iron and manganese. Nothing remarkable, but still worth recording in his report. Guy was wondering what might have been in those smoke bombs Thayer had mentioned. He decided that he would track that down in the morning and then find a diver to get some further samples at varying depths near the mouth of Howard's Creek.

The results of the River water samples were just coming out of the mass spectrometer and liquid chromatograph. Guy watched the print outs as they were emerging from each piece of equipment. He was seeing the basic expected levels of many minerals, however, he was also seeing traces of sulfur and silica which he hadn't expected. He knew that silica was present in some volcanic rocks and quartz structures. Dacite ash from a volcano or volcanic vent would be highly alkaline and full of silica, but he hadn't seen such material since his post-graduate research at Mount St. Helens. Most likely it was due to the high levels of quartz in the region and perhaps some had started to leach out as a result of the extremely high waters reaching soil and rock that had never been this deeply saturated. He suspected that there could be many reasons for new data considering the floods this past spring.

Water would have washed across farm lands, including poultry and cattle farms, and illegal dumps of all sorts as well as licensed landfills. There were many alluvial fan landslides around the lake which would introduce higher concentrations of various minerals and particulates. It's a wonder the whole ecosystem hadn't turned completely upside down. He remembered seeing photos of the Lake from the spring time showing the massive amounts of floating debris and the pictures of the lake literally turning chocolate brown overnight. Every expert and environmental amateur watching this flood believed the amount of decomposing material on the lake bed would be significantly higher than ever before. He was sure they were right.

The biggest threat could be within the next two years as the decomposing material would make the lowest levels of the deep water dangerously anaerobic, or oxygen deficient. Extremely low oxygen levels near the Dam's penstock inlets could result in poor oxygen levels in the river and hurt the Trout waters below the dam, particularly threatening the spawning areas of the Brown Trout. The Arkansas Game and Fish Commission and numerous unsanctioned environmental groups like the Friends of the White River were watching the dissolved oxygen levels closely.

He believed these levels would become most critical after the lake reached normal pool and the Dam's discharge was reduced back to minimum flow. With high water and all the generators open, the water would aerate as it passed through the wicket gates and turbines. This aeration would keep the river oxygenated near the Dam.

Guy started his laptop to check his email and send his preliminary report to his secretary. She would know which departments would need his data and exactly what to do. He added a note to let her know to send the data to his counterpart at the United States Geological Service. He knew the USGS would be interested in the silica levels and that they would have the best data showing locations of old mines in the region that could possibly leach out these soluble levels of minerals. There's a chance that some of the old mines still had blast and drilling materials that were now washing into the lake from somewhere within the six thousand square mile catch basin surrounding this huge Lake. There may never be any way to determine a source, but he would rather have someone else helping rather than never asking the question. It was a simple tried and true tactic for most government employees called covering your ass.

Chapter 9

Guy was up at daylight. He planned to get a couple of hours of fishing in before breakfast and his nine o'clock meeting with Thayer Davis and the press. He wasn't sure how much info he had that was worth sharing. Most folks wouldn't understand the basic science about differential pH levels or the significance of soluble mineral levels that had been found so far. In fact, he wasn't sure if what he had really told any story at all. He decided to stick to the basics. Guy would share the ADEQ's concern for ensuring everything was okay with the quality of the Lake and River. He could share that everything he had seen so far seemed to be within reasonable expected ranges given the massive amounts of rain runoff from the early spring floods and the saturated soils now under water throughout the region. He knew that he could assure everyone that he was working closely with the Arkansas Game and Fish Commission, the Corps of Engineers and local citizen groups as it related to the safety of the water for both humans and fish.

Guy was just putting his gear into the boat that Gaston's Resort had reserved for his professional, as well as personal use when his cell phone rang. He looked to see who was calling and then answered. It was Thayer Davis.

"Mornin' Guy, I hope I didn't wake you? There's something I think we both need to see."

"Actually, I was just getting ready to do some research in the River when the phone rang. Where do you need me to meet you?"

"Meet me at Jerry's office at the boat dock in twenty minutes."

"I'll see you there."

Guy was disappointed that he wasn't going to get out and do a little early trout fishing, but Thayer's call seemed urgent enough. The fishing would wait a while. He left his gear in the boat and walked up the steep stairs from the dock to the resort office. He let the attendant know that he would be out for a while and that he would be back for the gear in the boat later. He grabbed a courtesy cup of coffee and fresh cinnamon roll and headed out the door to his waiting Suburban.

It only took about twelve minutes to get from Gaston's to the Bull Shoals Lake Boat Dock. It was a little over six miles. No traffic, no lights, a fairly good road and beautiful scenery. It just didn't seem real. Sure, he thought the town could use a facelift and some improving. But why do anything that might cause it to lose the quiet charm it had. The signs were old; most of the buildings were old, except the flower shop and new grocery store. There was no real downtown. Most little towns seemed to have a town square, not Bull Shoals. You enter the town from the east over the Dam and leave town traveling southwest on the same road you came in on. The center of town is loosely defined by the new grocery store. One block south and behind the grocery store was city hall and the police department, neither one on the main road. The prettiest part of town, he thought, was near the Dam and it belonged to the State. The new visitor's center overlooking the Lake, the Dam and the White River was named the James A. Gaston Visitor Center. A gorgeous facility with meeting rooms, theater, museum and natural history displays, souvenir store, offices and other facilities for visitors and State park employees.

Guy arrived at the boat dock and parked his Suburban next to the boat shop and walked to the floating walkways that led out to the dock office. Parking was limited since the water was so high. The floating walkways were nearly reaching the back of the boat shop anyway. As he walked out across the water he realized just how flooded everything was. The propane tank serving the boat dock would be floating on one end if it hadn't been chained down. There were electrical service cables running in along the walkway since the service poles were almost all under water. Every picnic table was under water and there was no visible sign of a boat ramp anywhere.

FRACKED!

He was amused to see that the local school of pet Carp wasn't lost in the high water. They had adapted well. They swam lazily around in the water below the entrance area to the boat dock store waiting for their usual hand outs. It had been going on for years. Bags of food were available for twenty-five cents inside the store. In fact, the bags had been twenty-five cents for as long as he or anyone else could remember. Moms and Dads from everywhere would buy each child a bag and send them out of the store to feed the fish while the business of renting boats was completed. These Carp were enormous and always seemed hungry.

When he entered the store he saw Thayer and Jerry already talking at a table over by the food service area. He said a quick "Howdy" to both men and then sat down to listen. Jerry was explaining to Thayer that there had been a couple of landslides on the Lake reported by some fisherman who had gone out to fish before dark last night. He had the locations marked on a GPS unit and wanted Thayer and Guy to see them. Guy knew that small landslides weren't uncommon around the Lake, particularly during heavy rains. He wondered why these were getting so much attention.

Thayer explained to Jerry that he and Guy needed to be back before nine o'clock because of a press conference. Jerry assured them it would take less than an hour to run out to these slides, look around and then get back.

The three men loaded into Jerry's waiting boat and headed to the first spot which was about half way up Noe Creek. This area was a sparsely populated part of the township known as Promised Land. As they got closer they could tell this landslide was significantly different than the normal little slides that occurred occasionally around the Lake.

It appeared that a section which had been a five hundred yard long sheer limestone bluff had split open by about a hundred yards and the land behind the rock liquefied and slid into Noe Creek. The creek channel was now about half as wide as it had been. The other strange issue was that there was evidence of what must have been a barn above the bluff, but it appeared that the barn was now buried in the soil and only part of the roof was clearly visible. All three men were speechless at this point.

Jerry turned the boat and headed back to the main channel. He went north and then turned into Barne's Bay. He drove the boat all the way to the back of the Bay to the raised road bed that accessed Ozark Isle Recreation Area. If it wasn't for the raised road bed, Ozark Isle would only be accessible by boat, even during normal water levels. As he reached the back of the Bay the men could see that part of the rock bed had slid away and there was now a five to seven foot gap in the road way. The guard rails along the roads edge had sheered and were jaggedly hanging along the same gap. This was an engineered rock road bed that shouldn't be able to slide like other land. Something was seriously wrong somewhere.

The men were quiet on the way back to the boat dock. It had only taken about forty-five minutes to make this tour. There was still plenty of time to make it to the press conference. Guy and Thayer agreed that they would not discuss the landslides this morning with the press. They just didn't have enough information to fill in any questions that they were sure would come up. Jerry was on their side with this and he wouldn't share any info until he was told he could. Guy and Thayer agreed to call the USGS and fill them in as soon as the press conference was over.

Chapter 10

Guy followed Thayer back to the powerhouse entrance at the Dam. They parked and walked together to meet with the Press. Neither of them talked about what they had seen. Both of them knew they would be talking about it after the press conference.

Thayer had prepared a statement for the press, "Good morning, I'm Thayer Davis, manager of the field office for the U.S. Army Corps of Engineers in Mountain Home. This is Guy Fredricks the Director of the Arkansas Department of Environmental Quality from Little Rock. We have been investigating some events surrounding two recent accidents on the Lake and multiple reports of sightings of strange fog and odors in different areas. We believe that there is a connection between the fog and the accidents although we haven't discovered anything conclusive at this point. I'm sure that you have already been briefed by Sheriff Johnson from Baxter County about the boating accident and the condition of the boaters. He is also pursuing information and getting statements from citizens concerning the fog and odors reported particularly in the Howard's Creek area.

Our preliminary analysis of water indicates nothing specifically out of normal ranges. The water is safe for recreation, power generation and to convert to drinking water. There is no indication of any harm to animals or fish in or around the areas where the fog or odors were reported. Our investigation is ongoing and we will give you more information if it becomes available. We are working with both the Baxter and Marion counties Sheriffs and have passed some preliminary water analysis data to the United States Geological Survey to assist us in determining if there are any changes in our huge water shed and catch basin area that could account for these anomalies.

I want to assure the public that we are working diligently to discover what, if anything has happened and that our primary concern remains with the security of the Dam and safety of our population. If you have any questions we will be happy to try and answer them."

There were only two questions. A staff reported from the Mountain Home daily paper, the Baxter Bulletin asked, "Have you determined what might have caused fog and odors?"

"No, I'm sorry we haven't yet. We are collecting information and hope to know something soon."

The other question was directed at Guy by a reporter from KY3 TV out of Springfield, Missouri. She asked, "Mr. Fredricks, is there any reason to believe that these occurrences will affect our trout population in the River?"

Guy wasn't anxious to talk yet, but he was glad to answer such a simple question with a simple answer, "No, the trout are fine. I did some preliminary water analyses last night and the condition of the River water is still as pristine as ever."

The press conference was over. No hoopla, the members of the press simply said thanks and walked away after a few handshakes and pleasantries were exchanged. It was obvious that Thayer was respected in this area. He had always been very straight forward and plain spoken with the press. He had never tried to avoid them or baffle them. The press members were escorted to the Visitor's exit and then they left.

Thayer and Guy headed directly to the Powerhouse Operations Control Room. They each helped themselves to a cup a coffee. Coffee was always available in the Control Room. They sat quietly at one of the small conference tables in the middle of the room and started to discuss what they had seen on the Lake. Both men had already agreed that they needed the USGS to get involved. Thayer phoned his supervisor at the Little Rock District Office of the Corps of Engineers to brief him on what they saw and then called Dr. Ben Owens the Director of the USGS Central Region in Lakewood, Colorado.

"Dr. Owens, this is Thayer Davis with Army Corps of Engineers in Mountain Home, Arkansas. I hate to bother you;

however, I've got a couple of geological anomalies at Bull Shoals Lake that you need to know about."

"Hello, Thayer. I remember you from a meeting in D.C. about two years ago. We were at a conference put on by the EPA concerning ground water pollution and control. How are you?"

"I'm fine, but we're concerned about a couple of very unusual landslides that occurred sometime yesterday evening before dark."

Thayer described what he had seen and the facts concerning small pressure spikes on the Dam inlets. In fact, he was handed this morning's readings while he was still on the phone. The pressures spiked again about the same general time they believed the slides had occurred. He also passed on information about the fog and odors, and trace minerals like sulfur and silica that they were investigating. Thayer was afraid that mentioning the fog and odors might sound too much like a bad episode of some ghost hunting TV show, but he let it all out anyway. He described the boat accidents, particularly the one concerning the houseboat that was apparently lifted and dropped back on the water in the middle of one of these fog areas.

He wanted the USGS to commit resources to help investigate the landslides which was already in their job description and mission statement. Any other help they could bring would be a bonus at this point. Dr. Owens agreed to send a small team out to research the slides and asked Thayer to make sure the Corps of Engineers and local

Sheriff secured those areas to keep out unauthorized visitors. Thayer agreed to secure the areas and would call Sheriff Wilson and Sheriff Johnson for help as soon as he got off the current phone call. Thayer thanked Dr. Owens and assured him that he would send an email as soon as possible with details for the USGS team to use to contact his office and others when they arrived in the area.

Guy was more than a little interested at this point about the landslides. He had studied and taught geology for years, he understood this kind of stuff and really enjoyed what the rocks would tell him. He knew what the USGS investigators would do and wished he could assist. As reality slowly came back into focus for him, he knew he would remain on what caused the odor and fog.

Guy had a quick thought and suggested, "Perhaps we should plan to have daily meetings until this thing is settled. You, me and the USGS rep ought to meet daily at about seven o'clock in the evening. What do you think Thayer?" Thayer quickly agreed and then turned his attention to the pressure spike data.

The pressure spike had grown this time. It was on the statistical edge of what the Corps believed was within normal limits. Thayer didn't like it, he wanted answers. His boss would want answers. The next step, if there was another spike and if it were to go outside normal, would be full core inspection of the Dam's lake side face. Basically, the tests would use a ground penetrating radar to scan

74

the concrete and steel internal composition of the Dam to check for structural problems. That would mean lots of money and lots of time.

Guy called his office and had his secretary put in a call to the Governor's Executive Assistant. He wanted the Governor to know what they were doing. He made sure they had his cell phone number. He expected the Governor would call him directly as soon as he was able. Guy's next call was to ALS Technologies. He needed the technical data for the stink grenades.

Chapter 11

Guy was able to reach the CEO's secretary at ALS Technologies right away. He explained a little about what he was doing in town. He only talked about the odor and fog at this point, no need to give her too much information, so he asked if she could put him in touch with someone who could help him. She immediately passed the call in to her boss, the CEO Jack Simms.

"Mr. Fredricks, this is Jack Simms. How can I help you?" Mr. Simms seemed cordial and curious.

"Mr. Simms, thanks for taking my call. As I explained to the secretary, I'm investigating a bit of a mystery concerning some strange fog and associated odors on the lake a couple of nights ago. I did some analysis of the water in the areas of the reports, nothing very conclusive I'm afraid. I know that Sheriff Johnson has already checked to see if you had any stink grenades go missing. He felt that they might be capable of creating the occurrences." Guy was deliberate and sincere.

"I told Sheriff Johnson that we haven't missed any grenades that I'm aware of. The Sheriff mentioned that you might need to know what we put in them. I'll get my technical expert to give you a call." Simms had nothing to hide and even if the grenades had been used, there was nothing illegal about setting them off in unpopulated areas.

"That would be great. They can reach me on my cell phone…" Guy went on to give him the cell number but he really didn't think there was much about the stink grenades that would really help at this point. They certainly couldn't be blamed for the landslides, but he would pursue it anyway. Better to know too much than not enough he thought.

Guy headed back to Gaston's Resort. As he was driving, he thought about needing to pick up his gear from the boat and putting it away and the fishing that he was missing. Lost in his thought, he was startled when his cell phone rang within a mile of leaving the Powerhouse. It was the Governor.

Guy quickly summarized what had occurred so far. He explained what was being done and who had been contacted so far. He wanted the Governor to know that he had agreed to call the USGS, a federal agency, to assist. Having more agencies usually meant more bureaucratic tangles and there would be issues with jurisdiction. Guy stayed calm with the Governor and shared his belief concerning who had jurisdiction. This was a federal problem so far. If whatever was happening started polluting the lake or river with methyl-ethyl bad stuff, his favorite catchall name for harmful chemicals, then he would share jurisdiction. For now, he was an assistant and he was okay with that. The Governor knew if things escalated with landslides it would be joint jurisdiction.

Guy had just walked down the steep concrete stairs below Gaston's Restaurant to the boat dock on the River when his cell phone rang again. His caller I.D. showed that it was the number he had dialed a couple of minutes ago to reach ALS Technologies. The caller was Jenny Simpson, manager of the manufacturing facilities for ALS. Jenny explained that she was at the corporate offices and just about to head back to her facility near Fairview, south of Bull Shoals when her boss hollered at her when she neared the main door. Guy thought perhaps a quick drive over to Fairview would be a good distraction. He had nothing to do for now. He was waiting for the USGS people to arrive before he could start sampling water near the landslides and he still needed the deep water samples from Howard's Creek. He asked Jenny if he could meet her at her facilities after lunch. She agreed.

Guy finally put his attention back on getting his fishing gear from the boat. He stood there and stared at the gear and boat for a moment and realized his fishing might have to wait for another day. He climbed into the boat to pick up his rods and tackle. As he stepped out of the boat and back on to the dock he happened to notice a strange thin grayish stream in the water under the dock. It looked like a thin line of smoke wafting from a chimney on a cold morning in winter.

FRACKED!

He thought it could be any number of things. Usually a riffle in the water caused by a disturbance up stream would show a sediment flow. He knew that most sediment flows were usually brownish or red like the surrounding clay soils. This line was clearly grayish tan, almost the color of ash from a fireplace. He decided to get a sample of the water.

There was an empty plastic Coke bottle in the boat, it would have to do for now. He cut the top third of the plastic bottle off and used the bottom to scoop out a sample. He was satisfied that he had a fair sample of the colored water so he headed back to his cabin without delay. His fishing gear would have to wait, again.

Guy prepared three samples using the water he now held in the Coke bottle. The pH was quickly checked with a quick test strip, it was surprisingly low and in the acidic range. This was a significant issue and could affect trout. The good news was that it was a thin ribbon of water and would probably dissipate easily without lowering the pH of the surrounding water. He needed to know where this was coming from. He had about an hour before he would need to meet with Jenny Simpson.

The mass spectrometer was loaded with the new sample and turned on to begin an analysis. Guy headed back to the boat. He intended to make a quick run up River to see if he could find a source for the colored water.

Guy's boat motor started quickly. With a quick flip of the wrist on the outboard, he was out of the dock and heading up River against the current. He maneuvered the boat and stayed close to the east bank of the River and tried to keep his eye on the color stream while he navigated the high water. It didn't take long to find the end of the stream. As soon as he reached the Bulls Shoals-White River Park about two miles upriver the color ended. He slowed and drifted backward until he saw the color again. He knew where the color was coming from, it was Big Spring.

Big Spring is a large underground spring which bubbles up and out of the rock about one-hundred-fifty feet from the edge of the River. The spring has a constant flow year round and streams into the River at a near steady rate. The spring was explored some years ago and the geologists that did the research finally found that the water actually came from Bull Shoals Lake. They conducted several dye tests in the Lake. The idea was to see if the dye would ultimately show up at Big Creek. The source of the spring, as it was discovered, is an underground stream which originates in the Jimmy Creek arm of the Lake. The water drains from Jimmy Creek via an underground cavern running beneath Bull Mountain, then under the river where it finally comes up through the ground and out at Big Spring. Guy knew the history of the spring. It had been one of those trivial, but interesting, geological things that he thought added one more layer of uniqueness to the area.

Another deep water sample would be needed. He would add Jimmy Creek to his list. He let the boat drift back to Gaston's, no hurry at this point. Guy's brain was whirling. The color of the sample reminded him of the injection well water samples from many of the natural gas company drilling and fracturing sites he had recently been reviewing. Fracking and earthquakes to the south and now landslides, pressure spikes at the Dam, slightly unusual minerals in the water, and now a strange color coming out of Big Spring. He decided he was going to find a common thread. Something was seriously wrong, he was sure of it.

Guy decided he would get his fishing gear put up, grab a sandwich and then drive over to the ALS plant in Fairview. He was definitely looking forward to meeting with the folks from the USGS more than some bomb builder. In fact, he hoped there might be a post-graduate doctoral candidate in the USGS group. Guy expected that would be intellectually stimulating and he was anxious to see if there were new techniques or theories that he had somehow missed in his private reading and research.

Chapter 12

Jenny was waiting in the gravel parking lot outside the main building at the ALS manufacturing site a few minutes before one o'clock. She knew to look for a white Suburban with the ADEQ logo on the doors. Jenny was visibly bored. Being the plant manager was a good job and she was needed there, but she was still bored. Most of her workers were pretty good at what they did but she suspected they were generally living below poverty levels, had no vision, and no clue about where they would be or what they would be doing next year and probably thought Social Security was a great retirement plan. Cigarettes and beer were a significant part of their families' budgets and they would think that insurance, of any sort including a government plan, was for rich people. She often wondered what made people so different. She knew it must be hereditary. Jenny perked up once she saw the Suburban pull in.

Guy parked and got out of his vehicle. He did a quick scan of the plant. It wasn't much more than an old house, trailer, pole barn and Quonset hut. There was a rail road tie reinforced dirt bunker on one end and fence around the entire place. The best looking part of the facility was across the road. It was a new looking concrete bunker buried on three sides by pasture dirt and grass. The steel door and blow out vents on the roof of the concrete structure gave away its purpose.

"You must be Mr. Fredricks. I'm Jenny Simpson." She smiled and held out her hand to shake his. Jenny had thought she would be meeting a pudgy, pale, middle aged, office dwelling government bureaucrat. She was pleasantly surprised to see Guy wasn't any of those things. He was about her age and seemed very fit.

"Hi Jenny. Thanks for meeting with me on short notice. Your facility looks different than I expected. I thought it would be something different or bigger." Guy was surprised that Jenny was basically gorgeous. She acted like she didn't know it and he thought that added a bit of girl next door charm that he found very sexy.

"I'm not sure that what I need is really going to be that helpful anymore, but I want cover all my bases. We had reports that someone may have seen and smelled something that resembled your stink grenades being detonated out on the water. A list of ingredients for the grenades will give me something to compare to my water analysis data." He seemed distracted as he explained what he wanted.

"I can give you the ingredient list, but not the quantity or composition of the grenade; that would be a bit of a company secret. I could have just emailed the list to you. Was there something else that you needed?" Jenny could tell he was distracted. "How about a quick tour while my assistant emails the list?" Her offer seemed to fall on the wind, he hesitated a second longer than was comfortable to answer.

"Sure, a tour would be good. Forgive me please, I'm a bit preoccupied. We've had a couple of other weird things pop up over night. There were two landslides across the lake and now I've got some kind of effluent running into the river from an unknown source. I need to get back and start making some calls to find a diver. It looks like I'm definitely going to need some deeper water samples." He felt like he had just overloaded Jenny with his rambling. He didn't have answers yet, and that was clearly bothering him.

"For what it's worth, I got my explosives training in the Navy as an Underwater Demolition Team member. I'm a master diver, hard hat qualified still. Let me help if you don't mind. To tell the truth, I could use a bit of field trip. Don't get me wrong, but basically I'm babysitting here all day. I would love to get out. Besides, I've got an old pontoon boat that I use as my dive platform and plenty of gear that needs to be used." Jenny was clearly excited about the prospect of helping, especially since it wasn't going to involve stealthy incursions into enemy territory with the threat of getting shot.

"Wow. That solves my first problem and takes a load off my 'to-do' list. If you're sure you want to do this I'm not going to say no. It will probably be simple deep water sampling, nothing very tough for

84

someone with your qualifications. How soon can you start?" Guy was pleasantly surprised that she could solve his first problem. He was suddenly overwhelmed with the feeling that he liked the idea of seeing this woman in a skin hugging wet suit as well. Something about her was comfortable for him. He could tell she like being outdoors instead of being penned up in a factory making explosives. Guy suspected she was a bit older than she looked, and he clearly thought she looked great. She seemed savvy, smart and easy to talk to.

Jenny gestured to one of her employees and told him to get the stink grenade ingredients list, what she wanted done with it and where to email it. She pulled her cell phone out of her cargo pants pocket and made a quick call to her boss. She explained that she was going to take the rest of the day off to help the ADEQ Director get some deep water samples and watch to see if the contents of the samples resembled any of the ALS products. She felt it was the prudent thing to do. After all, considering the kind of materials they stored and work with, it was probably a good idea to make a friend in Little Rock. The CEO quickly agreed.

Jenny turned her attention back to Guy quickly and asked how soon he wanted to get out on the water. Guy said he was ready except for some sample bottles. Jenny explained that she needed to get home for a minute to change clothes and pick up her dog, Buck. Buck always went on the dive boat with her. She hoped the dog wouldn't be a problem for Guy, but she wasn't going to ask. Buck was going no matter what.

Guy asked where he should meet her and when. Jenny said she would be at the dock by the time he could get to Gaston's to pick up sample bottles and get back to the boat dock. They agreed to make the quick turn around and meet as soon as possible at dock number three of the Bull Shoals Lake Boat Dock.

Dock three still had a ramp reachable by patrons walking out from shore. This was the only dock not attached to the store and fuel dock that had its own ramp. All of the other docks could only be reached by a shuttle boat. Jenny liked the fact that her dock still gave her independence to come and go. Waiting for someone to shuttle her back and forth was more than her usual patience would allow when she was anxious to get out on the lake.

Jenny drove her Jeep out of the ALS parking area just ahead of Guy. Within just a couple of minutes, she was signaling to turn left into McDonald Meadows where she lived. Guy made a mental note and kept on going toward the other end of town, the Dam and on to Gaston's.

He made it to the room and decided to change into shorts and a t-shirt before heading back. He checked his email. Nothing significant, but he was pleased to see the grenade ingredients had already made it to his inbox. He could save that for later. He pulled the latest water sample results up on the mass spectrometer and printed them out to carry with him. He could see right away that the ingredients resembled something familiar. Something he couldn't believe he should see in this area. "Dacite? Fracking liquids don't migrate this far… do they?" Guy wondered silently.

Guy got back in his Suburban and drove back across the Dam to Bull Shoals Lake Boat Dock. How many times had he been over the Dam today? He didn't care, it was still impressive, and he sincerely loved the view.

Guy parked by the boat shop and made his way to dock number three. He could see that Jenny was already fussing with gear and had several items lain out on the deck of her boat. She was making a mental inventory, professionally inspecting every item, and conducting a nearly religious assembly process. Nothing was overlooked, no detail too small. Jenny was obviously a pro and would never take an unnecessary risk when relying on life saving equipment. Her boat could use a little attention and cleaning, but her diving equipment was immaculate.

Guy gave the courteous call, "Permission to come aboard skipper?" Jenny grinned and said, "Permission granted." Guy stepped aboard and was immediately greeted by the big, wet tongue of Buck. Buck had never met a stranger. He was your friend until you deserved something else. Guy acted like a kid for the first few seconds after being greeted by Buck. He grabbed Buck's head and rubbed him up and down while saying the normal stuff that dogs probably never understood, but clearly loved to hear. "Good dog, you like being rubbed don't you, what's your name you big hound?" Jenny thought Guy sounded like a dog lover. So far, so good. He passed the Buck test.

Guy repeated his thanks for Jenny helping him with the sampling. He went on to explain a little more about the effluent flow he had observed in the River and the fact that it was coming from somewhere between Big Spring and Jimmy Creek. He also talked about the landslides, explaining that the slides typically occurred on alluvial fans which weren't uncommon in this area.

"Alluvial fans", he explained, "were areas where sediments and top soil would wash off and down through valleys in mountains or hills where streams would flow after rains. If there was a particularly heavy rain and the area was already saturated then the land, particularly the land over rock shelves like much of that surrounding Bull Shoals lake, could actually liquefy and flow down the stream into the area of built up sediments or the alluvial fan. If the flow were heavy enough it would push the material and cause a landslide. Sounds kind of geeky doesn't it?"

Jenny had started the outboard motor and was untying the boat all the while that Guy was talking. She was obviously interested, but geology wasn't really her cup of tea. What she found amazing was the sheer power of rain and that over time it could do what several pounds of TNT would do. Jenny asked about the landslides wondering if they would keep happening. After all, the rains had stopped; we were just dealing with high water now. Everything was basically stable as far as she could tell.

Guy was clearly concerned. He went on to explain that he didn't have a good reason for the landslide happening at the road bed in Barne's Bay. It wasn't an alluvial fan. It was man made from limestone rock, it was not expected to move because of rain and above ground hydrologic pressures. Water wouldn't be moving sediments and top soil from this structure. This was something else.

Jenny was just clearing the outer marker buoys of the marina's no wake zone. Guy explained where they needed to go for the deep water samples. She eased the throttle up and headed into the main channel and then took a course toward the mouth of Howard's Creek. Guy was pleased to be on the boat and moving quickly over the water. He felt at home here. Buck was as far front on the boat as he could get and then extended his nose as far into the wind as he could reach. Surely, Buck was guiding the boat.

Chapter 13

Jenny set course for the open part of the main channel. As she cleared Pinehurst Point she turned east. The boat glided past the Marion County Water District intake facility on a private bluff on the south shore overlooking the main lake. As Jenny passed the facility she drove on to the big bluffs near Evergreen Cove.

The big bluffs were sheer limestone cliffs cut out of the mountain eons ago by the flowing waters of the White River before it was dammed. These bluffs held unique formations of multiple ledges under the water. Each ledge was about eight feet below the previous and would jut out just enough to give it a saw tooth appearance. Jenny really enjoyed spear fishing this bluff because the ledges would typically hold plenty of large fish.

During the summer, there would normally be several boats either anchored or tied off from the bluffs during the day. Vacationers would snorkel around the rocks while the more adventurous kids and adults would climb the rock bluffs to varying heights and then either jump or dive off. Jenny knew that more boats and more swimmers would mean more treasure for her later. She was always amused at what she could discover under the bluffs.

Jenny had found all sorts of watches, jewelry, combs, brushes, snorkel sets and coins. She had also found more unusual items. There was the portable barbeque grill, lawn chair, innumerable cans and bottles, pocket knives and even an old gun. The gun had been in the water for decades she imagined. It was covered in algae and a thick layer of rust. Nothing on the old revolver moved anymore. She had tossed the gun back to deeper water for future treasure hunters to find. Of course she sent it to a depth where only an experienced diver would dare go and certainly out of reach of kids doing some simple snorkeling.

The boat cleared the bluffs and Jenny turned north east to make the last two and a half mile run across the largest open part of the lake to the mouth of Howard's Creek. This open water was beautiful but it could also get very wild. West winds could blow down the main channel of the lake and seem to intensify down its sixty-five miles of channel bouncing along every point on the way to the open water. Wind speeds of fifteen miles an hour would feel like thirty and could stir up waves and white caps across the lake making the drive treacherous. In a storm or with winds at twenty five miles an hour the lake could have waves of two or three feet, plenty to capsize small boats and scare the wits out of an unqualified boater.

Jenny handled her boat like a pro. She had been caught out on the lake during sudden pop-up summer thunderstorms and knew how to protect herself. Even though she was capable of taking on the storm, she definitely preferred not to. Always, better safe than sorry out on the water.

Jenny slowed the old boat as she entered the mouth of Howard's Creek. Guy was watching and studying the bank to determine a good spot for his samples. He wasn't surprised that this area seemed more populated than most others. The little town of Lakeview had numerous subdivisions, and all of them seemed to crowd the banks of Howard's Creek to maximize their view of the lake. These houses were as close together as allowable while still maintaining their individual septic system drain fields.

Lakeview didn't have a city sewer system like Bull Shoals. There was some talk about developing a system, but the residents would surely stifle the plan. These residents, much like those in the sister city of Bull Shoals, were predominantly retirees who had moved here from other places. The majority were from Chicago, St. Louis, Green Bay and Detroit. Many of them moved here to get away from big city rules, crowded neighborhoods, ethnic issues and high property taxes. They liked the fact that most other people thought the Ozarks was full of bare-footed hicks resembling something from an Al Capp comic strip and not a place worthy of relocation. This would be their little secret. These immigrants enjoyed watching the Bears or Packers, most were members of various clubs, including the Wisconsin Club. A club for folks who moved from Wisconsin but wanted to be with others from their home state to talk about whatever they thought might have been the good old days.

These transplants would either die here or eventually move back to where their children and grand children lived. But while they were here, no one would raise their taxes or create new government rules without a fight. The sewer system would likely never happen, at least not in Guy's lifetime.

Guy had sent his technicians up here numerous times over the past couple of years obtaining water samples near the shoreline looking for sewage contamination. Likewise, he had them sampling around and near the Bull Shoals sewage treatment plant located at the base of Bull Mountain on the north bank of the White River just below the Dam. The plant was just through a thicket of trees in a beautiful area at the far end of Rivercliff Golf Course's front nine.

A leak or major system failure on this sewage treatment plant could contaminate the entire ecosystem of the River from the nearby spawning grounds all the way to the Mississippi River. Frequent visits and checks would keep city officials and maintenance crews vigilant. It was a small way to remind them that this was more than just a city problem if it should ever fail.

Guy signaled for Jenny to stop the boat. She eased back the throttle to let the boat drift to a stop. As soon as she saw eighty feet on the boat's sonar she hollered at Guy to toss over the anchor. As he was lowering the anchor, Jenny was already getting into her neoprene wetsuit. Guy did a quick double take over his shoulder and quickly realized that he had definitely made the right decision to let Jenny help. Director or not, he was still an all American red-blooded, testosterone pumping man.

Jenny rechecked her equipment as she geared up. Tanks, buoyancy compensator, regulator, dive knife, fins, weight belt, mask, dive computer and mesh bag to carry the sample bottles, she was ready. Guy gave her the sample bottles and helped her clip the mesh bag to the bottom of her weight belt. He told her to get the samples at about sixty-five feet to be sure they were well below the thermocline. She nodded her understanding and then hollered at Buck to get him off the front of the boat. He obediently plodded back and hopped up on the vinyl couch at the back of the boat in the shade of the canopy. Buck knew that when Jenny was diving, he was supposed to guard the boat. Of course he could nap while he was guarding, that was the deal.

Jenny waved and with a little hop she disappeared over the side of the boat into the water. Guy watched her descend for what seemed like a long way until all he could see was bubbles coming from her tank. He decided to call Thayer Davis while Jenny was underwater and he had nothing better to do. Thayer was in his office.

"Thayer, this is Guy. Just thought I would check in with you. I'm out on the lake with a diver getting some deep water samples. I was wondering if we have an ETA on the USGS folks yet?"

"As a matter of fact, we don't know exactly when they'll be here, but they should be here sometime late this evening. I'm glad they're coming, we are still having some strange pressure readings at the Dam." Thayer was still worried that his Dam was showing stress from the record high waters. He wanted the engineers in Little Rock to recalculate everything using up to date and state of the art computer simulations. He was sure that engineers from 1950 were probably off on their load variances. After all, with billions of cubic feet of water straining against this structure in a way that had never been done, anything could happen. The load might seem within normal ranges, but he was worried about the amount of load over such an extended period and its effect relative to time and the age of the structure.

"I'm anxious to meet with them. I used to teach environmental geology, so this will be a good ....." Guy wasn't able to finish his sentence. "Holy shit, you should see this! Bubbles everywhere in front of me, the water looks like it's boiling up from a spring and... whoa, the smell! Thayer, we've definitely got hydrogen sulfide gas coming out of the water. My diver is down there in this. It looks like the bubbles are stopping. I'll call you back in bit." Guy was more than a little rattled by this. There was definitely something wrong.

Buck jumped off his couch and barked just about the time Jenny popped back up to the surface. It had only been about two minutes after the bubbles stopped. She pulled her mask off and then spit out her regulator. She appeared tickled and a little bit giddy. "You won't believe what just happened! I was putting the sample bottles back in the bag and all of a sudden I was surrounded in bubbles and then the bottom just fell out." She took a quick breath, "I did a freefall to the bottom of the lake. I was in about sixty feet and the next thing I know, I'm on my butt at around eighty. The bubbles were coming from everywhere around me and the water suddenly felt like I was in a hot tub. As soon as they stopped I popped back up to about sixty feet. My buoyancy compensator couldn't keep up with the sudden changes. What a rush!" She was almost laughing, until she saw the expression on Guy's face.

"Well obviously you're okay." He was already taking her dive gear up from her as she handed them over the side of the boat. "Something is wrong here, very wrong. We don't normally see huge pockets of gas just release from under water like that. This lake has been here over fifty years; most of the trapped gasses were released early, after initial ground saturation from the early stages of the lake filling." Guy was clearly concerned.

Jenny had climbed back onto the boat and unzipped the front her wetsuit while he was explaining. Guy realized he wasn't enjoying this as much as Jenny had. He realized that if he wasn't the Director

96

of the ADEQ he probably would have been thinking about the unique geological episode rather than the environmental issues. This was clearly not a manmade event. He could regulate municipalities, people and businesses, but he couldn't regulate nature. Whatever was happening wasn't going to change with a citation or court order.

Guy hurriedly hauled in the anchor and asked Jenny to get the boat underway. She was already out of her wetsuit and stowing her gear on a make shift rack at the back of her boat where she could air dry here scuba equipment. Most of it would be completely dry after a run back to the boat dock, especially on a hot September day. Jenny obliged and fired up the motor. Buck quickly took his position on the front of the boat, nose into the wind.

Thayer was still in his office when Guy called him back to finish his conversation. Guy explained what happened from what his diver had described. Thayer was concerned about the gas escape. He knew there were always trapped pockets of gas below the water which would occasionally escape. He also knew that dead and decomposing animal and plant material could create gas. But these were always very small; most of them never seen. Thayer and Guy agreed to meet later in the evening. Guy thought seven-thirty would be good and told Thayer to meet him at the boat dock. Thayer said he would contact the USGS team and have them meet at the boat dock as well. He figured the team would be close by then and that he and Guy could wait there for them if needed.

Chapter 14

The USGS was sending Dr. Ben Owens, the Regional Director who happened to also be their best field geologist from the Denver office. His team, as it turns out, would be a group of two grad school Master's Degree candidates and two post-grad doctoral candidates from the Geology Department at the University of Oklahoma. The Fall semester was already starting at the University and they were only a few hours car drive away when the call was made. They were all excited about field work. Labs were mind numbing, fresh air would be a great way to start their Fall semester.

Dr. Owens looked like Indiana Jones' uncle. Ruddy complexion covered in two week old whiskers. His clothes were clean but eternally wrinkled. He always wore a tie. He blamed his British ancestry for the neck-tie. He kept a pipe clenched in his teeth although he had given up tobacco something like fifteen years before. Dr. Owens would make excuses in his offices and in conference rooms saying the pipe helped him think. He was old enough to merit the respect and attention of younger geologists. When he spoke, however, the respect was instantly earned. He was extremely bright and exceptionally seasoned with years of field experience.

Thayer called Dr. Owens to check on arrival schedules. Dr. Owens would be flying directly into the commuter airport in Harrison, Arkansas by charter. There was already a rental car waiting. He expected to be on the ground by six-thirty that evening. His team wasted no time getting on the road. The kids, as he called them, were in an University of Oklahoma Ford Expedition pulling an eight by fifteen utility trailer loaded with every geological research device they could think of on short notice including, rock hammers, Geiger counters, seismographs, ground penetrating radar, core sample drills, the latest in GPS, surveying lasers and many other toys. They didn't know or care what the mission was, it was a road trip and they wouldn't leave anything behind. The kids weren't inconspicuous either. Their whole rig was painted crimson red and cream with the University logos on all four doors and had the University of Oklahoma mascot, the Sooner Schooner, painted on the sides of the trailer. Quite a sight, especially since it would be driving right through the heart of Arkansas Razorback country.

Dr. Owens gave Thayer the cell number to the team vehicle coming from Oklahoma. He would have to call them to find out where they were and what time they thought they would arrive. A quick call to the crimson and cream Expedition and Thayer found out the kids were already crossing into Springdale on the northwest border of Arkansas. They would be in Bull Shoals by seven-fifteen. Rooms had been reserved at the Lighthouse Resort overlooking the Bull Shoals Lake Boat Dock. They would check in at the resort, drop their personal gear in rooms, park the equipment trailer and be ready to meet the rest of the group. He expected that Dr. Owens would be pulling in about the same time if his flight went well. It was only a fifty minute drive from the Harrison airport to Bull Shoals. Thayer told them to meet him and Guy Fredricks at the Boat Dock office at around seven-thirty. He explained that Guy was the Director of the Arkansas Department of Environmental Quality and that he had already started some preliminary work with water sampling.

Guy had a quick burger and drink at D's Beacon Point with Jenny. While he was treating her to dinner, a small reward for helping him today, he asked if she wanted to tag along and see where this next meeting would lead. It didn't take much to convince her. It was something new that didn't involve making grenades and rubber bullets. She was in! In fact, she offered to help as much as needed, she could use sick days from work if needed. She admitted that she would really be sick if he didn't let her stay on this project. He explained that it might be a bunch of geological tech talk and didn't want her to feel uncomfortable. She reassured him that she was a quick learner and, besides, she had a boat they could use.

Guy and Jenny arrived at the Boat Dock a little early. They checked in with Jerry and asked how the injured fishermen were doing

100

after their accident. He said both were fine and home already. Bill had been hurt the worst. Several broken bones in one arm, one small break in his other arm and lots of abrasions and bruises, only a few deep cuts on his head and back that required any sutures. Jim was mostly sprained from head to toe. Nothing broken. He had more cuts and bruises than Bill though. Mostly to his hands and knees. Bill wouldn't be able to cast a fishing rod for several months. That might be the worst part of the ordeal for him. Jerry wondered and asked Guy if they had found out anything about what was happening on the lake yet?

Guy explained a little about the bubbles they had seen earlier and the colored stream of water he found coming from Big Spring. He also talked about the landslides and what that might mean. He realized that Jerry didn't know yet that the research team would be coming to his dock within the next thirty minutes, so he also explained who was involved and would be helping starting tonight.

Jerry was pleased that this was getting so much attention. He suspected there was more going on than could be explained away by myth or legend. He offered the use of one of his houseboats for the research team. Jerry knew Jenny and could trust her to drive the boat and take care of it and the passengers. "What a great idea," Guy thought. He was extremely grateful and accepted the offer. Of course he also assured Jerry that the Department could reimburse him for the use of the houseboat. Jenny was also tickled by the offer. She had never used one of the houseboats, but had always wondered about living on one full-time. This adventure was getting better and better as far as she was concerned.

Thayer arrived at seven-fifteen and found Guy, Jenny and Jerry sitting at one of the round dinette tables at the snack bar area of the store. Thayer grabbed a Mountain Dew from one of the refrigerators and then paid the attendant at the counter. Guy stood up as soon as he saw Thayer at the counter. He did the quick introduction of Jenny and explained that she was his diver and would also be piloting the houseboat that the team would be using. They sat and started comparing notes from the previous day and a half.

Guy and Thayer agreed that the smells and fogs that had been reported were probably from the same kind of gas release that Guy and Jenny had witnessed. They also speculated that the houseboat which had been damaged was probably lifted and dropped by one of these enormous gas releases. The landslides were still a puzzle. They could kind of understand the loose soil slide on an alluvial fan, but they couldn't figure out the road bed being damaged by a slide. They still had not answered the question concerning the colored water streaming up through Big Spring and what appeared to be volcanic dacite in the samples taken from the site.

Thayer explained that he had asked for more engineering analysis of the Dam to see if the load stress pressures were really out of tolerance. He didn't know if the specs needed to be changed given

102

current engineering practice and technology or if there was really a problem. With this quick list of issues they went ahead and marked up a map of the lake to show where each incident occurred. They had just finished with the map when the University team walked in. They weren't hard to spot, t-shirts with University logos galore.

Thayer introduced everyone at the table to the kids and then they introduced themselves. Lennard was a first year grad student working on a Master's in Petroleum Geology, Kristi was a doctoral candidate with degrees in Geophysics and Geological Engineering, Brad had his Master's in natural gas and was working toward a Doctorate in Petroleum Geology, and his identical twin brother Brett had a Master's in Geology and was working on a second Master's in Geophysics. Lennard and Kristi looked like poster children for the best fraternity and sorority couple on campus. Brad and Brett were the definitive all American pocket protector wearing geeks. Those two would be equally comfortable in a University lab or at a Boy Scout Jamboree. They were very young and very bright.

Thayer and the kids pulled up another table and chairs to join the conversation already in progress. There really wasn't much to share. There certainly wasn't much real data for the kids to start hypothesizing about. They were just gathering around the map, which was now taped to the front of one of the big refrigerators, when Dr. Owens walked in. A quick round of hand shaking and name exchanges and then right back to the map.

It only took Thayer and Guy five minutes to run through what they knew as facts up to this point. They fielded some basic questions from the group about the history of the lake and general data concerning age and composition of the Dam. This group brought every USGS map, fact sheet, data book, survey map and soil morphology report they could gather. If there was such a thing as a geological baseline for the area, they would have it. They already knew more about the geology of the area than anyone around, except perhaps Guy. Guy finally allowed the group a small peak at his academic pedigree. He shared with them that he had a Doctorate in Environmental Geology and that he had been a professor for several years before taking the position at the ADEQ.

The kids suggested setting up seismic monitoring equipment at five locations. Dr. Owens quickly concurred. In fact, he wanted them up now. No time to waste. The group agreed to split up and start right away. Guy suggested using the houseboat to hold the remote monitoring equipment. It would always have electric power, either from a dock side connection, generator or batteries with solar charging backup. The houseboat living room was easily used as a conference room and the dining area would accommodate the myriad of computers and remote monitors.

Chapter 15

The map was marked with the five locations where the seismographic equipment would be placed. Each monitor was equipped with a radio transmitter which would send a signal to a receiver and computer located in the dining area of the houseboat. The first seismograph monitor would be located out on Ozark Isle. This would have to be placed and checked using a boat to get to the point and then walking up the hill. Since the road bed had partly collapsed with the rock slide, this would be the safest option. Monitor number two would be placed at the James A. Gaston Visitor Center on the west side of the Dam. The third would be placed at the Welcome Ridge Volunteer Fire Department building, located almost due west of Ozark Isle on the south side of the main lake channel. They had decided to place two distant monitors, one at Theodosia, Missouri and one at Lead Hill, Arkansas. The team had also managed to use the Boat Dock's wi-fi connection to get a link to the USGS permanent monitoring station in New Madrid, Missouri. This was the closest major fault line and it had frequent small tremors. Dr. Owens had agreed that it might be helpful to know if there was any correlation on an event with those of the New Madrid fault. There had been multiple quakes at New Madrid over the years but nothing seemed to shake this part of the Ozark Mountains with any significance.

As the team took off to grab more of their equipment Thayer decided to get back to his office to email his boss in Little Rock an update before heading home for the night. Guy and Jenny took Dr. Owens in her boat to go place the seismograph at Ozark Isle. The rest of the team headed out to set up the other units. Kristi and Brett took Dr. Owens car and headed to Theodosia and the Visitor Center. Lennard and Brad took the U of O vehicle and headed to Lead Hill and Welcome Ridge. Given the distance to both Lead Hill and Theodosia, Guy figured it would be about eleven-thirty p.m. before the kids finished placing monitors, testing signals and getting back to their resort for the night.

Jenny piloted her boat up the main channel of the lake past Barne's Bay. She slowed and then eased in to an old road bed between some thick trees on the northwest side of Ozark Isle. The boat stopped against the bank. Buck was the first one off. He needed a private moment.

Guy offered to help Dr. Owens with placing the seismograph. He carried the unit up the narrow road to the crest of the hill until Dr. Owens motioned to stop. At this point, Dr. Owens took over. Guy hadn't been around this kind of equipment in a couple of years and was envious of his counterpart's dexterity with the unit. He finished the set up in just a few minutes. These were state of the art field seismographs which had strong, long lasting battery packs, digital transmitter and GPS tracking chips. They would broadcast there exact location and any other data every few minutes. If the unit detected movement, the transmission would be constant until the event ended.

Buck wandered up the hill and inspected the setup. With one quick sniff, he was satisfied that they had accomplished their mission. He looked at Guy as if to say, "What's so tough about this?" Then he turned and jogged down the hill and back to the boat. Jenny hollered at Buck and diverted him to the deck of the boat just before he was prepared to jump into the lake for a quick swim. She really didn't feel like having a wet dog in the boat tonight, not with company riding. She finished tinkering with the equipment she had used earlier in the day and started putting them into their appropriate storage places. She looked up and saw Guy and Dr. Owens walking down the hill.

As Guy was getting back on the boat he couldn't help but remark about the beautiful sunset happening behind them. Everyone agreed. It was magnificent. There was a streak of brilliant yellow on the horizon; on top of this was a layer of light tangerine glowing into a burnt orange with a small scattered layer of gray clouds making beautifully odd shapes against the orange colored sky. You could almost imagine a forest fire raging far into the distance. Above the orange, the grayish clouds seem to blend smoothly into a blue-violet layer and on up to a deep purple. Darkness would be on them within minutes. The half moon was already peaking over the distant hills to the east.

The aluminum pontoons of the boat scraped as Jenny backed away from her temporary berth on the old road. She turned the boat and headed back to the east. In the distance they could already see the Top of the Ozarks tower on Bull Mountain. It was lit up as usual and was a great landmark for night time boaters. The tower was originally an oil derrick. It had been purchased by one of the town's early businessmen from a company in west Texas. The tower was dissembled in Texas and reassembled at its present location. There was a tourist shop built at the base of the tower and an elevator to take folks to the top observation deck. From the top you could see for hundreds of miles in all directions.

As the boat slid across the glassy calm lake Jenny was the first to comment that the air temperature was dropping quickly. Late September was a favorite time for locals. You could enjoy the sun and warmth during the day and then take a dip in the lake at night when the water temperature would be higher than the surrounding air. It was a wonderful treat. The cool evenings were always considered the early sign that autumn was just around the corner. They were all beginning to notice that the ride back was certainly a bit cooler than they had expected.

As the boat cruised the main channel Dr. Owens and Guy were engaged in what appeared to be a geological game of Jeopardy. One would state an observation and the other would state a possible reason for the occurrence in the form of a question.

"Massive gas bubbles and the smell of hydrogen sulfide," pondered Guy.

"What can be caused by a large pocket of decomposing material opening up from deep under the water?" Dr. Owens asked.

"Fog and light was seen, some people reported the smell. These happened over unseen bubbles at night," Guy was stating facts and filling in the blanks. Witnesses at night had seen fog and lights, they couldn't see bubbles. He suspected that was because of the darkness, the fog and confusing light.

"If the outside air had cooled then, like it is now, the fog was clearly formed from warm water and heated bubbles coming from the bottom. Jenny described the water as being like a hot tub. The lights, well, that's a bit more confusing. We don't have enough evidence yet for good speculation on this. It was probably just moonlight reflecting on the fog." Dr. Owens didn't want to go too far with the speculation. He knew from experience that too much speculation was more akin to telling ghost stories. You could stir up emotion but not have anything meaningful to prove from research. He hated wasting emotion.

Guy and Dr. Owens agreed that what had happened over the last couple of days could be the result of deep ground saturation by flood waters. The pressure of the water in deep parts of the lake was now nearly three atmospheres greater than normal. That much water weight could make the bottom of the lake do strange things. They also considered the possible reach of injection well pressurized fracturing fluids from natural gas drilling that was happening many miles south of their current location.

Jenny made the turn south past Frost Point and pointed the boat at the gap near Jimmy Creek island and on toward the marina. Passing Frost Point brought an additional chill to Jenny. She shined a spot light over to the rocks and could still see pieces of the destroyed bass boat. Guy pointed at the debris and told Dr. Owens a short story about the wreck and that it was the first occurrence of what they were now investigating.

They were quiet the remaining five minutes of the ride back into Jenny's slip at the marina. With the boat tied up and gear stowed, the three made plans to meet at the Village Wheel for breakfast with the entire group at seven in the morning. With that, they departed and went in separate directions. Dr. Owens decided to go to the houseboat to check his computers and to see if his seismograph was transmitting okay. Afterwards, he would walk up the hill from the marina and two blocks over to Lighthouse Point and his room at the resort.

Guy had almost forgotten about his water samples. He ran them through the spectrometer as soon as he returned to his room. He also re-verified the results of the sample he had taken from the gray stream at Big Spring. He did a quick check of the mineral profile and

110

was now more certain than ever that it was consistent with dacite. He watched the current sample impatiently and started thinking out loud. "If this is dacite, it had to come from a volcanic source. There are no active or dead volcanoes for hundreds and hundreds of miles. It has to be prehistoric." Guy decided he would take all of his water analysis print outs to the morning meeting.

During his doctoral program, Guy had been given the opportunity to travel and do research around a lake formed in a volcanic caldera formerly thought extinct. He was beginning to put several pieces together in his mind about this previous experience and didn't like the picture that he was forming. He was certain this couldn't be the same kind of event. After all, they were nowhere near a volcano.

Chapter 16

In January about fifteen years ago, Guy had been on a research expedition at the Karymsky volcano in Kamchatka. There had been an eruption early in the month which had been preceded by quite an uptick in seismic activity. Seismic activity grew throughout the year before prompting Russian volcanologists to make some threatening forecasts that an eruption would most probably occur. Just two days prior to the eruption, in the early evening, an earthquake with a magnitude of five point eight on the Richter scale occurred in the Kronotsky gulf about forty miles northeast of the volcano. The next day, just over twenty-four hours from the last earthquake, a quake measuring five point two was felt in the Karymsky volcano area. This quake was followed within an hour with another, larger quake occurring at a remote monitoring post about twenty miles south of volcano. Over the next two days there were more than ten earthquakes measuring over five point one. The largest quake was six point nine at what was believed to be the epicenter near the volcano.

FRACKED!

Karymsky Lake, which filled the caldera of the volcano, showed the first sign of an eruption. The eruption began with the formation of a vent with a diameter of approximately fifteen to twenty feet that was located nearly one-hundred twenty feet below the surface of the lake. There were reportedly very violent expulsions of gas filled with ash. These gas releases would raise to almost three feet over the surface of the water and release steam into the air with visible ash rising to almost three feet above the bubbles. Steam and hydrogen sulfide gas jets were noticeable. They contained black and gray colored matter and were pushed into the air from what was estimated to be several hundred feet from beneath the water of Karymsky Lake.

The center of seismic activity was calculated to be approximately four hundred feet from the shore of the northwest part of the lake. As the activity intensified, there were violent steam and gas releases rising several thousand feet above the water surface. The gas vent was approximately five hundred feet in diameter at this point. The winter ice covering the lake had entirely melted by now. Within the next forty-eight hours the eruption of the Karymsky volcano increased. Two eruptive vents had been formed. One on the summit of the volcanic crater forming the lake and another on the southwest slope. There were frequent ash explosions from these vents. Gas, steam and ash would erupt from the vents with enormous force. These events lasted only a few minutes and then the gas and ash would drift on the wind toward the southeast and on to the ocean. The surface of Karymsky Lake steamed like a Yellowstone hot spring. Clouds of steam rose several hundred feet above the surface of the lake. The surrounding air temperature was typically near zero this time of year, so the fog created by the warm lake was eerily beautiful.

The lake was changing rapidly. A newly formed black volcanic ash beach was visible on one side of the lake. In the northeastern part of the lake a narrow spit of land was beginning to form. What had been the lake's natural inlet, the Karymsky River now had a naturally forming dam that extended for several hundred feet to the center of the lake. There was a noticeable drop in the water level. Within just a few hours the level had receded by about six feet and the upper reaches of the river were also drying up. The volcanologists assumed that the water was falling into a newly formed vent and were bypassing the lake. There were also waves created in the lake from the underwater eruptions. These waves could get up to twenty feet high before spilling over the north shore. These huge waves would eject massive amounts of water down the mountain and flood the valley below.

The vents that developed during this period seemed to follow a well documented fault zone. There were now thousands of volcanic funnels with diameters ranging from a few inches to several feet. These were created by intense material ejections around the lake. Areas to the southeast were rapidly being buried by ash, tons of it in fact. The ash was of a light gray color and was dacite in composition. Guy remembered that dacite had a very similar mineral makeup to that of his sample. It was composed mainly of quartz, lime, silica, and sulfur dioxide.

The temperature of water in the lake rose abruptly and a huge fish kill occurred. There was nothing that could be done. This was a natural disaster and fish were only part of the sacrifice. A portion of the lake's shoreline about five hundred feet long and forty feet wide east of the river entrance to the upper lake sank and disappeared into water. Results of air inspections showed drastic changes around the shoreline of the lake and all the while, the level of the water continued to fall, probably due to intense evaporation.

The landscape was inescapably changed forever. Guy remembered thinking that this area seemed to look like the downhill side of Mount St. Helens after that eruption, without the trees of course. There was a river of ash for as far as he could see. Yet the new hot spring created by the death of the lake was strangely beautiful. The virgin landscape around the lake was changing shapes by the hour and he suspected that the best was yet to come. Guy often wondered about his study of geology and the fact that the geological clock could almost be reset by volcanic activity. Since the earliest beliefs about the Earth's formation revolved around molten formations prior to the oceans and then volcanic activities forming mountains and continents, Guy believed that a new volcanic eruption was like resetting the clock for the region. Something new was born and now laid over the old.

Chapter 17

The morning light seemed to stab through the curtains as Guy readied himself for his breakfast meeting with the USGS team, Thayer and Jenny. He couldn't help think about Jenny's face as she broke through the surface of the water after scuba diving through the bubble storm. He was also probably a bit more anxious to see Jenny than he thought he should be from a purely professional standpoint.

The Village Wheel wasn't busy this morning. In fact, it seemed there were no vacationers in the restaurant. Guy arrived several minutes early only to find that Thayer Davis was already at a table and on his second cup of coffee. Guy knew Thayer was worried, it seems he was right, and it was getting worse.

"Mornin' Thayer, can I join you?" Guy was pleasant enough, almost cheery Thayer thought.

"Sure, sit down. I haven't seen Dr. Owens or his kids yet, have you?"

"I'm sure they'll be here shortly... listen, Thayer, before the others get here, I need to tell you about one of my water samples. It's the only one that really bothers me, and it's not from the lake. I took a sample from Big Creek, over at the state park. It contains dacite, a mineral combination we usually only see from volcanoes. I know that sounds bizarre, but I'm going to have to share this with the USGS team. I've already arranged for samples to be retested and confirmed by my labs in Little Rock. But I'm positive the results are accurate." Guy was concerned and a bit confused as he told Thayer about his findings.

"Dacite? Volcanoes? Guy, what the hell are you saying? Have we got a Mount St. Helens starting up here?" Thayer was getting a little loud. He obviously had a lot on his mind and this wasn't helping him. "You know, this area was shaken in the early 1800's by a large earthquake which occurred along the New Madrid fault. That fault is still active. Maybe we're just seeing the results of some earthquake activity."

Guy looked around and realized no one was close enough to hear much of Thayer's comment. He held up a hand as if to hush Thayer and said, "Don't panic, that's not what I'm saying. But we've got something geological happening here. Personally, I hope it just quits. Maybe the gas bubbles will run out and the landslides will stop on their own. But I think I have to share this with the USGS team.

Hopefully, they will have all the reasons why this is probably nothing to worry about."

Dr. Owens and his team came through the restaurant door right on time. The hostess just missed them as they paraded past the main dining area and back to the tables that were occupied by Guy and Thayer. The kids were obviously hungry and in a hurry. Guy had almost forgotten how impatient he had been as a student. He was always anxious to learn something new and to make exciting new discoveries. How could something as mundane as meals get in their way?

A quick round of good mornings happened simultaneously with sloshing of coffee into mugs all around and a flurry of orders for food thrown out to the extremely patient waitress. There were no concerns about trans-fatty acids, or low-density lipids, or calories for that fact. The kids were hungry and it was a long time until lunch. Guy had ordered a rather large breakfast himself. Truth be known, it was his favorite meal of the day.

The waitress rushed the order back to the kitchen just before Jenny came through the restaurant's main dining room. She said "Howdy y'all" to the group and pulled up a seat and sat next to Guy. He waived for the waitress and Jenny stopped him, explaining that she had already eaten. In fact, she had added that she had already had a quick four mile run and then breakfast consisting of a large bowl of fresh fruit, yogurt, walnuts, all sprinkled with a few flax seeds. She

118

only wanted a cup of coffee and a glass of water for now. Guy's amazement of Jenny seemed to grow a little more.

Dr. Owens told the group that he had made a quick trip to the houseboat and checked the monitoring of all the seismographs and was pleased that all sites were reporting without difficulty. He laid out the plan for his team quickly and efficiently. He would take them to each of the landslide areas and conduct various tests, collect samples, get photos, and survey the slides and surrounding landscape. He asked Jenny if she could drive the houseboat to each location to transport the team and equipment. Jenny anxiously agreed. Dr. Owens also asked if Thayer thought it would be permissible for them to take two small ATVs on the house boat to use on the Corps of Engineers property surrounding the lake. Thayer assured him this would be fine, as long as the houseboat could accommodate the ATVs. Thayer made a cell phone call to Jerry at the marina office and asked Jerry for help. Thayer was told that they could modify the houseboat's bow deck area and guard rails anyway needed to accommodate their gear.

Guy shared his findings about the Big Spring water sample and the dacite content with the group. They were all instantly sure there was probably a mistake. They concurred that there was no way a volcano could be causing any of this and that there had been similar samples found in several natural hot springs at Yellowstone and everyone knew that there was very little mineral concentration in the forty-seven hot springs around Hot Springs, Arkansas. It had to be an anomaly, perhaps prehistoric volcanic matter leaching into the water as Guy had thought. Definitely not volcanic.

Guy also explained, with Thayer's help, that witnesses had seen lights at night around what he was now calling "bubble storms". The team looked a bit puzzled for a moment and when Brad, one of the twins, said "Maybe it was Tesla lightning, you know static electricity. If there was any Earth movement under the water, maybe it created a static charge which was seen as it became airborne." The group looked at him like he was from Mars for a moment, and then almost nonchalantly, nodded in agreement. The students were easy, they could believe almost anything. They hadn't yet been hardened by real world failures where theory and practice were governed too often by profit motives. Quite frankly, the best answer, albeit not the one anyone considered technical enough, was that it was reflections of moonlight. If the twins were right, then there would have to be some seismic explanations for what was happening.

Thayer was clearly the most nervous person at the table. He told the group to keep him informed of all their findings as soon as they knew anything. He explained that the pressure readings on the Dam had increased again for the third day in a row and were now outside of so called normal. His District boss was in the process of briefing the U.S. Army Corps of Engineers headquarters staff in Washington D.C. via teleconference this morning. Thayer feared that a bureaucratic storm was getting ready to land on the Bull Shoals Lake Dam.

The group finished breakfast and headed out. Thayer was going to the Dam Operations Center and planned to get an update about what his boss had discovered in his teleconference with D.C. Guy, Jenny and the USGS team headed for the marina and the waiting houseboat. Dr. Owens made a quick call to a local ATV dealer and had two used ATVs scheduled to be delivered later in the morning.

Within minutes of arriving at the houseboat the twins were on the bow and making plans for modifications. They borrowed a welding unit from the boat shop and helped themselves to one of the several metal ramps laying around unused. Since the flood waters rose, the ramps couldn't be used on each of the various boat docks, so this was a good use in the mean time. After cutting out about six feet of life railing from the center of the bow, they mounted to crude brackets which would accept one end of the ramp. With two large cotter pins, the ramp was mounted. They mounted a small pulley on the bow canopy and with a length of rope they had rigged a convenient draw bridge style landing ramp for the ATVs.

While the rest of the kids began checking monitors and loading additional equipment for their expedition, Jenny loaded diving gear. Her dog, Buck, was happily following her from dock to dock as she carried various items from her pontoon boat over to the houseboat. He had waited patiently in the Jeep outside the Village Wheel while she met with the group. Now that she was on the docks, Buck knew he was needed, constantly guiding her from dock to dock. Of course the occasional stop to bark at the ducks was his little reminder to Jenny about his genetic makeup.

Guy sat in the houseboat dining area with Dr. Owens while the crew was busy with gear. They had pulled out a large USGS sectional map of the area. It showed elevations and was color coded to show the Ozarks Plateau Aquifer system. They also had an overlay map that showed the location of mapped or known caves and caverns in the surrounding the area. Dr. Owens had commented that the entire forty or fifty mile wide band of the northern part of the state was literally peppered with the aquifer system and that it was unique compared to other parts of the country. The limestone substrate was literally honeycombed by caves, caverns and aquifers. He also commented that having such a honeycomb on the edge of the New Madrid fault zone seemed a bit ominous. "Ominous indeed," Guy thought as he absorbed this refresher in geological formations.

Guy added some additional geological primer by reminding Dr. Owens that the area was once a bustling mining region boasting numerous Lead and Zinc mines and that there are literally hundreds of caves, caverns, and mines throughout the hills surrounding the lake. He explained that one of the largest privately owned commercially operated Caverns is located in the 1890's Mountain Village, a tourist attraction in the city limits of Bull Shoals and that within a seventy-

122

five mile radius there are over four hundred caves with the largest, Blanchard Springs Cavern designated as a National Park hosting year round tours.

Dr. Owens explained how the seismographic equipment would work for them. Since they didn't have the benefit of long term monitoring to establish the normal thresholds for real earthquake monitoring, these units were being used as ground movement detectors. They should show high levels of earth noise if there were any significant ground changes in the area. A landslide, sinkhole, or cave-in of a cavern would show up as noise above background. This would help them determine times and relative magnitudes of any event that may be monitored.

Guy's cell phone rang, it was Thayer. "Guy, hey, its Thayer, I just wanted to let you know that my headquarters has decided to send their top people in Dam construction, engineering, and hydrology. They are already on their way. The General's staff at the Army Corps Headquarters put them on a transport jet. They should be here by three this afternoon. I have to pick them up at the Mountain Home airport. They have rooms at Gaston's and should be working within about an hour of touch down. Give me a call around four o'clock and we'll catch up."

The ATVs arrived shortly after the twins finished their customization of the houseboat bow. They had found a little extra paint in the boat dock maintenance closet and managed to paint the ramp to look like a small road. Mostly black, with a yellow line down the middle and a white line on each side. It was sloppy, but it covered the welding and cutting slag and might keep the rig from rusting for a day or two. The twins lowered their ramp, ran down to get the ATVs, and drove them up and around the main dock, across their freshly painted ramp and onto the houseboat. They were clearly pleased with themselves, high fiving each other as they got off the ATVs.

With Guy's assistance on line handling duty, Jenny maneuvered the sixty foot house boat away from the dock, made a backward u-turn and then headed out of the marina area. She was extremely pleased with how this large boat handled. It had two outboard motors, one on each side of the stern that could be operated independently or together. It made the task of making tight turns reasonably easy given the size of the houseboat. The small helm area was inside the main deck cabin. It was outfitted with enough gauges to know the status of the motors, auxiliary generators, fuel tanks, water tanks and sewage tank. There was a master electrical panel which controlled every exterior light on the boat and showed a status of all batteries. A two-way radio was installed above the helm area which was the main way to communicate with the boat dock. There was also a ten inch wide GPS unit gimble mounted above and just to the right of the steering wheel. Jenny thought she could get spoiled with this setup, but kept it to herself as she smiled and steered the giant boat out into the main lake channel.

Guy and Dr. Owens had decided to visit the sight of the landslide in Noe Creek first. Guy hollered over at Jenny and told her where to head, she happily nodded her understanding and made a small course change to give them a straighter line to the mouth of Noe Creek. As the boat was turning into the creek channel, one of the kids at the computer station who had been watching the seismograph monitors started hollering, "Dr. Owens, you might want to see this, we've got a noise spike on station number one. That's the one at the Dam's visitor center!"

Chapter 18

Guy was on his cell phone half a second after hearing that the seismograph had recorded something at the Dam and was dialing Thayer Davis. "Thayer, everything okay?"

Thayer wasn't in the mood for idle conversation, "Yeah, Guy. Why?"

"There was a spike in noise on the seismograph that was installed at the Visitor's Center. It was fairly significant; did you or anyone feel any unusual vibrations or movements?" Guy was trying not to sound condescending.

"Not down here. We only feel major vibrations when generators fail or when we open and close spill ways. We haven't had either event today. What do think it is?" Thayer was showing signs of nervousness again.

"Well, we don't know. Something made the noise. If it wasn't a manmade event, then it has to be subterranean. Any change in pressures in last few minutes?" Guy wanted correlation, but was afraid of what the answer might mean. Guy could hear Thayer on the other end hollering at the Operations Center watch supervisor to get a pressure reading.

"You guessed it. There was another spike, again slightly higher than the last. What the heck does this mean?" Thayer was clearly nervous. Pressure readings had never been out of the normal range before. He decided at that moment to activate his damage control protocols.

"Guy, keep me posted. I've got to go. I'm going to order implementation of damage control protocols. I can't afford to wait for more information and I can't afford to be wrong. Call me later."

Thayer got off the phone and ordered an internal inspection of all bilges, interior main structure walls, penstock pipes, wicket gates and generator rooms. He also ordered an inspection of the road deck and spillway gates. Within minutes he had recalled all shift workers to report for work assignments and was on the phone with the supervisory staff at the Little Rock district office. Thayer explained that he hated to be in the middle of this emergency inspection when the D.C. team arrived, but it couldn't be helped. He knew he had to act. The district office agreed.

Within the first hour, Thayer was satisfied that there was no water seepage in the bilges above that normally observed. There were not obvious stress cracks, fissures, or lines showing up on any of the interior concrete walls. The spillways were intact as was the generator room and all the penstocks and wicket gates. The road deck, however, had what appeared to be a newly discovered crack.

There were frequent inspections of the road deck and every crack was filled with a sealant. New cracks were reported, marked on the maintenance map and then had sealant applied. That was the routine. Cracks weren't unusual, but this one was new and had a jagged half inch wide gap across the width of the road deck. It was about sixty feet from the west end of the Dam closest to the Visitor Center. This is an area of the Dam with no interior spaces. Concrete and steel go straight to bed rock on the sloping surface of the west wall of the old river canyon.

Thayer ordered an exterior inspection of the concrete structure below the road bed and all the way to the ground. He knew they wouldn't be able to inspect all the way to dry ground on the lake side, not with the flood water level as it was. This area was normally dry when the lake was at normal conservation pool or about forty feet lower than where the water was today. However, they would be able to see all the way to where the concrete disappeared into the dirt on the river side.

It didn't take long. The first report was being radioed back to the Operations Center as soon as the crack was spotted. There was a stress fracture from below the road bed along the lake face of the Dam

128

which disappeared under the surface of the water. More noticeable was the small landslide that was evident along the shore adjacent to the Dam. The dirt and rock had slid down enough to undercut the asphalt parking area of the scenic overlook just above this new landslide area. Thayer had one of his supervisors contact the Arkansas Highway and Transportation Department maintenance office over in Yellville to let them know about the impending damage to the overlook. They offered to get right over and put up barriers and inspect the damage.

Thayer called Guy and filled him in on the current findings, he knew that Thayer would agree that this was significant. Thayer's nervous sounding voice added a level of foreboding that Guy hoped he wouldn't have to consider. These structures could handle lots of stresses and still be safe and functional even if other structures were crumbling. A Dam of this magnitude was built to withstand most of Mother Nature's fury and the eternal test of time. Guy passed on the information about the crack and small landslide to the USGS team. Dr. Owens shared Guy's worry. The kids, well, they were having a great adventure, another little landslide was just another mystery barely worthy of their intellectual talents. Another mark was placed on the working map to show the latest landslide and to record the seismic reading associated with the event.

Dr. Owens studied the overlay maps closely. He seemed more interested in the aquifers at the moment, noting that there appeared to be a small chance that all three landslides had occurred along what could be described as a connected small group of branch lines from the main aquifer. The worst slide had occurred at Noe Creek and it was the one closest to a recorded outcropping of the aquifer. Non-geologists refer to these outcroppings as natural springs. The lines also zigzagged across the main lake from Ozark Isle to Little Sister Creek, back to Noe Creek, and then it branched again, one going to Jimmy Creek, the other to Howard's Creek and the main lake channel to the Dam. He connected each of the known occurrences and found that the only place that had not had a reported issue was Jimmy Creek. Guy added his two cents and reminded Dr. Owens that there was the strange water sample from Big Spring and that the spring fed from somewhere in Jimmy Creek. Dr. Owens put a mark on Jimmy Creek and a note: "unknown event, specific location unknown".

They were fairly sure that there was some correlation between the aquifer network and everything that was happening. What they needed now was proof and answers. This didn't appear to be an earthquake and it was far from the known central line of the New Madrid Fault. There are no active volcanoes in the area. The team agreed to take one step at a time as already planned, however, the landslide near the Dam had now become the second area they would investigate.

Jenny eased the houseboat into Noe Creek and slowed the engines. Guy and the twins went on deck to assist with tying off the large boat to a bank a couple hundred yards away from the landslide area. The boat slowed and passed between submerged trees and bushes as it scraped its bow against the gravel and brush embankment. The twins jumped to shore with mooring lines and quickly tied off each side of the houseboat securely to trees up the bank. Then, like two kids showing off a new toy to excited parents, they lowered the ATV launch ramp. They were smiling and giving each other high fives and fist pumps when Dr. Owens started handing out orders.

Dr. Owens said there would be three teams. He assigned one team to do a quick survey. He expected them to get GPS coordinates of the landslide widths, top to bottom; he wanted the starting point identified, where the ground initially separated and its GPS coordinates. The second team was assigned to take a map and GPS unit and identify the exact location of the closest outcropping, and get water samples for later analysis. The last team, which would be led by Dr. Owens himself, would take the portable electromagnetic induction generator and conductivity probes up to try to locate the subterranean boundaries of the aquifer. This equipment was something still categorized as experimental proprietary property of the university. Dr. Owens had been involved in its development. His equipment was more sensitive and accurate than other equipment used to date and didn't require digging test pits or laying out induction coils in numerous locations. Early tests had been extremely good; he expected this outing might be a grand validation of earlier testing.

The first team was the two graduate students, Lennard and Brad. They headed out on one of the ATVs to begin mapping the slide. The second team was Guy and Jenny, and Buck of course. They headed off on foot to locate and accurately map the closest known aquifer outcropping. It should be a natural spring coming out of an exposed limestone ledge somewhere on the land above the slide area just northeast of the old barn that had been partly destroyed by the landslide. Dr. Owens would be assisted by the two Doctoral students, Brett and Kristi. Brett fired up the second ATV and loaded the portable EM equipment to be hauled up the hill.

It didn't take the teams long to reach the top of the hill where the slide originated. From there, they went in different directions as planned. Dr. Owens was making his first EM measurements at the top of the slide, while the grad students headed down the north side of the landslide to begin charting the GPS coordinates which would later be used to calculate the volume and magnitude of the slide. Jenny and Guy were hiking toward the old spring, following what they believed to be the small creek bed where the spring should be flowing. It didn't take them long to reach the limestone ledge where the outcropping was.

Chapter 19

The spring was nothing like Guy imagined it should be. It was a trickle of water at best. From the looks of the outcropping's natural rocky cistern and rocky creek bed, the spring should have been giving up several hundred cubic feet of water per minute. Something more peculiar struck him right away. This water had a faint smell of sulfur.

"Jenny, do you smell that? It kind of reminds me of the smell from the bubbles during your dive in Howard's Creek." Guy was already digging in his pack for water sampling bottles and test equipment. He needed samples for mineral analysis and he wanted a quick pH level as well as temperature. Jenny watched Guy as he reached into the rocky cistern for his first sample. It surprised her when he suddenly yanked his hand back from the water. "Damn, this water is hot! Hand me the temp probe." Jenny handed him the probe and knelt down to touch the water. "Jenny, it will scald you, be careful. In fact, the temperature probe says this water is about one-hundred sixty eight degrees. That's way wrong for this kind of spring. It should be closer to forty-eight degrees, even in September." Guy carefully gathered his samples and did a quick pH test. Like the water at Howard's Creek, this was a bit acidic as well. He looked at his first sample bottle and realized sediments were already beginning to form at the bottom of the bottle. It had the same basic color of the dacite material he had seen at Big Spring.

Guy had Jenny get several pictures of the surrounding limestone ledge and the spring. He also insisted that she get pictures of the thermometer reading and probe while the measurement was being made. It was weak proof of the temp, but still proof none the less. They began to gather up their gear when suddenly the ground was shaking beneath their feet.

Guy and Jenny looked at each other while Buck started barking wildly. The tremor only lasted a few seconds, but Guy called Dr. Owens anyway. "Ben, did you feel that tremor?" Guy was almost hollering in the phone.

"Yeah, we felt it. We're about a quarter mile from the where the landslide started. I think we need to get back to the boat to check our monitors. Meet me there as soon as you can. I'm going to call the other team." Dr. Owens was very concerned. He had been in earthquake zones many times and felt hundreds of tremors. This was more like the tremor from an underground explosion. He had been around numerous strip mines to observe huge blasting operations for various minerals and raw ores. This felt more like the orchestrated and sequentially timed blast that was used to displace large masses of overburden that miners would create.

Dr. Owens had tried several times to reach the grad students on their cell phone. He wasn't having any luck. Perhaps it was just a poor signal, or maybe the cell phone was on the ATV while the guys were on foot doing surveys. Either way, he was still upset that they didn't answer. From now on Guy would make sure everyone carried a small two-way radio while in the field. He kept trying to call as his assistants gathered their gear and loaded up the ATV for the trip back.

Dr. Owens and his team reached the landslide area at about the same time as Guy and Jenny. The landslide was different. It had slid again and they were pretty sure that's why they felt a tremor. The slide was now about two hundred yards further up the hill than it had been. They started down the south slope toward the houseboat. Jenny was looking down the hill toward the houseboat and was pleased that she had tied it off far enough away from the original slide to avoid the debris field. Buck took off running down the hill. He started barking about half way down and was now struggling to climb out and across the lower edge of the new slide area. Guy was watching Buck and then noticed what seemed to be part of an ATV sticking out of the fresh loose soil, rock and trees.

"Ben, look! I think that's the other ATV over there." Guy was pointing and starting to trot across the hill toward the edge of the landslide. Dr. Owens looked where Guy was pointing and then told

135

his team to get their ATV and EM gear down to the houseboat and to grab some rope and a couple of shovels and picks and come back up to the slide.

Jenny was the first to reach the area where Buck had stopped. She could see two feet and most of one side of a leg sticking out of the dirt below the ATV. It appeared that whoever it was had been caught in the slide while riding the ATV. The ATV probably rolled and trapped the rider and then was covered in rapidly sliding debris.

Jenny was digging with her hands to try and reach the person's head and face. She hoped that perhaps he was still alive. What she found was something she had regretfully seen before during combat and she knew the ashen look. He was already dead. As Guy reached Jenny's side he could see the young face of Brad covered in dirt. Jenny looked up at Guy, "His neck is broken, probably happened when the ATV flipped. Poor kid, I wonder where his partner is?" Jenny was looking around and scanning the area for Buck. Buck had already moved off and seemed to be searching again.

Jenny heard Buck start barking and moved quickly across the slide to see where he had gone. She was glad to see that he was jumping up and down around someone who seemed to be sitting up on the dirt and rocks close to the water. Jenny and Guy moved across the slide area, both now struggling to keep their footing. The fresh landslide was loose and fragile. It moved easily under each foot step. They were shocked by what they found.

136

The other grad student, Lennard had been caught up in the landslide and partly buried by large slabs of limestone and tree trunks. From a distance he looked like he was sitting, but in fact he was buried up to the back pockets on his jeans and couldn't move. He was nearly unconscious and bleeding from several cuts and abrasions on his face, head and arms. The bleeding was minor compared to the pain he was feeling below his waist.

Kristi and Dr. Owens were carrying the rope, shovels and picks and were just coming over the crest of the slide. They had already seen Brad.

Brett had been horrified by seeing his twin brother like this and had broken into tears instantly. They felt helpless there and decided to leave Brett to sit and cry at his brother's side. Dr. Owens felt that they would deal with the rescue first and console Brett later, everyone would need time to deal with this in their own way.

Guy and Jenny were trying to move rocks and debris away from Lennard. Dr. Owens put down the shovel and pick he was carrying and grabbed his cell phone to make a quick call for help. He really didn't know for sure who would respond, but he decided to call Jerry at the boat dock for help. Jerry listened to the quick description of what was happening and told Dr. Owens he would take care of getting rescuers and paramedics to him. That was enough to satisfy Dr. Owens. He had turned it over to the right person after all.

Jerry called the Bull Shoals Fire Department and they notified the paramedics by radio. Within minutes they were loading a small team into the Fire and Rescue Boat at the marina. Jerry decided to personally drive the boat over to the landslide since he knew exactly where it was. The rescue boat was fast and they were at the slide within fifteen minutes from the first call.

Guy and Jenny could see that Lennard's left leg had a compound fracture above his knee and had been bleeding badly. Jenny was able to get a makeshift tourniquet around his leg to slow the bleeding while they continued to try and free him from the slide. It took about fifteen more minutes to get Lennard free of the debris. His other leg seemed intact, although they suspected that he could have additional fractures since there was already some significant bruising and swelling. Just as Guy and the others had finished freeing Lennard the Fire Department rescue team arrived. The professional team had back boards, immobilizers for every extremity, neck braces and stretchers. They would get Lennard wrapped up, stabilized, start an I.V, radio his condition to a waiting ER doctor and deal with transporting him back to a waiting ambulance. One of the paramedics and a fireman remained to assist with Brad. Guy and Jenny were exhausted and glad to be finished digging. Dr. Owens' age was showing and Kristi became an emotional wreck as the rescue boat pulled away.

By the time Lennard was being carried off the slide Brett had stopped crying and was looking up just as the others approached. The fireman, paramedic and Guy started digging and freed Brad within just a few minutes. With an extra stretcher, they loaded the now extricated corpse. He was zipped into a waiting body bag and then carried somberly down to the waiting houseboat.

The ride back to the marina was quiet except for the occasional sobs coming from Brett and Kristi. Kristi had huddled by Brett and was holding him like a mother holding a small son who was hurt. Brett was going on and on about his brother and how close they had always been. They had been together every day of their lives. He couldn't remember a time that they had been separated for any reason. He shivered as he sobbed. Brett's parents were both dead and he didn't have any other relatives as far as he knew. Brett was suddenly overwhelmed again at his loss and became nearly hysterical. He started screaming, "WHY BRAD? Why Brad? He didn't deserve this. He shouldn't have been the one to die." Then he leaned forward and sobbed violently into his open hands. Kristi felt helpless but continued to rub Brett's back and try to console him.

Dr. Owens was wiping tears from his own cheeks after watching Brett. He decided to refocus on the problem and occupy himself with his phone. He called his colleagues at the USGS office in Denver to discuss what he and his team had learned and just observed.

Clearly, there was a geological puzzle unfolding right beneath them. Guy too, was on the phone. He had called Thayer Davis.

"Thayer, this is going to sound irrational at first, but hear me out. We just had another landslide at the Noe Creek site. This time it killed one of our college kids and injured another. One of the springs up there has lost most of its flow and become almost superheated. You know we have a fairly extensive system of caverns, caves and aquifers in this area. I believe a branch of the aquifer is collapsing. I'm not sure why yet, but I'm starting to think it may have something to do with what seems like a deep core magma vent." Guy could tell Thayer was taking him seriously and he expected Dr. Owens would start arguing as soon as he overheard this, but he didn't.

"Guy, what does all that mean? What am I supposed to do?" Thayer felt that knowing this had now somehow put new pressure on him to do something radical.

"I don't know yet. My fear is that the area below the slide at the end of the Dam may become even more unstable. We could be seeing a collapse in that weird honeycomb of caves and whatnot that we have underground. If we do, then I'm afraid there will be significant structural damage possible in the area, maybe even the Dam. As radical as it sounds, you guys might want to consider a downstream evacuation order. Better safe than sorry." Guy ended his call with that time tested cliché. He didn't want to come across as

Chicken Little, but he was certain that no matter what was happening so far, it could still get worse.

As the houseboat slowed to enter the marina area Dr. Owens was busy checking monitors. He had verified that the new landslide was captured by the closest monitor. But his attention was now drawn to the Dam site monitor. He could see the signal starting to waiver. Not a dramatically changing signal, but at least perceptible. He knew something was happening again so he hollered at Guy and motioned to the monitor. Guy walked quickly to the monitor, saw what was happening and didn't hesitate to call Thayer Davis again.

"Thayer, we're monitoring subterranean movement near the Dam. It doesn't read like an earthquake, but there is something happening. It's smaller than the last reading I told you about. You need to alert your people again." Guy was very direct and obviously nervous. The phone went silent as Thayer hung up to begin warning his staff. Guy felt helpless at this point so he refocused his thoughts on the hot water spring he had just seen.

"Ben, I think the aquifer is collapsing. I know I don't have any good scientific evidence, but I believe we're seeing something new here. I've had dacite minerals show up now in a couple of water samples. You know, Volcanic Dacite... the same minerals found in actively flowing lava. I had an opportunity once to do some deep earth core sampling near a volcano. We used a geyser site to penetrate a magma vent and pulled samples resembling these minerals. Look,

141

here's what I'm thinking. This whole area is dense in limestone, most of the aquifer system and caverns are Precambrian limestone tunnels. Limestone dissolves easily with water and if you raise the acidity and heat even a small amount it dissolves quicker. By introducing magma minerals and heat to the water you will find any and all weaknesses in this labyrinth of tunnels. I really believe the hot spring we found at Noe Creek was just a small indicator that water from the aquifer has penetrated a deep core magma vent. That water will superheat and eventually blow like Old Faithful. We know we have a relatively localized problem. It seems to be just the south quarter of Bull Shoals Lake. I don't know why this is happening, but I would bet it has something to do with the record lake level and pressure changes underground as well as the earthquake swarm south of here that could be caused by the natural gas drilling and fracking." Guy started feeling like a professor again and stopped just before he felt as if he were lecturing to Dr. Owens.

"Look, Ben, if this was some isolated part of Yellowstone or Siberia, we might not even notice the change. But this is a tourist area; the economy revolves around the Lake and River. The Dam provides flood control for thousands of farms, businesses and residences downstream and generates electrical power for millions of customers. This could be devastating." Guy's passion for this area was showing. He wanted Dr. Owens to know that whatever happened it would have huge emotional repercussions for hundreds of thousands of people, even though hundreds of thousands of people were not in direct peril.

"Guy, I agree with you about the collapse. Our EM reading went crazy during the tremor that caused that last landslide. We were getting the aquifer boundaries marked fairly clearly until the tremor. Then the readings changed remarkably, like the aquifer had literally moved. If what you're guessing is true, that would explain the EM reading. Part of the aquifer must have collapsed in on itself. We know where the various problems have been so far, so I agree with you that this might be isolated to just this quadrant of the aquifer branch. We need to know the source of the vent." Dr. Owens seemed tired as he strained against his own emotions to make sense of all that was happening.

"What is going on with that monitor?" Guy was focused on the Dam Site monitor, it was showing stronger fluctuations, the motion was evident and would likely be causing problems. Guy's phone rang almost as soon as the apparent tremor stopped. It was Thayer Davis.

Chapter 20

"Guy, the lake side scenic overlook parking area and half the road below the entrance to the Visitor's Center are gone." Thayer was calm but his voice was strained. "It slid into the lake a couple of minutes ago. I was on the road deck of the Dam looking at the new crack and heard a horrible crunching sound and looked up in time to see the rocks and road just slide off into the water. Thank God nobody was in the area and there was no traffic. The crack in the Dam isn't any worse. I'm worried for the Visitor Center though. If this slide gets bigger it could bring down the hill across the road and threaten the Visitor Center."

"We just saw the reading from the seismograph. You beat me to the phone call. I'm glad no one was hurt. We'll stop by and look at the slide later. I've got to check a couple of things first." Guy wasn't surprised by the call. He passed the news on to the rest of his team. Dr. Owens said that he and what was left of his team would have to go and make arrangements for Brad's body and go to the hospital to check on Lennard. He felt obligated to personally notify the

University and the families of the students about what had just happened.

Jenny hollered at Guy to help with mooring the houseboat. She was starting to pull into a vacant slip on the main dock next to the store. Guy ran to the bow and with a little help from the boat dock crew, he had the houseboat tied up in no time. Before he could finish tying off the lines he was being questioned by waiting reporters. He asked them to wait until the body was moved and then he would talk to them.

One of the Springfield, Missouri network TV reporters was in the area with a camera crew filming a short report on the record high water and its effect on this year's tourism business. They heard about the death on the landslide via an emergency radio scanner in their van so they hurried over to the boat dock for a "breaking story". Jerry was on the dock waiting also, "Guy, I haven't told the press anything yet and the paramedics only gave them a quick condition of the injured student and confirmed that you were carrying someone who had died out there. Also, we've got the County Coroner standing by to take the body."

"Thanks Jerry, tell the Coroner to come on, we'll help him if needed." Guy was very matter of fact in his approach with the press watching. Brett left the boat with Brad's body and rode with the Coroner. Dr. Owens and Kristi ignored the press and walked off the boat and back to shore to get their car and head to the hospital where

Lennard was by now. Guy moved out onto the main dock and started talking with the press. He gave a brief statement.

"Some of you may already know me, I'm Guy Fredricks, the Director of the Arkansas Department of Environmental Quality. You probably also know that we've started an investigation into some unusual occurrences happening around the lake. It started with some fishermen getting hurt and various reports of mysterious fog, lights on the water and strange smells. What we have found so far is that this area is indeed experiencing some geological changes. We don't know yet what is causing the changes nor do we know what the extent may be at this point. We believe the geological events involve the labyrinth of caverns, caves and aquifers in the surrounding area. We were investigating an area in Noe Creek where a landslide had recently occurred. While two members of our team were mapping the slide area there was a second larger landslide. This new slide caught two of our graduate students by surprise. The younger student was killed when he was caught by the slide and buried under the ATV he was using to survey the area. The second student was severely injured by the slide and trapped for some time until he was rescued by the remaining members of our team and local paramedics who arrived within about fifteen or twenty minutes of being called.

We are continuing to investigate what is causing the landslides. In fact, a second slide has also just recently occurred near the James A. Gaston Visitor Center. I will be checking this slide next. As soon as we know anything substantial we will share it with you." Guy was professional and cordial to a fault. He had nothing prepared, but he sounded almost rehearsed. Jenny was watching him closely and realized that he was suddenly more charming than she expected him to be in light of what they had just been through.

Mary Snider of KY3 TV was the first to start asking questions, "Mr. Fredricks, are the Dam or any area residents in danger and who is on your team?"

"Our investigating team is Dr. Ben Owens from the USGS district office out of Boulder, Colorado. He is being assisted by graduate and post graduate students from the University of Oklahoma, Geological Sciences Department. We are also working closely with Thayer Davis, the local Officer in Charge of the U.S. Army Corps of Engineers Field Office. In fact, we have been in constant communication with Mr. Davis about the geological issues and possible risks related to the Bull Shoals Dam and the Lake. Mr. Davis is currently investigating some anomalous issues at the Dam. He held a press conference earlier about this. If you need any more information about his efforts you will have to contact him personally. We are also being assisted by Miss Jenny Simpson. Jenny is our team diver and skipper of the houseboat." Guy was succinct, no drama, no speculation and didn't release names of the students knowing that the injured and deceased deserved to have families notified first.

"Mr. Fredricks, you said geological events. Are we having earthquakes that are causing these landslides? What do suspect is causing them?" Miss Snider's questions were still on target.

Guy wanted to tell them about his speculation concerning the aquifer collapsing and a possible deep core magma vent. This was potentially very dramatic news. He was sure of one thing though, too much drama and too many unknowns could really panic people. He had no proof yet and knew better than to knowingly cause immediate panic. His speculation would remain guarded for now. He also knew he needed to brief the Governor and local officials first and this had to be when the facts were available and the time was right. "Miss. Snider, we are far from the closest known active earthquake fault line, the New Madrid fault. We don't believe this has anything to do with an earthquake. We believe there are changes happening in the layers of rock immediately surrounding and beneath the lake. Perhaps like sinkholes. However, we don't have any specific evidence yet. Something is causing the ground to collapse and we're anxious to find out why.

I really need to contact my office and check on the members of my team. Please excuse me; I know we'll probably talk again soon. Thanks." Guy was finished. He had politely told them to get out the way so he could do his job. Smooth and efficient.

Guy asked Jenny if she wanted to ride over to the Dam. She asked about Buck going with them and with a nod from Guy, she was loaded up and heading off the boat dock to his waiting Suburban. Guy was already emotionally past the death of Brad. Jenny could tell he was more determined than ever to find out what was happening.

As they were driving to the Dam, Guy mentioned to Jenny that he would probably give up his room at Gaston's Resort and just take up a berth on the houseboat. He could easily move his portable lab equipment. Sleeping, eating and working on the houseboat would be more efficient. After all, the houseboat could accommodate ten people if needed and his department was paying for it anyway. Jenny offered to help him move the lab equipment. She also asked about moving her diving equipment on to the houseboat. He quickly agreed that having her gear available would be a great idea.

"I just realized that I'm hungry. It seems like it's been a long time since breakfast. Let's get something to eat before we get to the Dam." Guy looked at Jenny with a little smile and waited for her answer.

"I'm hungry too, let's eat!" Jenny smiled back at Guy and held her gaze for a second longer than Guy expected.

"Beacon Point's burgers sound good to me, how 'bout you?" Guy really wasn't expecting anything except an agreement.

Chapter 21

Guy and Jenny found a booth at the back of the D's Beacon Point to a have a quiet lunch. It was already after the main lunch hour rush so except for two old fishermen drinking coffee and eating pie near the front of the dining area, Guy and Jenny were almost alone. They ordered iced teas to drink and both ordered burgers with the works and extra fries. The drinks were on the table within the first minute.

"Jenny, I know this sounds cliché, but you're not like other women I've worked with. I mean, I've had female research partners in the field before, but they always seemed a bit uncomfortable when things started getting edgy. But, you seem to like edgy. In fact, when things started going to hell in a hand basket out there on that landslide, you just jumped in the middle and started making things happen." Guy was looking directly into Jenny's eyes as he commented and when he finished he just stared at his tea.

FRACKED!

"I never could just sit and watch when something was going on. When I was a kid I was into everything outdoors. The other kids would see a big bug and scream and I would grab it to prove it wasn't a big deal, or they would see who could climb the highest tree, or who could swim underwater the farthest, and I was always the one that seemed to try the hardest." Jenny was enjoying telling a little about her childhood. "Don't get me wrong, I was okay in school too. I happened to like history and science, but never thought about going on to college. In fact, I tried a couple of years of junior college. I actually thought I wanted to be one of the crime scene investigators you always see on TV now.

What I really wanted was to get out and explore the world. I guess that's why I ended up joining the Navy. You know 'see the world'; 'it's not just a job, it's an adventure'. After I had been enlisted a couple of years I found out about UDT and decided to try out. It suited me." She was playing down how easy it really was for her to get in UDT and graduate with a promotion because she was number one in her class.

They were obviously both hungry, the burgers disappeared within minutes of coming to the table. The conversation had nearly stopped while they ate. Guy had clearly been deep in thought. Jenny figured that he was thinking about the aquifers and where the problem might be. Guy was actually thinking about Jenny. He hadn't been impressed emotionally by a woman in quite some time. He had seen that Jenny was a complete package. She was emotionally controlled but clearly driven by her heart when people were in need. She was physically strong, very strong for a woman he thought. He also found Jenny to be extremely attractive.

About the time Guy was down to his last bite of burger he became aware that Jenny was watching him finish. He suddenly felt embarrassed, wondering if Jenny could have read his mind over the last several minutes. Jenny was the first to break the silence.

"Guy, do you have family…you know, wife and kids?" Jenny seemed more nervous at that moment than she had been in two days.

"Actually, no. I guess you could say I'm a widower. I got married in grad school. Broke, infatuated, desperately in love. It was quite the adventure as I look back on it. I don't know what we were thinking. Anyway, her short life was ended by a drunk driver." Guy's expression was nearly blank and he was staring at his empty plate.

"I'm so sorry, I didn't mean to…." Jenny was cut off by Guy.

"No, no, listen. I haven't mentioned this to anyone in years. I took up fishing as a kind of therapy to get past the emotional issues that I had back then. The solitude and quiet it provided was therapeutic. Problem is, I think I've made fishing my companion. Most of the time, I escape from work and find myself fishing or thinking about fishing. Honestly, this trip has been so far out of the ordinary that I haven't had time to think about much of anything,

152

including fishing. Seeing that poor kid killed out there made me realize that I still have emotional needs that fishing obviously hasn't fixed." Guy was as unarmed as he could be. He was opening up to her in a way he hadn't done with anyone that he could remember.

"Guy, I've seen friends and workmates die in war and training. That's the kind of risk my work involved. Every incident was painful for me, but they weren't personal if that makes any sense. I've never had anyone that I loved, except maybe grandparents, who died unexpectedly. I can't begin to understand what it must have been like for you to lose a wife so young." Jenny was sympathetic and honest. She had seen death but had no idea how much it could hurt if it involved someone you were deeply in love with.

"Tell you what, let's get out of here and go check out the landslide at the Dam. This day is slipping away quicker than I want and there are several things that still need to get done. Are you sure you can stick around on this project for a while? You have no idea how much this means that you're helping." Guy was ready to change the subject and get back to work.

"I'm glad you asked me to help. So far this has been more exciting than anything I've done since Iraq. I just hope no one else gets hurt." Jenny was upbeat and ready to move on.

As the Suburban pulled away from the restaurant, Jenny slipped Buck a couple of hamburger patties that she had ordered before leaving. Buck made short work of them, basically swallowing them whole. His stomach would do the real work.

Within just a few minutes they were at the damaged area of road near the Dam. There was a crowd of on-lookers and road repair workers.

Guy called Thayer with his cell phone to let him know they were at the landslide area. Thayer was on the Dam side of the gaggle of people just out of sight from Guy and Jenny. Thayer told them to walk over to meet him. The local cops stopped Guy and Jenny from crossing their make shift temporary barrier and with a few seconds of discussion and identification they were cleared to go.

Guy walked the line of the actual break in the road bed so that he could see the magnitude of the damage. He was picking up faint traces of sulfur odor as he walked the area. He had become sensitive to this smell after all the previous encounters. He suspected that most folks wouldn't even realize the smell and landslide were remotely connected. He was right of course, no one seemed to notice.

Guy and Jenny walked across the break until they reached Thayer. Thayer was busy talking to other engineers from the Army. His headquarters had already managed to get an engineering team on site and they appeared busy evaluating and calculating. Thayer excused himself from his engineering posse so he could talk to Guy.

"Guy, I need you to show these guys the geological maps which outline the aquifers, springs, caverns, caves and mines. I know you're probably not formally ready, but I also think you should explain the sampling you made at those springs you told me about and what your theory is regarding the landslides. Can you do that?" Thayer was looking for anything that could help at this point.

"I don't mind sharing anything. I just want folks to know that its theory and that's all at this point. In fact, getting solid proof isn't really an option under the circumstances. I mean we can't very well crawl up an aquifer and look." Guy was ready to share his theory, but he hated staking a reputation on it without good proof.

"My problem is a Dam with an unexplained crack, a landslide next to one end of the Dam where the crack happens to be and pressure changes on the Dam we've never seen before. I've got a bunch of engineers trying to calculate hydraulic load stresses and now the public, especially living below the Dam and downstream on the White River are starting to fill up my phone lines with questions about the Dam breaking. I need something to force some action. I don't want to be the guy waiting until the water is rushing out between the cracks to admit that we might have a problem. That's too late!" Thayer was losing what little patience he had been saving. He felt like Guy could help.

"Let's get them together. I have the maps we've been using, including markings indicating the geological phenomena we've encountered. I need to call the Governor first. He needs to know that I'm fixing to uncork this information and what effect it might have on the public. I suspect he'll send up some reinforcements." Guy was more than a little certain that the Governor would take some action. In fact, he was going to suggest that the Governor notify the Arkansas National Guard, the Disaster Preparedness Office, and his public relations team.

Chapter 22

Guy decided to go back to the Suburban to make the call to the Governor. He didn't want any bystanders over hearing this conversation. He dialed Gretchen, the Governor's secretary, on her private office line. "Hi Gretchen, this is Guy Fredricks. I've got an urgent issue which needs the boss's attention. Can I speak with him?" He was cordial and upbeat with her. Gretchen knew that the various appointed Directors would only call the private line when it was not only urgent, but also serious. She had been the secretary for four different incumbents and knew her position with these calls was to get the Governor immediately. She patched the cell call through the computer switch to a private cell phone carried by the Governor. Within about twenty seconds Gretchen had connected Guy with the Governor.

"Guy, what's going on? Gretchen said it was urgent." The Governor was at an Arkansas Naturals baseball game sitting with friends in a private sky box behind home plate.

"Gene, I hate to interrupt your fun, but we need to talk. You know I came up to Bull Shoals to check out some environmental phenomena, what I found is turning out to be bigger than what I expected." Guy was serious and firm and didn't intend to give the Governor time to interrupt until he was done. "We seem to have some kind of geological instability in this region. It doesn't appear to be earthquake generated but we're having some significant landslides, including one that has now damaged the Bull Shoals Dam and continues to threaten the integrity of that structure. With the fracking going on near Conway and all the earthquake reports we may need to consider the effect that hydraulic fracturing may be having on the limestone shelves in the areas. We've seen some hot spring formation in one, maybe two places. I have a geology team from the USGS that has confirmed the structural failure of at least one part of a deep subterranean aquifer and there are probably more of this same branch failing. I know this sounds strange, but I believe we have a deep core magma vent which may have formed somewhere under part of this branch in the aquifer. If the water temperatures and acidity change as a result of superheating then it's very possible that these limestone lined aquifers are rapidly destabilizing and collapsing." Guy paused for a breath and to listen for any reaction from the Governor.

"Guy, it sounds like we have the right person in the right place for a change. With your background and education I can't argue with anything your saying. I think we need our Disaster Preparedness Office clued in so if this gets worse maybe they'll be ready. Do you think its going to get worse after all that's happened, maybe it's over?" The Governor was all business, no hint of worry.

"I really don't think this is over. The water from the damaged branch in the Aquifer must be going somewhere; it's not flowing freely from area springs at this point. Until we find out what the water is doing down there we won't know for sure.

Gene, I want to recommend that you let your National Guard leadership know what's happening. In fact, we may need some help with the public up here if things get worse. Also, can you get you PR folks on this? It might be good to have some experts dealing with the media. We've already had a couple of interviews.

By the way, one of the kids from the USGS team that the Corps of Engineers brought in was killed a few hours ago while investigating one of the landslides and another was injured." Guy paused for a second waiting for the Governor's reaction. It was silent.

"Gene, with your okay, I'm going to give this same geological theory to a group of engineers from the U.S. Army Corps of Engineers? I think they need to put their full emergency plans in effect at the Dam." Guy was finished and waited for the Governor's response.

"Guy thanks for telling me about the USGS loss. If there's anything I can do for them, please don't hesitate to ask. Go ahead and do your briefing and from what I'm hearing, tell the Corps to consider a voluntary evacuation downstream with assistance from Sheriffs in both counties there and perhaps they can pass the word to adjacent counties all the way to the Mississippi. I'll call the National Guard leadership and give them a head's up. You're right about the PR person. I'll have them get something going and to be prepared to deal with the media, especially following the Sheriffs making their notifications. What else can I do?" The Governor was being proactive as usual.

"Thanks Gene. I'm not sure there's anything else to do at this point. I look forward to hearing from the PR guys and I'm meeting with the Corps in a few minutes. I will pass on your words to them as well. I'll call you later when I know more." Guy ended his call with the Governor. He was pleased that it seemed to go well. The more he talked about his theory, the easier it was for him to believe it himself. He knew he was ready to share the theory with the Army Corps of Engineers.

Guy backed up his Suburban on the shoulder and hill side away from the landslide to make his way to the entrance of the Visitor's Center. Thayer had told him to meet them at the conference rooms up there. Guy and Jenny parked at the front of the building and walked into the main entrance of the Visitor Center. The nearly new James A Gaston Visitor Center was beautiful, roomy and bright and full of volunteers and U.S. Park Service Rangers who were busy working the front desk, gift shop and museum. It appeared that since the road had temporarily closed some of the east bound traffic decided to tour the Visitor Center rather than just turning around and waiting for the Dam to reopen to traffic.

Guy and Jenny were hastily greeted by Thayer Davis as they entered the conference room. Thayer immediately introduced Guy to the group of waiting engineers and then offered to help Guy by putting the geology map up on the white board for everyone to see. After they finished with the map, Guy began his monologue with the short story about the anomalies that caused him to come to the area in the first place and then progressed to landslides and calling in the assistance of the USGS. He explained their findings relative to aquifers, springs, location of the landslides and changes in water and appearance of dacite. He pointed to the various events on the map and showed the relationships to aquifers. Guy showed the group of engineers the location and cross sectional relationship of mapped caverns, caves and mines in the area. He could tell by their nodding and expressions that they were seeing the correlations.

Guy felt a bit nauseous as he began explaining his theory about the aquifer collapsing and the potential of a deep core magma vent being breached. As he explained the dacite, or volcanic materials, he found and the extremely high temperature of water he found trickling from one spring it seemed to once again reconfirm his own belief in the theory. He was already thinking about the questions that a group of engineers might have as he was finishing his presentation.

"Mr. Fredricks, is there any reason to believe that these events are going to continue and if they do, what can you predict about additional damage in the area from the aquifer chart?" The first question was on target and probably covered everything they were all thinking.

"I can't predict what will happen next, however, I believe the aquifer is failing rapidly now. We've seen more landslide activity today and I don't think it's over. What really scares me at the moment is that we don't know what's happening with the water from the aquifer system. Where ever it's going you can bet it's becoming more acidic as it gets hotter and mixes with volcanic chemicals. Our limestone thatch work of shelves that we call mountains around here is very vulnerable to rapid erosion and liquefaction. If we dissolve areas between the shelves, the top shelves can shift quickly and violently. So far we've only seen landslides resulting from what appears to be underground changes from a collapse in the aquifer. It could be worse. I've spoken with the Governor and he recommends at a minimum that you order a voluntary evacuation downstream and that he'll support greater measures if needed." Guy didn't want to cause a panic, but he really believed people needed to plan for the worst. Again, he was thinking better safe than sorry, as the old expression goes.

Thayer and the group began discussing options. Nothing was going to be easy or popular with the public. They decided to ask their

Headquarters in Washington for permission to begin mandatory evacuations below the Dam to an area just south of the confluence where the Northfork River joined the White River. This would protect the most vulnerable populace in case there was a breach in the Dam. Then they turned their attention to engineering reviews and structural analysis data from the 1950's. The group needed to know if the Dam could withstand more shakes and the growing pressure changes on the deep water lake side face of the structure.

Guy cornered Thayer and told him that he was leaving. He and Jenny left quietly and headed back to the Suburban. Jenny had been quiet for the meeting and so far hadn't pushed Guy about his theory. She was worried. This kind of threat was foreign to her and she was feeling helpless at the moment. She needed an enemy, something she could see and fight.

"Before you make the trip back to Gaston's to get your stuff, can you drop me back at my Jeep? I need to get home for a short breather. You know, shower and fresh clothes." Jenny's voice was tense.

"Sure. Don't mind at all. I'm going to get my gear and go back to the houseboat as soon as I can get myself loaded. I'll call you later if we need to get the boat going. You've been a great help. In case I forget to say it later – Thanks." Guy made the trip back to Jenny's Jeep as quick as possible. He was deep in thought. Jenny didn't interrupt and sat quietly wondering what the next move would be.

Chapter 23

Jenny was glad to be home. She needed some quiet time to collect her thoughts. The day wasn't over and it somehow seemed longer than normal. She couldn't help but think about the students and the landslide. Jenny was beginning to think that she was getting more tenderhearted the longer she was away from daily duties of UDT. She had almost grown numb to her own pain and discomfort during that time and in the UDT other people's pain only meant she had to carry more load or do more work. This time it was much different. These kids were still in school, learning about their environment and certainly not expecting to go in harm's way. Casualties without an enemy just didn't make sense in Jenny's world. She couldn't make herself get mad at nature, and she couldn't fight back. Jenny was beginning to realize that she was more vulnerable to hurt, both physical and mental, than she had been for most of her adult life. She supposed that living involved risks regardless of the type of hobby or occupation and that real life meant facing some uncontrollable risks. Her new enemy, it seemed, was risk.

Jenny decided right then that she would be the risk manager for the group. Every situation in the field would require a quick assessment and directions from her about the environment and how each member could reduce their risks and stay as safe as possible. She was perfect for the job. She knew she couldn't fight nature, but she could certainly improve the odds for everyone in a dangerous environment. Jenny was beginning to feel better. She had her enemy. She could help defend herself and her group by being smarter about the risks they faced.

Jenny's shower was long, hot and soothing. She tried to relax. As she did, she kept finding herself drawn to thoughts about Guy. She thought he was kind of a paradox. How could an ex-professor turned bureaucrat be so comfortable in the field? She saw a side of him that was more than a little comfortable in the outdoors. He was handsome, tanned and appeared fit, almost muscular. Jenny found it refreshing that Guy hadn't been the least bit chauvinistic and hadn't questioned her strength and ability like so many other guys. She suddenly embarrassed herself and thought of him in a more personal way. She hadn't been close to a man in years. In fact, Jenny had overheard a couple guys at her work site talking about her and wondering if she was a lesbian. Strangely, she found it comforting at the time to let them think that way, after all, there would be less stress if guys didn't hassle her about dating and relationships. Jenny let herself fantasize briefly while she finished lathering, slowly rubbing, soaking in the warmth and wetness of the moment.

Jenny was starting to shiver, she had been in the shower long enough for the water to cool off. She grabbed a large clean soft towel and patted herself dry. She stood in front of the bathroom mirror nude, taking inventory of herself. She knew she was in good shape and she worked hard to stay that way. As she was dressing she thought she might grab a bottle of wine, some bread and some leftover lasagna and take it to the houseboat. She hoped Guy wouldn't think she was being too forward.

Guy managed to move all his equipment and personal gear to the houseboat within an hour and a half of dropping Jenny off. He was finishing calibrating the equipment when he heard someone coming aboard the boat. It was Jenny. He was more than a little pleased to see her, perhaps too pleased he thought.

He was almost staring as Jenny came through door. He saw that her hands were full and he jumped up to help her. He never said a word; he just looked at her face as he reached to help take the bags from her hands. He finally found a few words.

"Wow, what a surprise! You look refreshed and whatever you're carrying smells great. I hope there's enough for two." Guy was suddenly overwhelmed with feelings he hadn't allowed himself to have in a long time. He decided he better get a grip on himself quickly, otherwise he could easily lose focus.

"As a matter of fact it's dinner for two. I hope you don't mind. I was getting something out to eat and realized I had enough leftover lasagna to feed a couple of people. I figured you might be here getting unpacked, looks like I was right. Thought you might prefer not having to go out to eat again." Jenny was being a bit coy. Guy could tell.

"Honestly, it sounds wonderful. This houseboat is very comfortable and has lots of room. Let's eat on the back deck. We've got about an hour before the sun sets and it gets dark." Guy fumbled for dishes, silverware and glasses in the galley while Jenny carried the lasagna and wine to the back deck.

Jenny thought Guy was right, the back deck was great. There was a slight breeze, the evening air was cooling off and the western sky was already orange and yellow readying itself for night. The marina dock lights were beginning to come on and the whole area seemed to be a perfect setting for a private dinner. Guy set the dishes out and helped Jenny serve the lasagna. They sat down together and she poured them both a large glass of red wine. Dinner was quiet. Jenny would occasionally stare at the sunset and Guy would stare a Jenny while she was looking away. He enjoyed the meal and poured a second glass of wine. He realized that Jenny was already on her second glass.

Guy had been so preoccupied with the events of the past couple of days that he hadn't taken any real personal time. He was enjoying this moment. He thanked Jenny for the wonderful dinner and started

168

picking up the dishes. Jenny got up with her glass of wine and stood at the railing on the back deck to watch the last few minutes of the sun disappearing behind the distant hills. He dropped the dishes in the galley sink and rejoined Jenny on the back deck. He stood next to her by the rail and watched the sun disappear as night began casting its shadow from the east.

Jenny turned and looked up at Guy. He moved closer to her and put his hand on her bare upper arm as he moved slowly to kiss her. Just as their lips were about to touch, one of the seismometer monitors began to alarm. It was at the Visitor Center… again.

Chapter 24

The alarm indicated a ground movement in the area near the Dam again. Guy had quickly moved back to the dining area to see the monitor and called Thayer Davis. Thayer was still at the Operations Center with the engineering team. As far as he was concerned there hadn't been any movement. He told Guy that he would radio the road crew to check for new landslides and to check the Dam's road deck for any more cracks. Within less than ten seconds, Guy had his answer.

"No changes on this end." Thayer was happy to report.

"Please call me right away if there are any ground changes, otherwise I'll just plan to see you on the houseboat early in the morning."

Guy's next call was to Ben Owens. He wanted him to know that the alarm had sounded. Dr. Owens had finished at the hospital and was already on his way back to the resort for the night.

As Guy was putting his phone back in his pocket he heard sirens blaring from up the hill toward the middle of town. As he listened he could hear additional sirens, now it sounded like three or four emergency vehicles. "I'm going to take a ride to see what's causing the sirens. You want to go?" He was still staring at the monitors intently. Jenny was quick to answer, she certainly wanted to see what was going on and she offered to drive.

Guy and Jenny jumped in the Jeep and headed up the hill to town. They saw a pickup truck with flashing lights go by, most likely a volunteer fireman, so they followed it. Within a couple of blocks they were in front of the 1890's Mountain Village. There was an enormous cloud coming from down the hill below the entrance to the village. Jenny guessed that the cloud was coming from the entrance to the caverns. It was already dark enough that they couldn't make out very many details.

Guy was surprised by the cloud. He assumed at first that it was smoke, but it wasn't. "Jenny, that's steam!" As they watched, they realized the steam was diminishing quickly and they also realized there must have been several injuries. There were two ambulances on scene and numerous stretchers being taken out of the fire department rescue rig.

Jenny walked up to the first city policeman she could find to ask what he knew about what was happening. All the local cops and county deputies knew Jenny. She was a regular instructor at all the training seminars held where she worked. Within a minute, Jenny was waving at Guy to join her by one of the patrol cars.

There had been some sort of explosion deep in the cavern and everyone in the cavern at the time of the explosion had been affected. Six people were dead, including the guide. The rest of the folks had been burned, some severely. According to the owner of the Mountain Village and cavern, there was an evening tour of the cavern for people to watch the nightly migration of the local cave bats.

Bat watching had a niche that was surprisingly popular for young and old people. This part of Arkansas, including the Buffalo National River is the most cave rich area of the U.S. National Park System with more than three hundred sixty caves. Most of the caves were regulated in the park system and might not be open to the public, some required permits and almost all of them required experienced spelunking skills. The open caves include such places as Lost Valley, Eden Falls, Cob Cave, Indian Rockhouse, Panther Cave, Bullet, Sinkhole, Icebox and Twenty-Nine and a Half Cave to mention a few. Only one, Bat Cave, was considered closed to recreational exploration. The system is home to three bat species on the endangered list and four other species not currently protected. There are only a couple of caves that people can tour safely regardless of age and some physical limitations. This cavern, in the heart of the little town of Bull Shoals was a popular spot for bat watchers because it was easy to access and guided.

Guy was suddenly feeling a little panicky. He knew the cavern was only a mile from the Visitor Center where the latest seismic activity had been recorded. The subterranean rumble must have come from the area below the cavern. He knew from the aquifer map that there was a deep water source near the floor in the deepest part of the mapped cavern and he suspected that the latest movement breached the cavern's deepest pocket. Guy and Jenny watched as the injured were carried out, loaded into waiting ambulances and driven away. There had been eleven injured.

With the last of the injured removed, the recovery process was started to extricate the dead. According to one of the cops, the tour guide had been in front of the group and at the lowest point in the cave closest to the deep pockets that could be seen, but not toured by the public. Generally, tourists would be amused by the water in the lower pools, but this time the water apparently became lethal. One of the injured witnesses said the guide was surprised when he got to the lowest point to see that there wasn't any water in the pools. Jim Gentry, the cavern guide commented that it was certainly strange not seeing water in the lower pools and that it usually only happened during long drought periods. After that, he did his short talk about bats and other cave life. When he finished the talk, he dimmed the lights anticipating the nightly bat migration.

Just after the lights dimmed they heard a sharp, loud and sudden sucking sound and then something that sounded like a train.

The next thing Jim Gentry knew was that he was suffocating in hot steam and couldn't see anything because of the dense hot cloud. The people on his tour screamed and ran over each other trying to get back up the steps leading to the surface. One of the witnesses had been lucky because she had been knocked to the floor of the cave and had avoided the hottest part of the steam rushing in above her.

Jenny asked one of the nearby cops if she and Guy could go over and talk to the Mountain Village owner. He told them to be careful of the emergency vehicles and equipment, but to go ahead and go over.

Guy introduced himself to the owner and quickly summarized what he was doing in the area and what had been going on with landslides. He asked the owner for permission to explore the cavern in the morning with his geology team. The owner was obviously very eager to have someone check out the cavern and he was clearly devastated by the evening's event and wanted someone to find out what had happened.

Guy was on his phone calling Dr. Owens to set up a time to meet. It was agreed that they would meet at the Mountain Village parking lot at seven o'clock in the morning. Guy told the owner that his group would be back first thing in the morning and then he expressed his sympathy for the guide and tourists that were killed and reassured the owner that they would do their best to find out what happened.

174

Jenny drove Guy back to the marina and dropped him off next to the docks. She knew he was in what she thought was a trouble shooting mode and that he would probably be focusing on maps and data for the next couple of hours before he would try to get some sleep. Jenny was ready to check on Buck, he probably needed to get out of her house for a few minutes to take care of his own business before the night got much later. She planned to meet the group at the cavern in the morning, even though she hadn't actually been invited. After all, she had appointed herself as their risk manager and she wasn't going to let any of them get hurt again. Morning would come early, so Buck would only get a short walk before calling it a night.

Chapter 25

Six o'clock came early, or so it seemed to Guy. He had stayed awake fairly late checking maps and trying to pinpoint the aquifer's closest branch near the caverns at the Mountain Village. Guy had been able to find a great map showing all known parts of the cavern but it was a slightly different scale than his aquifer map, so a simple overlay wasn't helping him very much. He had tried to trace the aquifer map over the cavern as precisely to scale as he could. It was close, very close he assumed, and it would be the best map available for now.

By Guy's calculations the aquifer was something close to thirty-five meters below the lowest mapped pool in the cavern. He also believed that the cavern had been a natural outcropping of the aquifer at some pre-historical time in the past and that the two were now commonly joined by only thin ribbons of limestone crevasses which allowed natural overflow drainage from the cavern's many pools. He suspected the crevasses were numerous, indistinct areas that were not big enough for human exploration. Guy finished his second cup of coffee while making the last of his sketches and then left the houseboat to meet with the rest of the team.

It was a few minutes before seven when Guy pulled in to the Mountain Village parking lot. He was pleased to see Jenny's Jeep already parked there, he hadn't really thought about it until just now, but he hadn't actually asked her to come this time. He felt very good that she just considered herself part of the team and was there ready to work. As he was getting out of his Suburban he saw Dr. Owens and his post grad student Kristi. They were followed closely by Thayer Davis and Sheriff Wilson from the Marion County Sheriff's Office.

There was a quick exchange of "good mornings", but the group was mostly somber this morning. Without any signal, Dr. Owens and Kristi started handing out back packs loaded with cave exploring gear. Everyone, including the Sheriff, got one. These packs had helmets, knee pads, gloves, bottled water, carabineers, climbing rope, descenders, and head lights for the helmets. Once loaded, they headed for the entrance gate to the village and then on to the owner's office. They found the owner sitting on the front porch of the office cabin drinking a cup of coffee; he looked like he hadn't slept last night. As they neared the porch the owner stood up and without a word turned and led the group to the entrance to the cavern. Then he unlocked the front gate at the cavern's entrance and stood there for just a second.

"Be careful in there. There're extra flashlights and batteries on the table over in the corner if you need them." The owner backed away and allowed the group to pass into the cavern's entrance. "The lighting system melted at the lowest part of the cavern. I rigged up an extension with several work lights to make getting to the bottom a little easier to see, but you will need the flash lights for detail work. The lower pool is completely dry now and it smells like sulfur. I checked for hydrogen sulfide and didn't find any, the oxygen levels are fine though. Use the walkie-talkies on the table to stay in touch with me. I want to know when you get to the bottom and I want you to key the mike and talk to me every few minutes so that I know you're okay after you get to work." The owner showed no emotion as he gave instructions and then he stepped aside.

Jenny had carried a small duffel from her Jeep and was sitting it down and opening it as she started talking. "I'm taking point as we go down in the cavern. Guy will follow me, then Kristi and Dr. Owens. The Sheriff will bring up the rear. Also, compliments of some UDT friends of mine, take these ponchos and put them on. Make sure you put the hoods up and over your helmet, they're plenty large enough. These things are made from a microfiber that is fire and heat resistant. If you hear anything or see anything strange just pull the hood over and across your face and crouch down to protect your lower half as much as possible." Jenny had taken on a new role and she wanted everyone to know that she was going to protect them as much as she could.

Guy was impressed to say the least. He knew Jenny was an experienced climber and that she was basically fearless in just about any outdoor environment, but he didn't expect her to jump out front to lead the group down the cavern. He didn't say a word, he just smiled wryly and got in line behind Jenny. The rest of the group fell in like a scout troop and then Jenny started the walk down into the cavern.

The cavern was surprisingly enormous and beautiful. Blanchard Springs Caverns and Carlsbad Caverns were the usual places people heard about and wanted to explore. This was an easy cavern to walk around in had all the usual cavern sights. There was even evidence of cave dwelling inhabitants which had been carbon dated to nearly three thousand years ago. One part of the cavern includes what appears to be an underground river, which is actually a small exposed part of a branch in the aquifer.

The cavern has multiple rooms and numerous limestone formations bearing names such as Rotunda, Liberty Bell, Garden of the Gods, Cathedral Chimes, Garden of Gethsame and the Diamond Chapel room. There is even a man made rock feature in the cavern, a white marble statue of Christ carved in Italy and placed with reverence in the Cathedral Room.

The Cathedral Room contains the highest ceiling in the cavern and is home to natural columns formed when stalactites met stalagmites millions of years before. There is also a crack visible in this room that was reportedly formed by the New Madrid earthquakes of 1811 and 1812. Fissures, cracks, crevasses and small unexplored tubes and tunnels are visible in many places throughout the cavern. The lowest part of the cavern is the Diamond Chapel Room and Chapel Falls which are about ninety-five feet below the earth's surface and about six-hundred feet from the entrance to the cavern.

When the group reached the last part of the open cavern they were standing by Chapel Falls they were at the lowest known pool. Jenny was the first down the final set of stairs where she stood at the edge of the pool and waited for the group to catch up. Guy and the rest of the group sat their packs and ropes down and looked around the lower cavern with their flash lights. Guy pulled out his map and asked the Sheriff to hold it up for the group to study for a minute. They agreed that someone would need to climb down into the lower pool to look around for anything unusual. Guy was the best choice and had the most spelunking experience, he would go.

Jenny tied off two ropes and lowered them into the dry pool. Guy put on a harness and attached a descender from his harness to the first rope and then started a slow descent into the pool. The pool was probably close to thirty feet deep at the shallowest point, which is where Guy headed. When he reached the bottom he started to remove the rope from his harness when Jenny hollered and told him to stay attached. He would have to hold the descender open so that he could move with a little freedom but appreciated the fact that Jenny didn't want to lose positive control of him while he was in the pool.

Guy searched the pool for any evidence of passages and found an area of the lower wall directly beneath where the team was standing that looked like it had been recently scoured and was certainly large enough to enter. He stepped out into the pool area where the team could see him and told them what he could see. Dr. Owens wanted it explored if he thought it was safe enough to enter.

There was no steam present, although the area was hot compared to the normal sixty degree temperature expected in the bottom of this type of cavern. In fact, Guy suspected the temperature was close to ninety. He knew they were definitely getting some geo-thermal convection which meant his fears were most likely true. There must be a breach in the limestone mantle creating a deep core magma vent. He was beginning to see the puzzle much more clearly.

Guy thought for a moment that if the water from the aquifer had heated and caused the limestone to rapidly deteriorate it probably collapsed near the Dam, closing the natural path of the water flow. The water in the aquifer continued heating and as it did pressure probably increased in the system until other weak parts of the aquifer started to collapsed. That's probably why the spring at Noe Creek was running weak and hot. The system was probably venting a little at the spring, but the water usually flowing through this branch of the aquifer was probably stopped by the second apparent collapse at Noe Creek when the last big landslide happened. With both ends collapsed and probably sealed by now, the remaining heated acidic water ate away the limestone around the crevasses leading from the lower pool. It didn't take more than a couple of days for the remaining water to leak into the magma vent and superheat. "This is just like Old Faithfull in Yellowstone!" Guy hollered up at the group. "The water in the aquifer had nowhere to go; it found a crack in the Earth's mantle and blew like Old Faithfull. The difference is that we no longer have a steady supply of water and it shouldn't erupt again. The aquifer collapsed, sealing the upper part of the flow from the Noe Creek area and stopped the water. We should be okay to explore the openings." Guy had figured out the geyser, now he worried about the potential for more collapses in the aquifer beneath the already over pressurized bottom of the lake. With over forty feet of extra water depth pushing down on the top of the deepest section of the lake he knew there was the chance that it too could collapse. He couldn't guess what might happen if the aquifer collapsed beneath the lake and he really didn't want to guess at this point.

Guy asked Jenny to join him at the bottom of the pool and then told Sheriff Wilson to contact his search and rescue volunteer team. He wanted a couple of extra experienced climbers on standby to assist with getting himself and Jenny out of the crevasse if there were any problems. Jenny threw down two extra ropes and a pack of repelling and ascending gear, then she descended over the edge of the pool for the quick repel to the bottom.

"I want to go into the crevasse as far as possible to see what's happened if that's even possible. It's hot down here and I'm guessing it will get a lot hotter in the crevasse. Are you up for this little adventure?" Guy was surprisingly excited about peering into the unknown.

"I'm going because I like adventure and to keep you from falling into the great fiery abyss you think might be down there. This is now officially the strangest thing I've ever been a part of and I don't want you or anyone else getting hurt. Let's get a look at this big hole and get the hell out." Jenny wasn't kidding and Guy could tell she was very tense.

Chapter 26

Jenny had all the gear laid out on the floor of the dry pool that she thought they would need to do some more detailed exploring. She double checked Guy's harness and then made sure her back pack had extra lights and batteries. They were both ready to climb. "If you're ready, let's get this going." Jenny ordered.

Guy led the way into the narrow passage that had never been explored before today. He could tell where the superheated steam had eroded the narrow passages and literally opened up the passage below the cavern all the way to the aquifer. He had been right about the location of the aquifer. It was almost exactly thirty five meters below the bottom of the cavern. From the bottom of the dry pool it was only about twenty meters to the aquifer. He could clearly see the expansive opening below them. It was a dark bottomless hole that a small beam of light barely penetrated. He was anxious to see what the aquifer really looked like.

Guy and Jenny lowered themselves slowly into the darkness until they finally passed through the last narrow part of the thin crevasse and were now leaning against what was the side wall of the empty aquifer. They continued down for another fifteen meters and reached the floor of the aquifer. It seemed like a huge, empty, rough-cut, manmade tunnel to Guy.

Jenny was shining her light all around and seemed mystified by the enormity of the now empty huge tunnel. She was struck suddenly by the unusual heat and humidity. "Is it supposed to be this hot down here?" Jenny was curious.

"Actually, no. It should be closer to about fifty degrees Fahrenheit down here. It's also not supposed to smell like rotten eggs. By all rights, we should be underwater. We need to see if we can tell where the water went. Let's start looking." Guy was in awe of the environment. He had never been in an aquifer before. He had been in the cavernous openings at the mouth of a couple of aquifer outcroppings. Most notably, he had explored the caves at both Blanchard Springs and Mammoth Springs. Each of these gave him a small glimpse of what it might be like to be in a huge natural underground water system. This was uniquely different and, in many ways, very eerie.

Jenny tied a rope from her climbing harness to Guy's. She radioed the group above that they were going to be off the ropes and doing some exploring. She was going to leave the radio keyed on so that they could work and be constantly monitored by the group without having to constantly check-in. Guy and Jenny moved slowly around the huge tunnel, checking every fracture and crevasse for evidence of where the water might have gone. They both noticed that the floor of the aquifer seemed brittle, almost crumbly under foot and surprisingly fragile.

Guy moved methodically in a zig-zag motion across the open space. They moved across the floor from the crevasse where they first entered the aquifer to the far wall. The darkness of the vast space had been almost overwhelming and suddenly they both noticed that the heat had increased, as had the smell of sulfur. What captured his attention next was a glow near the base of the wall just meters from where they stood. It was like seeing the last dying ember at the bottom of a barbecue grill, faint, red and flickering just a bit.

Guy was moving toward the glowing spot and as he neared the point of light in the rock the floor beneath him suddenly crumbled and gave way. He fell grabbing at loose rubble and would have been lost in this newly opened pit if it had not been for Jenny's safety line and her quick reflexes to brace for his fall.

Jenny felt Guy falling within half a second of his initial slip and had managed to wedge herself behind a vertical limestone ledge on the wall where they had been walking. She groaned under the strain of Guy's weight. "Are you alright? I've got you, climb out of there if you can." Jenny hollered, hoping both Guy and the team in the cavern would hear.

"I'm fine. Get me out of here. I'm burning up. Hang on, I think I can climb up." Guy was already leaning over the edge of the broken rocks pulling himself up. His eyes were as big around as pie tins and he was obviously shaken. "You saved my life!" Guy was panting as he got to his feet. He took a look behind him and then a deep breath to calm himself. Jenny was starting to relax and move away from the wall where she had been wedged. "Look at this! It looks like this pit goes down forever. See the red down there? It must be a magma chamber. This is the deep core vent I was worried about. I bet that hole goes a mile down. We need to get out of here."

Jenny caught her breath and looked down the hole. She felt as if her face would catch on fire as she looked into the deep long tube. It had been nearly invisible until Guy had broken through the rock floor showing more of the narrow tube. She could see that he wouldn't have actually gone very far down the tube, it was certainly too small, but he would likely have burned and or suffocated if he had fallen and become wedged in the tube.

Guy and Jenny told the team up top that they were okay and would be coming back up as soon as they could get back to the ropes and opening of the crevasse. It took only a few minutes for them to get back to the ropes and hook up their harnesses to make the ascent back to the top of the narrow crevasse. The two of them were back to the lower pool within just a few minutes. Adrenalin seemed to make the climb a bit easier than it may have been otherwise. Once they reached the pool they were pleased to see a couple of search and rescue volunteers had set up a long ladder to get them out of the pool without having to use ropes to make the last part of the ascent.

Guy was still a bit out of breath as he began to tell the team what they had seen. He was marking the map with specific locations showing the crevasse leading to the aquifer and the location of the deep core vent. Jenny was collecting herself by replacing gear into the various backpacks they had used. She was ready for a cold drink and fresh air and believed that the sooner they left this hell hole and could see daylight, the better.

Dr. Owens was quickly assimilating everything they knew to date about the failure of the aquifer, the deep core vent and the lost water. He was satisfied that the threat to the area was probably over. The heated water had caused the collapses. The fissure between the aquifer and the magma vent had been there for millennia and had just been penetrated by the smallest of openings which grew rapidly as soon as the water and heat combined. He believed the water from the aquifer would release into the top third or so of the magma vent cooling the vent walls and creating a thin crust of silica from the dissolving limestone that would temporarily hold back the water over time. When the vent finally grew wide enough to not fill with silica the water rushed down, superheated and blew back through any opening it could find. The unfortunate folks that had been in the deep part of the cavern when the steam released were in the wrong place at the right time. He also speculated that if the majority of the superheated steam didn't escape back into the now empty aquifer, it would have probably blown out through the top of the cavern and showered most of the old Mountain Village and surrounding neighborhood potentially injuring dozens of other people.

Thayer Davis was breathing a sigh of relief after hearing Dr. Owens' conclusions. He was anxious to get back to the Dam to call his boss and to share what he knew with the engineers. He believed the damage to the Dam was most likely over and they could make repairs and get back to normalcy. Sheriff Wilson had everything he needed for his investigation reports concerning the accident last night and knew what to tell the families of the people who had died in the cavern. He also had what he needed to order the cavern closed to the public until further notice. The group loaded up the gear and headed up to the cavern's entrance.

Guy and Jenny were the last in line to walk back up. As the team was walking up Guy turned and without a word grabbed Jenny and kissed her firmly for just a second and as he let her go he simply said, "Thanks, I think I owe you my life."

Chapter 27

It was close to lunch time when the group exited the cavern. The September air was warm and dry as usual, but the group somehow felt that it was fresh and cool after being in the hot sauna the cavern offered. They were pleased to be back in the open air regardless of the current weather and each was anxious to leave the Mountain Village for their own reasons.

Dr. Owens and Kristi needed to start documenting the newly discovered vent and would need to start planning a small survey expedition back into the cavern with experts experienced in underground mapping. Dr. Owens was sure that the owner would allow the team access to conduct their surveying. Thayer Davis was in a hurry to call his boss and fill him in on their latest discovery. He was relieved to know the landslides had probably ended and that further threats to the Dam were most likely over. The Sheriff wasn't looking forward to making notifications to next of kin about what killed their relatives, however, he was glad to have an answer so that he could get on with the dreadful task. He couldn't hand off this task to someone else; he would do it himself in his usual tactful way.

Guy was satisfied that the volcanic minerals he had observed from numerous water samples were most likely caused by the back flow of superheated steam and hot water into the aquifer and then the water leaching into the closest outcroppings or springs. The gas bubbles and fog were clearly caused by venting of the steam from the aquifer into springs beneath the lake. His immediate concern was to notify the Governor and the public relations media team. He was anxious to start the process in Little Rock for cataloging the cavern and its newly breached magma vent. Since the cavern was privately owned, he feared that it would be hard to ensure any protection for the geo-thermal resource potential that this cavern offered or for the safety of the public going into the cavern or living around the site. It would take special interest groups or a real threat to public safety before legislators would get involved.

Jenny was anxious to get away from the hole in the ground and to go swimming. It had been an exciting morning. But she was hot and smelled like sulfur; a swim would be just the mental and physical therapy she required. She decided she would go home and get Buck and then head for the water.

The team reached the parking lot and Guy asked everyone to join him on the houseboat at six o'clock for hamburgers and beer to mark and celebrate the new discovery. The Sheriff was thankful for the invitation but declined and said his goodbye. The rest of the group eagerly accepted and there was the polite flurry of post-invitation questions about what they could bring or do to help. Guy assured everyone that he was a master at making burgers and his beer budget was superb and didn't need augmenting. The team scattered from the parking lot and left in different directions.

Guy was back on the houseboat within minutes and wasted no time getting undressed and climbing into the shower. He smelled like rotten eggs and wanted to be clean and cool before starting his phone calls to Little Rock.

As Guy was finishing his shower he heard knocking on the door of the houseboat and then heard the door swinging open. It was Jenny. Guy was halfway out of the bathroom before he heard her come through the door and barely had time to get a towel draped around his waist.

"Hey Guy, nice towel. Hope you don't mind if I take a swim off your back deck?" Jenny was spirited, almost animated. She was followed closely by Buck as she walked passed Guy. Her tiny bikini captured his attention and he stared purposefully.

"Please help yourself, admission is free. There's not a qualified life guard on duty, but I'll be glad to keep my eye on you just in case you get a cramp or something." Guy was happy to see her and it showed. Buck stopped long enough to sniff at Guy's towel and then he moseyed on behind Jenny.

Guy hurried to get dressed and then went out on the back deck to check on Jenny. She was floating aimlessly in the cool clear water behind the houseboat. Buck was sitting on the deck lazily watching

Jenny until he lost his focus for a moment as Guy came close to the railing.

"Can I fix you some lunch? I'm going to grab a sandwich and cold drink before I start making some calls that I need to take care of." Guy's voice was polite and inviting.

"No thanks." Jenny waited to see Guy's reaction and then added, "How about letting me fix lunch while you make your calls?"

"Sure, that would be great. I could use the company, but I still owe you for saving my life. Shouldn't I be fixing your lunch or something to help pay that back?" Guy thought it would be nice to talk about anything other than landslides and volcanoes with good company.

"I kind of like knowing you owe me, let's just keep it that way until I need something. Lunch is easy and I really don't mind." Jenny was playing him perfectly.

Guy hurried back to the make shift office in the living room and made a call to the Governor's office. He relayed the information via the Governor's secretary about the cavern and aquifer and then promised a full report via email by later that afternoon. He called the media team and invited them to the houseboat for a briefing. He expected the newspapers and closest TV stations would like to know a little about what they found and why the people died in the cavern. They would have their information in time to brief the TV folks and be prepared for a live "on the scene" feed during the six o'clock evening news.

Mark Dobbs

Guy sat at his computer and typed out his report for the Governor within less than ten minutes from start to finish. He had been through the pieces and parts of this geological event so many times in his mind that it took no time for him to compose his thoughts. The words flowed easily as he described the deep core magma vent and how the opening had been undetected and unopened for millennia waiting for the slow erosion of a relatively thin limestone shelf before millions of cubic feet of water from an aquifer would rush in and literally explode back through the aquifer and cavern. He explained how the aquifer collapsing had actually prevented more horrific steam explosions because the water source had been cut off by the collapse. He listed the casualties by name and location, starting with the grad students and ending with the cavern tourists and tour guide. He also summarized his belief that the deep core magma vent was a great natural energy resource that could be tapped for geothermal purposes if the site were made available for its development. Finally, Guy speculated that the magma vent was stable and since the water was gone he believed that further erosion would not be an issue and any danger to the area was unlikely for the foreseeable future.

Guy concluded his email with recommendations that the Governor recognize Jenny for her service and heroism, also a special commendation to the University of Oklahoma for its support, and a special personal letter of thanks for service above and beyond to the dead grad student's parents. Guy expected the Governor would appreciate his recommendations related to whom to thank.

Guy was sipping a cold beer when Jenny walked in from the back of the boat. She finished her swim and, as promised, went straight to the galley to make a couple of sandwiches. Guy decided to make one last call before lunch. He called his secretary and told her to clear his calendar for the next three days. Guy had decided that he was going to take a little vacation and do some fishing, which he desperately wanted to do at the beginning of this ordeal. Guy sat his phone down and got up just as Jenny came by with lunch so he picked up his beer and followed her to the back deck where she had a table set for two and lunch laid out ready for them to enjoy.

Guy was less hungry than he had been, the beer must have quelled his appetite a bit. Jenny was obviously starving and ate hurriedly for the first half of her sandwich. She had thrown together two very thick, mostly vegetable sandwiches. They were loaded with avocado, tomato, lettuce, sprouts, baby spinach and a bit of smoked ham and honey mustard dressing piled high on toasted hoagies. Guy thought the sandwiches looked like they came from a deli rather than the houseboat's refrigerator. He would have to remember to thank Jerry at the boat dock office for the great provisions.

Jenny finished her sandwich and then took a long drink from the cold beer that had been sitting in front of her waiting until she finished inhaling her food. The beer obviously tasted good to her as she drank lustfully until it was more than half gone. Guy couldn't help but stare as she upended the bottle, threw her head back and let the cool liquid flow down her throat. Something erotic ran through his mind and he squirmed a bit before realizing his lower jaw was hanging open just a bit while he watched.

"Thirsty? I'm getting another beer, do you want one?" Guy was up and moving before he let the high school boy inside his testosterone filled brain make him start acting a bit immature.

"Since you're up, yes I do." Jenny was feeling more relaxed than she had felt in a couple of days. She had beaten the odds today and prevailed over her new enemy – risk. Saving Guy from going in the magma vent gave her the focus she needed and made her feel a bit special for being the right person in the right place at that exact right time.

"Coming right up! By the way, if that bikini you are wearing was standard issue in UDT then I think I'm going to have to enlist; I mean, you really look great in it for a cave diving life saver and all." Guy was trying to give a compliment without sounding like he was trying to make an obvious advance on her. He didn't want her to think he was just another horny thirty-something man looking for the next short term memory.

Guy put the cold beers on the table and sat back down. Jenny was obviously daydreaming and watching some billowy clouds floating from the west against a deep blue summer sky. As she finished her last sip on the first beer she turned back to the table and stared briefly at Guy.

"Since I had to save somebody today, I guess I'm glad it was you. Of course, you know in some cultures that means you are now my slave and I can do whatever I want with you. How 'bout being my slave Mr. Big Shot, think that would get you away from kissing the Governor's butt for a while." Jenny was toying with him to see if she could catch him off guard.

"First of all, I don't kiss butt. I might cozy up to it a little, but I don't kiss. Secondly, I'm not sure anyone I know would be able to be your slave and live to tell about it." Guy was usually quick witted, but somehow felt off balance trying to take shots back at her even in fun.

"I might let you live, if you promise not to tell." Jenny leaned across the table as she spoke, completely disarming Guy by letting her cleavage take center stage for just a moment.

"You know, we've got a couple of hours before the rest of the gang gets here for burgers later. Maybe I could start working off my debt. I worked part time at a spa giving massages while I was in college. Perhaps a massage would be in order your highness." Guy hadn't given a massage in years, but he was clearly willing to pretend that his skills were still well honed.

"Honestly, that sounds perfect. Where do you...." Jenny was interrupted by the sound of a computer beeping from the bank of monitors set up for the seismometers. Guy kind of blinked twice before he realized what the sound was and in disbelief he got up to check what was happening. The monitors for the seismometers at Ozark Isle and the Visitor Center were both alarming.

Chapter 28

"It seems like every time I try to relax something else happens. What could this possibly be now?" Guy was pissed about this interruption. He clearly had other things on his mind and was hoping he would have some quiet time to indulge himself.

The alarms were sounding a seismic change, but they were not at the magnitude that had been recorded earlier for any of the landslide events. Guy was starting to settle down a bit after seeing that these events appeared to be very minor. The investigator inside him still wanted to know what was happening regardless of how slight at this point, so he picked up his phone and called Dr. Owens to ask him to come in and look at the monitors. In the meantime, Guy put his main map back up on the wall and started studying it intensely. The map had been marked up with all the information from each of the recent occurrences and the latest discovery of the magma vent at the cavern.

As Guy studied the map Jenny cleared the rest of the lunch dishes and then walked to the map to see what seemed to be puzzling

Guy. He was using a ruler and pencil and measuring equilateral lines along the path of the aquifer back to the monitoring stations that had alarmed. He found the point on the aquifer that he believed to be centered between both stations and marked it with a red circled X.

When he finished his marking he went back to the monitors to verify the amplitude of both variants. They were nearly identical. If the monitors were showing seismic activity of equal magnitude then surely whatever created them must be near the center point between the monitors. The center point he marked was nearly one hundred ninety feet below the surface of the water about a thousand yards northeast of Frost Point out in the main channel.

Dr. Owens came through the door of the houseboat about the time Guy was starting to tell Jenny what he thought. Guy's attention was immediately diverted to Dr. Owens who was already hustling over to the monitors to see what was happening.

"Hey Ben, see the spikes? They're on both stations, almost perfectly identical." Guy was watching Dr. Owens as he was starting to decipher the monitors for himself.

"These are significantly smaller than any we've seen. If this had been an earthquake event, I would guess that these were aftershocks. This isn't an earthquake and these aren't aftershocks. It must be a new event somewhere between both monitors." Dr. Owens was looking up at the map and beginning to see that Guy had already had the same thought. "Looks like you made the same assumptive leap that I just made. What do you think?"

"I think we just saw the collapse of part of the aquifer somewhere under the lake. It's probably far enough from shore that it won't cause any noticeable damage. No telling how much of this system could collapse after the contact it had with the superheated water. I'm hoping it's done. I want to believe that as more time passes the remaining aquifer will feel less of the effect since the water is basically gone from the part of the system that drained." Guy was succinct and matter of fact.

"Let's hope you're right about future events and, for what it's worth, I totally agree with your theory. We'll leave the monitors in place for a few days just to make sure of course. In the mean time, is it too early for one of those beers you promised us earlier? This trip has added more gray hair to my beard than I can count and I'm ready to take a short mental break." Dr. Owens paused for just a moment as his expression completely changed. Guy handed the older geologist a cold beer. "That poor, poor student. Brad had a lifetime ahead of him to explore Mother Earth only to be killed doing the work he was really passionate about. What a waste. I hope his brother can carry on for them both." Dr. Owens held up his bottle and proposed a short toast.

"To the young rock hounds, may they be fascinated and full of wonder each and every day and never grow too old to learn and explore." Dr. Owens made a toasting motion with his bottle raised in the air and then took a long sip. Somehow the idea of toasting future geologists seemed to make sense at this moment, so Guy and Jenny raised a beer and saluted skyward as well.

The three moved to the back deck and settled in to various lounge chairs to relax for a bit before they expected the other guests might arrive. Guy shared with them that he had extended an invitation to Thayer Davis's team of engineers who were nervously working on sensors and pressure readings, and he invited Jerry from the marina as well. He hoped to share a beer and burger with all of them to say thanks.

Dr. Owens began thinking aloud as they sat and watched the afternoon sun start its bend into early evening. "When we started out here to do this investigation I expected to find simple landslides caused by saturated top soil and loose substrate liquefying and then sliding off into the lake. You know, all the normal kinds of things we expect to see when a lake is rapidly raised to an historic level and allowed to percolate for months waiting for the 'all clear' downstream to let go of its load. Not exactly a monumental undertaking honestly. But contrary to Ockham's Razor, the simplest solution isn't the one that fits our situation. What we seemed to have found is a complex series of events where if any one of them failed to occur the sequence would have stopped and none of this would have happened. Basically, in simple terms, geological events aren't logical at all. They are mostly unpredictable and we are either victims or observers based solely on where we're standing when things happen. With the newly discovered opening to the magma chamber we have uncovered an uncontrollable beast laying in wait for whatever it may choose to do or become. Perhaps it will push up and erupt like a volcano, or it could seal up and lay dormant for the next millennium. Who knows?" Dr. Owens didn't want to appear to sound too prophetic and seamed to stop himself before guessing what the Earth could do next.

"Well here's to Mother Earth, beautiful, unpredictable, a life giver and life destroyer all at the same time." Guy was raising his beer to the sky signaling another toast. The others followed with a mock toast toward the sky and they sat quietly and finished their beers.

The first wave of visitors was coming through the front door of the houseboat. It was Kristi, the grad student and Jerry. They knew they were about an hour early, but they didn't really care. Jerry brought a twenty pound bag of ice and Kristi had picked up a refrigerator box of her favorite Chardonnay. She liked the boxes better than bottles because they didn't break, were easy to carry and she never needed a cork screw.

Jerry barreled through the kitchen dropping the ice in the chest near the sink, helping himself to a cold beer and grabbing three more for the gang on the back deck. "Hey y'all, hope I'm not too early. I saw you out here relaxing and having a beer and decided to join you." Jerry seemed unusually happy as he passed out fresh beers to the group.

"Hey, we're glad you're here. Grab a chair and make yourself comfortable. We were just talking a little about the strange series of events that brought all of us together." Guy was inviting and genuinely glad to see him. Jerry was obviously one of the main cheerleaders for all things related to tourism and recreation on and around Bull Shoals Lake. He was probably relieved that the team was winding down their work and that the threat of more events was most likely over.

"So what do you experts think? Are we going to survive? I have lots of lake front property for sale cheap if we keep having landslides and rumors of earthquakes and volcanoes, not to mention lots of extra boats to go in the 'going out of business' auction." Obviously thick with sarcasm, Jerry couldn't help allowing a bit of humor to hide his obvious penned up stress.

"Perhaps you should sell me all your property while it's so cheap, you pirate! Your precious lake is safe for now, I'll bet your next pay check on that." Guy was sparring with Jerry a bit to help cut the tension and to give Jerry a sense of reassurance that all was probably going to be okay for the time being. "Why don't you show me how to start that grill up stairs on this big bloated boat of yours and I'll get some burgers going." Guy and Jerry climbed the stairs to the expansive covered upper deck.

As they lit the grill, the rest of the party came on board. The team of Army engineers was following Thayer Davis on to the boat and through the front door. Kristi had opened the cooler and was handing out beers to the new group like a hydration station attendant at a marathon running event. Each of the five engineers, including Thayer, took the cold handout without missing a step and saying thanks to Kristi as they passed through and out to the back deck and then up the stair way to the top deck.

"Hey Thayer, good to see you! By the way, no slide rules or pocket protectors on the upper deck. Make sure your guys check their engineering gear at the door!" Guy was being jovial and reached out to shake everyone's hands as they came over and found chairs and a table to relax near. As they sat down, Jerry went down to the kitchen to help Dr. Owens prepare the burgers, condiments and buns for the coming feast.

Chapter 29

Guy turned his attention to Thayer and the engineers at the table. "How's it going at the damn Dam? You guys any closer to solving the pressure puzzle?" Guy was actually very interested in what was going on at the Dam since it was the only mystery left unsolved for now.

"As a matter of fact, we have solved the puzzle. The brilliant minds you see before you have concluded that all of the engineers working on the Dam in the 1950's were very brilliant, but lacked the benefit of modern computers. The pressure differentials are simply a combination of record high water and the continual curing of concrete in this massive structure. Believe it or not, concrete poured fifty years ago is still drying somewhere in the middle of the thickest parts of this Dam. So, concrete that is completely cured is obviously less flexible than concrete that is still drying and it gives a more direct pressure reading. There you are, complex math made easier with computers and once you know the curing rate of concrete as thick as ours then you can calculate all the pressures much better. I hope that's not too much engineering techno-babble for you, but that's the long and short of it." Thayer was definitely happier this evening than he had been in a few days.

"So all you have to do at this point is fix a crack and repair a road. Not bad considering everything horrible that could happen. You have to admit; when you were down in that cavern earlier today you were probably thinking that all kinds of much worse stuff could happen. There was a little fear on your face." Guy was looking at the other engineers as he commented about Thayer. "You guys should be proud of Thayer, he climbed down in the cavern without the protection of a super computer or slide rule and looked into the eye of a real monster today. Thankfully, the monster is quiet and we hope it will stay that way for a very long time." Guy knew engineers hated things they couldn't control and any talk of the magma chamber, especially referring to it as a monster would twist their collective psyches into a knot by reminding them of their inability to fix everything.

"What do you mean you hope it will stay quiet?" There was at least one nervous engineer at the table. "I mean, there really is an open magma chamber and that's like a volcano waiting to blow isn't it?"

"This is one of those good news, bad news kind of stories. What we actually have is a deep core opening, not really a vent. A vent would mean that the magma is coming to the surface, what we have is a stable pocket of magma that is not under any apparent

206

pressure. The only real venting is gas and steam and we wouldn't have that if the water hadn't eroded the rock over time. So the good news is that there doesn't appear to be any reason for this particular deep core pocket to erupt or vent out to the surface. In fact it could theoretically seal itself up over time. That's the good news. The bad news is that like so many other things in nature, this opening is unpredictable." Guy felt a little like the university professor he had once been as he explained a little about what was happening.

"So we're safe here... for a while anyway?" The nervous engineer didn't really seem to be any less nervous after the explanation.

"At least until you finish your burger and beers." Guy was kidding, but having a little fun at the nervous man's expense.

The hamburger patties were brought up from the galley by Dr. Owens. They were laid out on a large plate each individual patty surrounded by its own piece of waxed paper to keep it separated from the others. Jerry followed him up the stairs carrying a large tray of assorted extras for the burgers. He had everything you normally find for a burger and a couple you don't. He also had a large bowl full of potato wedges that were seasoned and ready to be put on the grill before the burgers started. Jenny and Kristi were left to carry the huge cooler of beer to the upper deck. The sight of the two girls carrying the beer on to the upper deck brought a loud cheer from the guys as a couple of them jumped up to help finish carrying the load and to grab fresh beers for themselves.

Guy started cooking right away. The potatoes were first, he knew they would take several minutes to cook and brown so he spread them onto the hot grill and closed the lid. He found his beer and made his way to Jenny's table. Jenny had seated herself next to Dr. Owens and Kristi and the two girls were discussing the differences of scuba diving clear fresh water and clear ocean water while Dr. Owens listened. When Guy joined them the girls were agreeing that clear fresh water diving was less colorful than diving the clear waters around a reef or wreck in salt water. They were blaming algae and decomposing plant material for making the fresh water have a grey or light greenish tint to it and for coating everything with a slimy cover. Guy knew all the environmental biology behind this phenomenon; he had to learn it because of his position.

Almost every year, the Arkansas Department of Environmental Quality would get hundreds of calls complaining about the green color in the water, especially at the end of summer. He always knew the complaints were coming from new residents who hadn't seen the annual algae bloom. It happened nearly every year; usually the hottest month and it could be a rapid obvious change. The new residents around the big man-made impoundments of northern Arkansas were the most upset. These folks had no idea that their clear lakes could look so dirty in such a short period of time. Guy's staff would answer emails, letters and phone calls throughout August and September satisfying the new residents that nothing bad was happening and that it was just a normal stage in the lake's cycle of life.

Guy was feeling relaxed, more relaxed than he had in several days. As the potatoes cooked Guy thought about getting a boat out on the lake tomorrow for a quick bass fishing trip. Jerry had already offered to let Guy use one of the rental fishing boats as long as he had the houseboat rented during his short unscheduled vacation. He was glad he made the decision to take a little time off and he was feeling anxious to explore the feeling that he thought was starting to grow between him and Jenny.

The grill was starting to hiss and smoke a bit, so Guy got up to go check on the progress of the potatoes. The engineers were getting up and pulling their table over to where Dr. Owens and the girls were sitting to be more social. He was glad to see them moving.

The potatoes were nearly done so Guy started moving them to an upper rack and then placed all the burgers on the hot grill covering nearly every square inch available with ground red discs. He put the grill's lid down and stayed close expecting he would have very little time before the burgers would need to be flipped. As he stood there, beer in one hand, tongs in the other he couldn't help but stare over at Jenny. He watched the group as they talked and was enjoying the fact that everyone seemed to be having a nice time. Guy was daydreaming a bit when the sound of fat dripping from burgers and hissing on the hot burners below erupted in flame and smoke. He opened the grill to fan the smoke and check the burgers. After choking a bit on the smoke and holding back the tears from the smoke burning his eyes, Guy decided it was a perfectly timed signal to flip the burgers and then started the process.

Jenny saw the smoke. "You okay over there, or do we need a fire extinguisher?" Jenny was getting up to offer any help that might be needed.

"Trust me, these are perfect. They'll be done in just a couple of minutes. Nothing but the finest charred cow for my friends. Drink up! There's plenty of beer and the alcohol will help you believe that I'm a world class Iron Chef." Guy was waving his tongs like a maestro conducting a philharmonic.

Jenny brought a clean platter to Guy for him to use to move the potatoes off the grill. She sat the potatoes on the table next to all the hamburger building materials and then took the buns back to Guy so they could be toasted. Guy was moving burgers to one side of the grill and ready to take the buns from Jenny when she returned. Jenny watched for a moment and realized Guy was actually quite good with the grill. He had the burgers stacked, medium rare on top, medium in the middle and well done at the bottom of each small stack so that they would remain hot and not overcook while he tended to the buns. He brushed each inner side of the buns with some olive oil and placed them on the grill for a quick browning. As each bun browned he

210

would load them with a burger and move them back to the waiting platter. Within just a few minutes he had the whole stack of burgers and buns stacked and ready for the crowd.

"Come and get it! Fresh sliders fit for kings and drunken sailors. Medium rare on the top, well done on the bottom. Eat up and enjoy." Guy was wiping his hands on a towel and closing the grill. It didn't take a second invitation, the engineers were already at the food and filling plates.

The food was finished and everyone was relaxing and chatting about different subjects while watching the western sky for what was sure to be a grand sunset. There were wisps of thin layered clouds close to the top of the distant hills and horizon where the sun would nestle in and spray an orange to indigo drape across the darkening sky. The eastern horizon was already a royal deep blue with the hint of a rising moon on its horizon. It would be a glorious night; peaceful, calm and soulful without a hint of the tragedies from the preceding days.

As everyone watched the final minutes of the sunset Jerry reminisced out loud and shared a little insight about Bull Shoals with all the out of town visitors sitting on top of his big houseboat.

"You guys, ought to know our little city is very young as cities go. Just started about 1954. Dad said it was a great time, ripe for exploring by the parents of the so-called Baby Boomer generation. It was the post war era. People were enjoying their well earned freedoms. The almighty American dollar was worth a dollar and even more overseas according to my Dad. Seeing the USA by family car was all the craze. You remember the jingle, *See the USA in a Chevrolet.* People were re-discovering the great outdoors. New superhighways were being built and access to major historic and recreational sites was making the country seem ever smaller.

My Dad said it was a boom time. People bought up property around the new shoreline, small family operated resorts began to spring up and every guy with a fishing rod and boat became a paid fishing guide for tourists destined to visit. Tourists from nearby states would flock to the area from Memorial Day to Labor Day to spend family vacations. The intrepid Trout anglers anxious to pit their skills with a fly and flimsy rod would visit throughout the year to wade the swift waters of the White River."

The beer was making Jerry seem like a fair historian. He continued, "Amazingly, the town doesn't lack for technological resources. Seems it's okay to not have malls and big box stores in the neighborhood as long as you have high speed internet access and can shop on-line. The little town has high speed DSL internet phone lines, cable TV and internet, satellite providers, and fiber optic lines. Shoot, some of you guys probably don't have all these services in the bigger cities where you came in from.

FRACKED!

Low real estate taxes, low insurance rates, no traffic and no stop lights. Mostly a blue collar and better Anglo-Saxon retiree population with no desire to see more expansion. When there's a report of a drug or alcohol related incident, the typical violator is the sixty year old Viet Nam Vet being charged with possession of marijuana or driving under the influence after just leaving the VFW post."

Jerry stopped for a moment to sip more of his beer and then continued, "We rarely have any real crime. Although last year, the Harp's grocery store manager, Jeff, was gunned down in his own office during the middle of the afternoon by the angry husband of an assistant manager who had been let go from her job for disciplinary reasons. The husband had recently lost his job to a downsizing, so with the mortgage due and his wife losing her job, the stress overwhelmed him. He decided to take it out on Jeff. After he shot Jeff and was sure that he was dead, the man turned the gun on himself and pulled the trigger, twice. First time purposefully, the second was a nerve and muscle reaction from the first bullet passing through his cerebellum. The town mourned for days. They were sad about Jeff and the family that had the tragedies leading up to the murder and suicide, but most of them were really pissed that their only grocery store was closed for a week pending investigations and obvious clean ups.

Anyway, it's a great little place to get away from the rat race. I'm pretty well locked in to it with the boat dock and all. But honestly, I don't think I would leave even if I could."

At about dark, the engineers were saying their thanks and good-night to the rest of the group and heading back to their respective hotels and motels. Dr. Owens and Kristi were the next to leave, they both seemed emotionally exhausted and appeared in need of a long night of deep sleep. Guy suspected full stomachs and a few beers would help the process.

Thayer Davis left after Dr. Owens. He wanted to get back to his family in Mountain Home, and likewise needed a good night's sleep. Jerry was the last to leave. He stayed long enough to finally realize that it was looking like Guy and Jenny might want a little private time. Jerry could tell, the subtle signs had been there most of the evening. He would see Guy staring at Jenny or vice versa and when the two found themselves staring at each other he could see the faint smiles. They hadn't let on in any other way that there might be something brewing, but he could tell.

Jerry grabbed his half empty beer bottle and graciously thanked Guy for dinner and drinks and then headed off the houseboat and back to his office. His evening crew would be ready to shut down the dock and leave within an hour of sunset, so his timing was perfect to make sure everything was buttoned down as it should be.

With the last of the guests gone, Guy got up and started collecting trash and straightening up the deck. Jenny was up and helping without a word. She grabbed the remaining dishes from the tables and carried them down to the galley and began washing the few items that weren't disposable. Guy carried a large black plastic bag of trash to the front of the houseboat and deposited it in the large trash can at the end of the dock. When he walked back aboard he saw Jenny was finishing drying the last platter. He walked up behind her and put his arms around her waist and gently embraced her against his chest. She laid the platter down and then slowly rotated to face him without allowing his embrace to loosen. Jenny was breathing slowly and deeply and the movement of her ample firm breasts against Guy's chest was erasing away all the stress of the past couple of days. They were both clearly ready for each other as the embrace turned into a deep, long, wet kiss interrupted only by short gasps for air. It was like a choreographed shuffle as they found their way to Guy's berth. They were drowning in each other for the moment and would make love quickly, passionately, and with great satisfaction for each. Both of them seemed surprised by their own sudden and spontaneous physical and emotional fulfillment.

They were both deeply asleep within minutes. Dawn would surely wait and not interrupt this needed sleep.

Chapter 30

Thayer Davis was up early this morning and was already headed to his office in Mountain Home, a place he hadn't seen much in the last forty-eight hours. The engineers he brought in would be finishing up their work at the Dam today and Thayer needed to spend some time in his office catching up on the usual paper work that he knew was stacked in his in box. Thayer's cell phone started ringing before he made it to the parking lot at his office.

"Good morning Mr. Davis, sorry to bug you so early." It was Jack Cole, the senior operations supervisor at the Dam. "I thought you needed to know that the lake level appears to be dropping quicker than we calculated. Normally, as you know, we lose about eight inches of water in a twenty-four hour period with all the penstocks fully open. Since about three o'clock this morning our lake level readings show the lake is dropping by about one and half inches per hour. At that rate we'll lose about two feet of water more per day than we should for some reason. Before you ask, yes the power plant and structure are within normal limits." Jack didn't sound worried. He was just doing his by the book required reporting for anything that was found to be outside of normal limits.

"Thanks Jack," was all Thayer needed to say. He was parking his pickup truck as he ended the cell phone call. Before he got out of the truck he decided to call Guy. He dialed the number and waited for an answer. There was only one ring before the call went to voice mail. Thayer left a message, "This is Thayer Davis. Call me as soon as you can, I need to talk to you about lake levels. We're losing about two feet of water today that we shouldn't lose. I have no idea why. I'm going to work in my office for about an hour and then head to the Dam. Thanks."

Guy woke up slowly this morning although something was causing an unusual early morning commotion at the boat dock. He got up and slipped into the galley to start some coffee and was looking out of the window and could see the dock crew was hustling around loosening cables on the docks so that the docks could move with fluctuating water. Guy knew the lake levels had started dropping since the penstocks had been open for quite some time. With the height of the water and daily drops the crew would be working extra hard to keep up with the movements and to prevent leaving a dock high and dry on a bank or road bed as the water receded.

The front door of the house boat opened quietly and caught Guy by surprise. He leaned back to look to see who was coming through and was suddenly surprised that it was Jenny and Buck.

"Hey sleepy head! Glad to see you're up. You should have gone running with me, it was great and poor Buck was ready to see some grass and dirt, if you know what I mean." Jenny woke up with enough energy for three people. She was smiling and glistening in the early morning sun shining through the windows.

"Those guys look busy out there. I guess the water levels are finally starting to go down." Guy was still a bit groggy and looking forward to his first cup of coffee. "You look refreshed and full of life and I feel like I slept hard enough to make up for a week."

"You were like a zombie this morning, so I checked for a pulse before I went running. When I woke up I wasn't sure what happened to me last night. I think I just passed out." Jenny paused. "Thanks for last night, I think I needed that." Jenny was getting two cups out of the cabinet above the coffee pot and began pouring coffee for them while she was talking.

"Looks like I missed a call on my cell phone. Thayer Davis called and left me a message." Guy punched in the voice mail codes and listened to Thayer's message. "You aren't going to believe this. Thayer says the lake is losing water faster than should be possible. He said the Dam is doing its thing correctly and that he may need help figuring out where the water is going. That must be why the boat dock crew is hustling so much this morning."

Guy had dressed quickly and rejoined Jenny for coffee and sweet rolls on the back deck of the houseboat. They were watching the commotion around the docks when a bass boat slipped in next to them and tied up at the dock. The guys were in a hurry and went straight into the dock office.

The fishermen were coming back out within a minute of arriving and they were followed out of the office by Jerry. Jerry watched the guys get in their boat and pull away from the dock and then he walked aboard the houseboat to see Guy.

"Mornin' y'all. Hey thanks again for the hospitality last night, it was a great break. Hate to start your day off with a mystery, but I need to tell you what I just heard. Maybe you can make some sense of it." Jerry was in very early supervising dock movements. He would be diving later in the day to move docking anchors so he wanted to make sure everything was going just right.

"We were wondering what the guys from the bass boat were doing, they must have passed on something interesting. What kind of mystery have you got?" Guy reasoned by now that Jerry already knew the lake level was dropping abnormally fast and he wondered what else it could be that he had just heard.

"The guys that just came in told me that they saw what looked like a whirlpool out in the main channel northeast of Frost Point. Sounds bizarre to say the least, however, we're also losing water faster than I've ever seen. Something is messed up somewhere." Jerry wasn't panicky, but he was showing more fear about this than he had with the landslides.

Guy reasoned that rapidly falling water could hurt the boat dock in a hurry; landslides hadn't been a threat since they had occurred away from this protected cove. "Thayer Davis called me this morning and told me the lake level was falling rapidly, maybe we need to do some checking." Guy thanked Jerry for the info and Jerry disappeared back into the office. Guy knew Jerry was going to be very preoccupied for some time to come.

"Jenny, I'm going to call Dr. Owens and invite him and his assistant to join us. Let's get this beast fired up and ready to cruise. I think we need to go look at a whirlpool." Guy was already giving up on getting a short vacation. Maybe this whirlpool would turn out to be nothing and he could get back to what he was hoping to do, like getting some deserved rest and recreation.

"Whirlpool? In a lake? They can't be serious. I've seen a few at river outlets to the ocean, seeing one in a lake will be a first. This should be interesting." Jenny was already keyed up for the new adventure.

"Dr. Owens and Kristi should be here in about fifteen minutes. I'm going to get the maps back out and tape them to the wall again. Do you need anything from shore before we head out?" Guy was sure

Jenny was ready to go, but he wanted to give her a chance to think about her gear before they left the dock.

Jenny did a quick mental check list while she checked her gear. Everything was in order and she couldn't think of anything she might need. "Nope, good to go. Anytime, anywhere is my latest motto."

Guy was already staring at the map again, like he had several times before. As he studied he was beginning to suspect something potentially horrible. The last seismic reading they recorded was located northeast of Frost Point. He wondered if what he believed was a collapse in the aquifer at that location was now draining the lake.

Dr. Owens and Kristi came aboard the houseboat right on time. As soon as they came aboard, Guy started casting off lines and Jenny got the big boat underway. Guy went back in as soon as the last line was let go so that he could share the latest news with Dr. Owens and to discuss the reported location and its possible connection to the last seismic reading.

Jenny piloted the houseboat out of the marina cove and into Jimmy Creek. The weather was perfect, there's was no wind and only a few clouds in the sky. There were less than a handful of boats on the lake this morning, so boat traffic wouldn't bother them while they investigated whatever this event was. The houseboat gained speed as it reached the middle of Jimmy Creek and headed north to the main lake. Jenny passed Jimmy Creek island and turned left out into the main lake and toward Frost Point. As she neared the point she slowed the big boat and let it drift to a stop near where they could observe the surface of the water in all directions. The group immediately started scanning for anomalies.

Kristi was the first to spot the water churning out in the channel. It was about a thousand yards out from the point, almost exactly where Guy had marked the map showing where the seismic occurrence had been. Guy asked Jenny to slowly move the boat closer where they could see the event better.

"For God's sake, THAT IS A WHIRLPOOL! Guy, what do you think? Is it draining into the aquifer?" Dr. Owens was amazed at the sight.

There were not very many geological events that either Guy or Dr. Owens had not seen at some time in their lifetimes. Staring out at the calm lake and seeing a small whirlpool disappearing below the surface and presumably going down to a depth of about one hundred ninety feet was bizarre to say the least. It was clear to both of these experts that the water was draining into the aquifer.

Chapter 31

"We need to find out where the water is going." Guy was stating the obvious. He knew where the water was going, he was just afraid of the consequence.

"You know as well as I do that it's going into the aquifer. We need to call the owner of the cavern and give him a head's up." Dr. Owens was obviously thinking like Guy. They knew this water could only go to one place.

Guy hurried back into the dining area of the houseboat and found his cell phone. The phone's screen showed that he had missed a couple of calls in the last ten minutes, probably while he and the rest of his group were on the upper deck of the houseboat watching the whirlpool. The missed calls both came from Marion County Sheriff's office. He decided to call Sheriff Wilson back first.

"Sheriff, this is Guy Fredricks. I missed your call earlier. What's up?" Guy was in a hurry and skipped the normal 'Good mornings and how are you'.

"Guy, thanks for calling me back. The owner of the cavern called me a little while ago. He's got steam coming up from the cavern entrance. He's not letting anyone get close to the place. He seems really scared. I think he sees his business going up in smoke, or steam in this case. Anyway, I thought you needed to know." Sheriff Wilson wasn't trying to be funny, it just came out before he realized what he was saying.

Guy went back up to the top deck and shared what he heard with the group. Almost instinctively, they all looked back to the southeast toward the town of Bull Shoals. They seemed surprised when they couldn't see steam rising over the hills. Their attention quickly returned to the whirlpool.

Kristi had started recording the whirlpool with a video camera she had brought and Dr. Owens was getting some digital pictures to record the event. Guy recorded the latitude and longitude from the boat's GPS and transcribed it to the overlay map he had posted on the wall inside the houseboat. Just as he suspected, the location was nearly identical to the spot he had marked as the estimated area of seismic activity. "X marks the spot." Guy quietly said to himself. Once he had the map marked he went back to the top deck.

"Jenny, what do you think? Would it suck the boat down to the bottom?" Guy was ready to break the tension.

"I don't think the boat would be affected, but I'm not sure I would want to be a fish around that thing. That vortex is deep. No telling what it might do." The amazement was showing on Jenny's face.

"Do you guys hear that?" Kristi was looking back toward town again.

Suddenly, what Kristi heard was loud enough for everyone to hear and it was getting louder. The whole group was now looking back toward town again. Something sounded like a jet engine afterburner firing up and before it peaked they saw a plume of steam blow up into the blue sky over the town. There was a time lag between seeing the plume and hearing the horrendous noise made as the geyser of steam blew into the air above town.

Guy called Sheriff Wilson within a few seconds of seeing the plume. The sheriff was already on his way back to Bull Shoals and the cavern. He had monitored an emergency nine-one-one call from a resident living across the street from the parking area and entrance of the Mountain Village and cavern. She called after the explosion had blown out her front windows and scattered debris all over her house and yard.

Within minutes, emergency crews from the city's fire department, police department and sheriff's office were on scene. The Mountain Village area looked like it had been hit by a bomb. The structure at the entrance to the cavern was literally gone. The rest of the Mountain Village was in ruins from rocks, building materials, and boiling water falling all around the property. There was steam still spewing from the area that had been the small building at the entrance of the cavern.

The emergency responders were searching through the debris looking for the cavern owner and anyone else who might have been trapped in the debris. They found the owner, buried under a pile of debris in the area that was previously his office. He was probably on the phone when the explosion hit. He was still alive but barely breathing and not responsive. Two firemen worked quickly to extricate him from the rubble where he was trapped.

As the firemen were getting the owner onto a stretcher they heard the jet engine noise again. The steam was starting to pump out of the cavern opening and was getting significantly denser within just a few second. Hot water droplets were now falling all around the emergency workers at the scene. Rescuers scattered from the cavern opening as quickly as they could to avoid the hot water. The two firemen working with the injured cavern owner quickly covered him with a waterproof blanket and then hunkered down crouching over the injured man to help protect him from the hot water by shielding him under their fire suit protected bodies. The owner looked really bad and probably wouldn't survive the ride to the hospital.

The noise intensified and roared again until there was an explosion of water and steam shooting over two hundred feet into the air and showering the area all around the village with boiling water. Dozens of people had gathered and were standing out in the parking lot of the Mountain Village and along the road way next the village watching all the commotion. They were now trapped in the path of thousands of gallons of falling boiling water. The emergency crews were on their radios calling for backup as soon as the geyser let up. They were going to need extra help and more ambulances to take care of the many new burn victims.

Sheriff Wilson was just driving into the parking lot and could see people running and screaming. He called his dispatcher and put out a request for mutual aid from the Baxter County Sheriff's office and Lakeview city police. His first order of business was to get people out of the geyser's fall out zone and to prevent further injuries. He started assisting injured people as quickly as he could while other emergency responders were arriving. Within minutes there were several new ambulances and EMTs on the scene helping with the burn victims.

As soon as the last victim was moved from the parking area the Sheriff had the police and deputies set up an evacuation and buffer zone of about a thousand feet in all directions from the cavern. They had about forty houses within the one thousand feet buffer zone and worked quickly to notify all the residents they could reach that they should stay indoors or evacuate and why, as if they didn't already know.

Sheriff Wilson called Guy and told him what was happening. There had now been two geysers within about twenty five minutes of each other. Thankfully, the newest explosion of steam didn't destroy any more buildings or throw deadly debris into the air, however, they had casualties from burns caused by boiling water. The Sheriff explained the safety perimeter he put in place and then told Guy that various reporters had just arrived and then ended the call so that he could get back to work.

As soon as the Sheriff hung up, Guy realized that he needed to call the Governor again. With reporters on scene it wouldn't be long before stories started hitting the national wire feeds. He didn't want the Governor to be caught off guard.

Guy's call was put through to the Governor almost immediately. "Good morning, I didn't expect to get through to you personally and certainly not this soon." Guy was surprised.

"I was in an early budget session and on a break when your call came in. Don't take this personally, but you're a wonderful diversion from state budget work. So what's going on? I thought you were on a much deserved vacation." The Governor was very attentive knowing that Guy didn't call just to pass the time.

"Well, I thought I was on vacation too, until I got going this morning. We thought our landslides and aquifer problem had ended. Turns out, the lake seems to have developed a leak into the aquifer somewhere deep under water in the main channel. The water is apparently going into and through the empty aquifer tunnel and feeding into the magma vent. We've had two geysers this morning at the Mountain Village in Bull Shoals. These geysers make Old Faithful look like a squirt gun." Guy paused for a moment to see if the Governor would react.

"You said two geysers this morning and the water is coming from the lake? What's the lake level doing? How much water are we losing? I need more info, I need to know what you can do and what you need from me." The Governor wasn't wasting words and was obviously concerned.

"We've heard that the local fire and police have cordoned off a safety zone around the geyser. They had to deal with several burn victims this morning, mostly spectators that had gathered around after hearing or seeing the first eruption. The cavern owner is badly injured and not expected to recover from his injuries and burns. The lake is okay for now, but the Corps of Engineers says we're losing about two feet of water per day at the current rate." Guy hated telling the Governor about more injuries, but it had to be done so he would be prepared to respond if reporters were able to catch him.

"So what can we do?" The Governor's tone had diminished and he seemed to be showing a bit of helplessness.

"Right now I've got my team on the lake at the site of the presumed leak. Believe it or not, we're watching a whirlpool. We've only been out here about forty five minutes and we're just starting to get some ideas about what to do. I'll have to call you back as soon as we come up with something. About all you can do right now is to get your public relations folks back up here to help deal with the reporters, residents and tourists. I'm sure the local Sheriff's would appreciate the help." Guy hated not having some kind of plan, even a rough idea would be better than nothing. All he could do was reassure the Governor that he was working on the problem.

Chapter 32

"We need to figure out what can be done to stop this geyser. If the water from this whirlpool is ending up in the magma vent then it looks like it may continue erupting every fifteen to twenty five minutes until we lose this lake." Guy wasn't going to let this get out of control. He wouldn't let this huge beautiful lake die like this.

"The Sheriff is evacuating the area around the cavern to get people out of the path of the boiling water. What we need now is a plan to stop the whirlpool and the draining of lake water." Guy had everyone's attention and was moving them back inside the houseboat to start working on ideas to help fix this problem.

"We need to see the hole in the bottom of the lake that's making the whirlpool. Maybe we can just plug it." Kristi was the first to shoot out an idea.

"Plugging the hole is a good idea. Although, I wonder what kind of plug would work since we're assuming the roof of the aquifer probably collapsed creating the hole in the first place. Plugging it could cause the rest of the aquifer to collapse as well." Dr. Owens wasn't being critical, he was concerned that one thing could lead to another and then they would have an out of control progressive collapse.

"I agree that we need to see the hole." Guy was starting to write on a large clean sheet of chart paper that he had just taped to the wall next to the planning map.

"Seeing the hole could be an issue. The vortex of that whirlpool is going to make getting close to the hole tricky no matter what you try. You won't be able to use a remote camera. The currents will ultimately foul the lines by the time the camera gets to the right depth. You're going to need a diver on a good tether." Jenny was the underwater expert and no one was ready to argue with her point.

Guy was writing on the chart as he spoke. "Jenny's right. We're going to need a diver willing to get the video that we need."

"We can't just plug the hole. The aquifer needs to be filled so that it will have a neutral pressure against the lake above it to keep it from collapsing again." Dr. Owens was staring at the geological overlay map. He believed that the aquifer would need to be refilled with water to ensure the stability of the whole part below the lake.

"We already believe the aquifer is sealed on the north and east end near Noe Creek. That's where the flow of water was coming from for this branch, that's why it emptied." Kristi was standing at the map now.

"So you're saying we need to seal off the aquifer somewhere between the magma vent and the lake shore." Guy was using his ruler to calculate distances and marking lines across the aquifer every one hundred feet from the location of the magma vent. "The aquifer crosses under dry land at Pinehurst Point and then turns south and goes back under the lake on the north side of Bull Shoals Boat Dock cove and turns back under dry land just under the east end of the cove closest to the boat dock office. It's about three thousand feet from the magma vent to the boat dock cove." Guy was still marking the map while he finished his description.

"We know the aquifer can't be filling up with water completely before the geyser erupts, and that hot water and steam is probably blowing back down the aquifer for quite a distance, kind of like what we see above the ground when it does blow. How are we going to seal the aquifer that far from either the whirlpool or the vent? It's not possible. We need another alternative." Dr. Owens was staring at Guy's recent markings on the map.

"Ben, we've seen part of the aquifer, we know it's a rough cut tunnel. I believe the area we need to get to is probably reachable on foot from the cavern, but we can't do it between geyser eruptions and while we have fairly deep water rushing through it from the whirlpool." Guy had quit marking on the map and had taken a seat around the table with the others.

"Why don't we just seal the aquifer as close to the cavern as possible. We can do a controlled explosion to make the aquifer collapse and seal this thing up so the water doesn't get to the magma vent." Kristi was thinking aloud and saying what the rest of the group was most likely thinking.

"We can't. If we collapse parts of the aquifer under that area of town we could cause a collapse in the ground above the aquifer causing severe damage to the town. Just like the landslides we've seen where we believe other parts of the aquifer first collapsed. We might be creating a horrific sink hole that would swallow up homes and businesses between the cavern and lake shore." Dr. Owens was right of course. They had seen how the previous collapses had impacted the land above. Any attempt to manipulate the tunnel under that much of a small mountain of limestone could be catastrophic for the town.

"Maybe we just need to collapse the part closest to the shore. If we get a landslide there it will be relatively minor and probably only effect one or two homes at the most." Guy was thinking about the collapses that they had already witnessed. It made sense to him that shoreline landslides would have the least effect on the surrounding areas. "The best shoreline bank to use is at Pinehurst Point. It's a large point and the Corps of Engineers property will probably absorb the biggest impact of any landslide." Guy was up and looking at the map again. He calculated the distance to the magma vent from Pinehurst Point, it was more than five thousand feet. "That's almost a mile from the magma vent and about a mile and half from the whirlpool."

"We can't just force a landslide and hope that it seals the aquifer below, we're going to have to collapse the aquifer first and plan for the likely landslide." Kristi was coming to grips with the geophysics of this puzzle.

Guy was standing at his chart paper now and had the following items written out for the group to see and discuss:

1. Observe and measure the hole at the base of the whirlpool

2. Plug the hole

3. Get in the aquifer and find the area to be sealed near Pinehurst Point

4. Seal the aquifer

5. Unplug the hole and refill the sealed off branch of the aquifer

"So here's what we have so far. The steps make sense. This is a straight line critical path plan if ever there was one. If any step fails, then we can't move on to the next step. So as they say in the movies, 'failure is not an option'. Jenny, we need some underwater video equipment and a couple hundred feet of tether. Do you want to dive on this?" Guy was willing to call for back up if Jenny couldn't or wouldn't do the dive.

"I'm ready. We've got good line for a tether in the anchor compartment of this houseboat and I always carry a small underwater video camera in my diving gear. You never know when you will need to record a Loch Ness monster or UFO or whirlpool after all. As long as I don't have to stay at that depth more than a couple of minutes it shouldn't be a problem with the gear I've got on board." Jenny was already getting excited to do the dive. This was truly unique and would require skills that she was anxious to exercise and very qualified to use.

Diving to the depth of the whirlpool was beyond the safe limit for all but the most experienced divers. Jenny had been this deep on regular SCUBA equipment before and knew that her stay time on the bottom would be less than eight minutes to avoid any real decompression issues. If she stayed longer, she would have to decompress for short intervals at varying depths all the way back to the surface. She was obviously hoping to make very short work of the dive. The only safe way to stay longer and avoid decompression problems would be to get a SCUBA tank filled with a more sophisticated mix of gasses to prevent nitrogen from building up in her body during the dive. She would need either trimix or heliox. These gas compounds contain higher amounts of helium which reduces the amount of oxygen and nitrogen found in normal compressed diving air. The lower portion of nitrogen would reduce the chance of nitrogen narcosis and the possibility of getting decompression sickness. Since these mixes weren't readily available, she knew she would have to make a very short dive and try to avoid the risk of deep diving injury.

"So, unless someone objects, let's get a close look at this whirlpool before we do anything else." Guy was picking up his phone as everyone sat and stared at the list. The list was short and at first glance seemed simple. Everyone knew that each step was a serious milestone in and of itself. No single step would be easy.

"Thayer, this is Guy. We found your leak. It's about mid-channel in the lake northeast of Frost Point. Believe it or not, we're watching a whirlpool. It must be draining the lake here and we think the water is making it back to the Mountain Village cavern and into the magma vent." Guy made quick work of telling Thayer Davis what they had found. He waited briefly for Thayer's response.

"What are we going do? I was worried that we might lose the Dam, I never thought about losing the water. That geyser is blowing water out on top of a hill which naturally drains to the White River just below the Dam. It may not be fast enough to start flooding land downstream, but we don't have control of discharge. That makes flooding possible and generating power impossible. I'm ordering the operations supervisor to shut down the penstocks and to stop generating. We can't stop the water from leaving the lake at this point, but we can at least slow it down a bit." Thayer was straining to hold back obscenities at every other word. He knew he had no control of the lake at this point and unless something changed, he would not be able to sustain his primary function and mission. This would be devastating to everyone in the area. The economic impact to local businesses and the families that support them would be life altering for quite some time.

"Thayer, we've got a plan. It's not great, but it could work. We're getting ready to put Jenny in the water to try and get some video of the hole causing the whirlpool. Once we know what it looks like we may be able to figure out how to stop this mess. We need to get your okay on what we're thinking about doing. Some of the plan might cause some lake front property to change. Can you get out here to help?" Guy hoped Thayer would join the team again. They could potentially use some engineering expertise and would definitely need him around if they had to make decisions that could impact the lake. Even though the lake was literally bleeding to death, it still belonged to the U.S. Army Corps of Engineers and the American tax payer. Thayer was the right person to clear everything through.

"Give me about an hour and I'll be there. I can get a boat at the dock and meet you out there." Thayer was anxious to get to work. Anything he could do was better than just watching the lake drain.

Chapter 33

Jenny was on the back deck checking her diving gear. She had also pulled out her video equipment and checked the batteries for both the camera and underwater flood light. Everything was in good order and she was beginning to slip into her wet suit. Guy walked out to the back deck and sat in a chair close to where Jenny was getting ready and watched her for a minute before breaking the silence.

"Are you sure you want to do this?" Guy didn't want to sound like he was questioning her decision, but he wanted her to know that he was concerned about her safety.

"I can do this. You won't find anyone around more qualified. I would prefer to make this a hard-hat dive, but we don't have the time or the equipment." Jenny was reassuring and firm. She didn't lack for confidence and made sure that Guy understood that she wasn't making this decision lightly or without the ability to carry through with the job safely.

"You're going to be on a long tether. I don't want you getting away down there. I need you to remember to give the rope two tugs when you reach bottom. I'm going to have you on a stopwatch. When you hit six minutes at the bottom I want you to give me three yanks to indicate that you're coming back up. If you don't signal me I'm going to haul your ass up at seven and a half minutes. I'm not taking chances on this." Guy was staring directly at Jenny as he spoke and was as serious as he could be without talking down to her.

"I'll be fine. The video equipment will be tied to my buoyancy compensator and I have extra lights if I need them. There is plenty of air in my tank even if I have to decompress for a while. This will be easy compared to hiking in that aquifer later. That's uncharted and unpracticed so its way scarier as far as I'm concerned." Jenny was right about the uncharted aquifer. No one in recorded history had been in a recently emptied aquifer, much less making plans to blow-up part of it to try and cause a controlled collapse.

Guy was coiling the rope tether onto the deck near Jenny when they both heard the now unmistakable sound of the geyser erupting again. As soon as Dr. Owens and Kristi heard the sound they walked out of the galley to the front deck to watch the plume of steam. When the geyser collapsed out of sight Dr. Owens and Kristi walked through the houseboat and out onto the back deck to see if Jenny was ready to dive.

Jenny was suited up and buckling herself into the buoyancy compensator vest and tank assembly. Guy was attaching the rope tether to a D-ring on the back and bottom of the vest. It was strong enough to handle five times the weight of its diver and all her gear.

Jenny inched her way to the railing gate, put her mask on, zeroed her diving computer and timers, looked back at the group and gave a quick thumbs-up and then stepped over the side of the houseboat and into the water. There was very little splash considering all the gear she was wearing and carrying and she quickly and quietly disappeared under water. Telltale bubbles were all that remained after just seconds of the small splash. Everyone watched the bubbles as they moved across the open water closer to the whirlpool.

Guy was feeding out rope to prevent it from impeding Jenny's swim. He passed every inch through his hands as if to feel each braid as a double check that the tether would pull her to safety if it was needed. Dr. Owens sat in a deck chair out of the sun while Guy watched the rope. Kristi was busy with her video camera capturing the latest eruption and now Jenny's descent into the water and bubble trail out to the whirlpool. Kristi climbed the back stairs to the top level so that she could get a better view of the lake surface while the dive progressed.

It seemed like an eternity waiting for the signal from Jenny that she had reached bottom. Two tugs on the line were strong and obvious, though any yank regardless of how weak would have been detected by Guy's steadfast handling of the rope. Guy started his stopwatch and then looked up for a second or two to watch the whirlpool. He was nervous for sure, especially since the bubbles from Jenny's SCUBA gear had obviously been trapped in the underwater vortex and comingling with the whirlpool so that they were no longer separate and distinct. The bubbles had been his only visible indicator of where Jenny might be.

Guy waited and watched. His stopwatch read five minutes and fifty seconds. He began counting down. "Five, four, three, two, one. Three pulls and she should be heading back."

There was no pull on the rope. Guy tightened the rope a bit to make sure it wasn't overly slack, still no pull. He was watching his stop watch again, very intensely. Dr. Owens was out of his chair and looking over the railing at the back of the large houseboat. Seven minutes passed.

Guy was tying off the rope to the back railing and getting ready to pull Jenny back up. "I told her I would haul her up at seven and half minutes. I wasn't kidding, she knows that I'll do it. Ten, nine, eight, seven, six, five, four...."

Without warning the rope started pulling away from Guy. He thought he felt several pulls and then the rope went taut. He pulled with all his strength but could barely gain any headway. Guy was panicking, pulling the rope fast and furious with as much strength as he could and not making any progress. Dr. Owens grabbed the rope behind Guy and started helping him pull. The two men were now pulling in unison.

Guy and Dr. Owens had been pulling for over a minute. They quickly tried changing positions around the back of the boat trying to get more leverage and their pulling was moving the boat closer to the whirlpool but clearly not bringing Jenny up from the bottom. Guy was certain that Jenny must have been caught by the whirlpool and was probably being pulled into the aquifer. He was sure that no matter what he did at this point she would require decompression and she wouldn't be able to manage it on her own if she was injured or, God forbid, unconscious.

Furiously they pulled but were still stalemated in their effort. The rope wasn't coming up. Kristi was videotaping their frantic attempt and she began sobbing uncontrollably. She watched the two men hoping that they would quickly and easily drag Jenny to the surface. In fact, Kristi expected that Jenny would pop up at the end of the rope and be cussing them for pulling her up like some giant halibut.

Kristi had seen enough death and injury for anyone in such a short time and couldn't stand the thought of Jenny being a victim. Her sobs turned to loud crying as she sat her video camera down on a nearby table. Kristi put both hands over her face and fell into a chair and wept.

As the two men were beginning to give up hope of making any progress on the rope they saw the unmistakable bubbles in the water showing the path of a SCUBA diver moving away from the whirlpool. Guy was hypnotized by the sight and watched without blinking. Dr. Owens was moving back and forth on the deck like a caged cat rubbing his hands together trying to eliminate the sting that came from pulling so fiercely on the rope. Kristi looked over at the water just in time to see Jenny surface about a hundred feet from the boat.

Guy just stood there watching Jenny swim to the boat. Dr. Owens sat back down in his chair and wiped his forehead after taking a deep retreating breath. Kristi's crying turned to laughter as she realized that Jenny was fine and had made it back from the bottom. She ran down the stairs and on to the back deck, wiping tears from her eyes as she went.

"ARE YOU OKAY?" Guy hollered at Jenny.

She answered with a wave as she swam the last few yards to the boat. Guy was on the ladder to grab her as she got close enough. Once she was next to the ladder she started handing up her gear for Guy to take. She gave him the video camera and her mask, then she unbuckled her buoyancy compensator vest and tank and let them slide off into his waiting grasp. With the big gear out of her way, she reached down and grabbed her flippers and then threw them on board as she started climbing up the ladder.

244

As Guy was setting the buoyancy compensator vest down he noticed the tether rope still tied to the D-ring although it appeared to have been cut three or four feet from where it was tied. "What happened? I thought I... we, lost you. You didn't signal that you were coming up and we started pulling. We couldn't make the rope come up."

"I did exactly what you wanted. At six and half minutes I was done and started to pull the rope to signal you that I was coming up. When I grabbed the rope to yank on it, I realized that the rope felt like it had started pulling back. I back tracked a few feet in the muck down there and found it wrapped around one of the big rocks at the edge of the whirlpool hole. That rock was starting to creep toward the opening of the aquifer. Thank God I carry a sharp knife. I cut myself free and headed back up." Jenny was out of breath and pausing mid-sentence to gulp air while she told her story. As she talked she saw that the rope had been tied off on the railing. She walked over, removed her diving knife from its sheath strapped to her calf and then with a swift movement cut the line and let it fall into the water below. "You guys were trying to pull up a thousand pound rock that was in the wrong place at the wrong time."

Guy didn't know whether to get angry or hug Jenny. He finally just smiled and asked if she could share the video and her findings with the group. Jenny unzipped her wet suit and slid out of it and into a waiting towel that Guy was now conveniently holding for her. Dr. Owens patted Guy on the back and walked inside to the living room. He was followed by Kristi who stopped long enough to smile and hug Jenny before making it back inside. When Jenny finished drying off she gathered up her video camera and headed into the living room to view the video. Guy followed her without a word.

Chapter 34

"Look at the bottom of the whirlpool! It looks like a waterfall, not a drain hole!" Kristi was completely shocked. She had expected to see something resembling a bathtub drain, not an underwater waterfall. The group agreed that it looked like a large section of rock had dislodged beneath a massive ledge rock and the water was draining out under the huge slab of limestone. It was an opening about four feet square tucked back and under the mammoth ledge probably six or eight feet back below the larger rock.

"Actually, I think we got lucky. If we can figure out a way to tip that ledge rock to plug the hole below it, we might have a temporary fix." Guy was sure that the larger rock could plug the hole.

"If we tip it we may just weaken the area around the ledge and open the hole more. I don't think we can just tip the ledge without significantly affecting the rest of the area." Dr. Owens was mesmerized at what he saw. He knew there were probably natural openings in the rock below the lake that fed springs throughout the area, but this one was pumping water under great amounts of pressure straight to a magma vent over two miles away and then creating a killer geyser.

"Why not pump concrete down there and fill the hole. It will…." Kristi's thought was interrupted by the sound of a motor boat pulling up along side of the houseboat.

"It's Thayer Davis." Guy got up and went to the front deck to greet Thayer. Thayer had used one of the Corps of Engineers speed boats normally used by their enforcement officers to get out to houseboat's location.

"Good to see you Thayer. We've got some video you need to see." Guy hustled Thayer into the living room and restarted the video. Everyone was silent as the video started again, still amazed at what they were seeing.

"That's crazy. How did that happen?" Thayer was shocked at the sight of the underwater waterfall and the huge volume of water that was pouring out of his lake.

"We believe it was another collapse in the aquifer. That whole area is apparently unstable. With the water gone from these underground tunnels and with the extremely high water in the lake, the differential in pressures is causing the roof of the aquifer to collapse. We could lose this lake if we don't do something to stop it." Dr.

Owens was the first to answer the question. He was hoping an engineer might see a way to stop the flow.

"How in the world do you plan to stop that? Even if we stop this one, what's to prevent another one from starting?" Thayer wasn't panicking, but he was close. His livelihood and the lives of thousands of people could change for a decade if the lake drained as a result of this geological catastrophe.

"We're not sure yet how to stop it. We just started throwing out ideas when you drove up. Kristi was saying something about concrete if I'm not mistaken. Go ahead and finish what you were saying." Guy was trying to get the group back on track and hoped that the mental gymnastics would keep the group focused and keep Thayer from a breakdown.

"I was saying that we should fill that spot with concrete. The right mix will set up quickly even underwater." Kristi knew that with enough Portland cement in the mix the concrete would cure underwater.

"We don't have the resources anywhere locally to pour concrete out in the middle of the water. That would take a barge. Or maybe a ferry. They still run a ferry service about thirty miles up lake from here." Thayer was finally out of his stupor and thinking about solutions. "The problem is, we don't know how much concrete it will take and it's not like we're pouring into a form that we can measure and calculate volume. We don't know how far the concrete will run before it starts to fill the hole." Just like that he was beginning to show signs of panic. This wasn't a measurable problem with calculable solutions. There were clearly too many unknowns for Thayer to cope with in his normal engineering world.

"What if we use the big ledge rock without trying to tip it or move it? We don't need to shift everything around, we just need to get part of the ledge to seal the hole. Let's cut it and let the top part fall onto the opening and seal it off." Kristi was thinking out of the box which is exactly what they needed now. Something quick that was possible and made sense.

"Thayer, can that rock be cut underwater?" Guy snapped the question to Thayer to get him back on task.

"I don't think we can with any equipment that is available within a thousand miles." Thayer was shaking his head and staring at the paused image of the hole still showing on the television set.

"I think I can cut that rock. We have the equipment to burn through almost anything. I think we can literally melt the rock, you know, turn it into molten rock and let it flow until the end of the ledge falls over the hole." Everyone was staring at Jenny. No telling what kind of thoughts they were having. Jenny was ex-UDT and she was the underwater expert after all. Maybe she could make something work.

Jenny knew that her office was experimenting with different packaging and uses for a very volatile chemical compound called Thermite. Thermite is capable of burning at very high temperatures, high enough to melt most rock and it would ignite and maintain ignition even under water.

Thermite is not normally explosive, so it is relatively easy to handle. It burns in a short burst of very intense heat that can be focused on specific points. In fact, in some applications, thermite with additional components is used to cut steel. The normal mixture has multiple metastable intermolecular composites added to it which turns it into a super compound called Nano-Thermite. It's hot enough to cut case hardened steel. Jenny knew this compound well enough and she believed it would be more than adequate for their needs.

"Can you get this super thermite?" Dr. Owens was more than a little intrigued. He wasn't the only one, the others were anxious to learn a little more.

"Yeah, we're experimenting with it at my office. We've been looking at different ways to package the material for use to create a new niche in the weapons market. In fact, we've got several prototype canisters put together that could do the job. They are basically shaped charge canisters which deliver the thermite in a specific pattern to burn through four inch armor plating. I think we can use them to melt the ledge rock and fill the hole." Jenny was punching buttons on her cell phone as soon as she finished her sentence. She was calling her assistant to verify quantities and to have them make up six more prototype canisters as a back up and to scrounge up some timers that would work to set off the canisters. After she gave the assistant the list she called her boss to fill him in on what was happening.

Jenny told her boss she wanted the materials within the hour and that she would be at the Boat Dock office waiting for them to arrive. The only question from her boss was, "Who's paying for the material?" She quickly said the State or U.S. Government would probably pick up the tab and looked around at both Guy and Thayer to see if they were nodding their heads in the affirmative. They were.

"Okay, we've got a plan... Anyone have any questions?" Guy was smiling as he asked. He really didn't expect that anyone would have a question. "Like I said before, this is a straight line critical path plan. If this step doesn't work, then we can't move to the next."

"Can someone taxi me back to the Boat Dock office? I've got the chemicals and timers coming. I also need to get a fresh tank of air and a new tether line." Jenny headed to the back deck to collect her gear.

Within less than two minutes Jenny was ready and waiting. She was pleased at how fast her taxi arrived. Thayer had already moved his borrowed speed boat around to the back deck and was ready to make the open water run. As Jenny was getting into the boat,

Guy ran out and decided to ride with them so that he could continue talking about the plan while they waited ashore for gear.

As they made the short run back to the boat dock Guy was able to fill Thayer in on the rest of the plan. He needed Thayer to commit to causing a landslide at Pinehurst Point because without his okay, they wouldn't be able to move forward. When the boat entered the marina cove, Thayer began using his cell phone to make the calls to his State headquarters. Just as he expected, he was told to wait before doing anything until the senior engineers could review the idea and get back to him.

Guy decided to use the time that Thayer was on the phone to also make a call. He called the Governor. He knew that the Governor could help expedite the decision process at the Corps headquarters. He was sure the Governor would be glad to make a quick call to the District Engineer, who was a regular active duty Army Colonel in charge of the district. Guy believed that the Governor's call would probably go a long way in getting the support he and his team needed. No offense to Thayer, but sometimes cutting through the normal bureaucracy could make quick work of a normally slow process.

He was right. By the time Thayer was docking the boat, his cell phone was ringing. It was the Colonel himself.

Chapter 35

Jenny headed to the fuel dock to see about getting her air tank refilled. Jerry was at the compressor station changing filter canisters and getting his own tank refilled when she walked up.

"Hey Jenny, what did you guys find?" Jerry had been very busy this morning moving docks and mooring anchors anticipating more dock movements.

"Believe it or not, there's a hole in the bottom of the lake. We found an area of rock that seems to have collapsed into that aquifer running below the lake. The same one that emptied into the Cavern. If you ask me, this place is turning into a weird bastard child of Yellowstone and really horrible things could happen to this lake and town." Jenny wasn't wasting words or sentiment; she wanted him to know it was truly unusual and bad out there. "We're hoping to plug the hole with a little help from my office. In fact, I could use some underwater help out there too, if you're up for challenge."

"How can I help?" Jerry knew that if the water was draining uncontrollably that he might as well leave the docks for his crew to finish and spend more of his time working on the main problem. The docks wouldn't be worth anything if the water was gone.

"I'm going back to the hole. This time I'm setting some thermite charges." Jenny did a quick explanation of thermite for Jerry and then continued. "The geologists and engineer think that if we can make part of the big rock break off and fall down then it will plug the hole. I need someone experienced with handling equipment underwater to help me. I'll set the charges, but I need someone to help transport and handle some of the gear to make quick work out of this. If anyone stays at the depth where this hole is for more than eight minutes then they have to decompress coming back up and I don't really want to be hanging around over the thermite or the whirlpool any longer than I have to." Jenny was hopeful that Jerry would help. She really hadn't thought about all the details of making this plan work until she started talking to Jerry. With his help, Jenny knew that she could make this plan work and do it quickly.

"Let's go! I've got several tanks already filled and anything else you might need. By the way, for what it's worth, I've had quite a bit of experience with deep dives. Most of the time, when there's a search and rescue or recovery operation around here I've been the guy most folks call. Now that I know a little about your background I may have to call on you for a favor after this." Jerry was smiling. It seemed obvious from watching her over the last few days, that Jenny would help if she was called no matter who made the call. He really liked the idea of helping with this project. His family's long time investment in this lake made him one of the largest stakeholders in the outcome of whatever was about to happen.

"Great, let's get this gear checked out and I'll tell you what else we'll need." Jenny was all business as she went over her list of needs. She doubled her need for tether since Jerry was also diving and she added several mesh diving bags to the list at the last minute. The bags would make easy work of transporting canisters and timers. She also grabbed two large underwater lights. Her light had been barely bright enough to film the underwater waterfall and she would need something better to make sure she could see where to set the charges. She also explained in great detail what she had seen at the bottom of the lake. She wanted Jerry to know what it was like and where the obvious danger zones were. Jenny also told Jerry that they would review the video tape a couple of times once on board the houseboat so that he would have a clear visual understanding of the plan.

Guy and Thayer were sitting in the boat waiting for Jenny and the gear to arrive. While they waited, they discussed the plan for sealing the aquifer under Pinehurst Point. Thayer finally decided it wouldn't really be that tricky. Causing a slide anywhere along the front edge of the point at the lake's edge would be enough to seal the aquifer. What they had seen at Noe Creek confirmed that it would work. All they needed now was a way to make the slide happen.

Thayer could arrange for explosives but Guy wasn't sure if they could mark the point to set the charges as accurately as they needed to ensure the aquifer sealed and to keep the lake from draining more. At this point, they both agreed that they could sacrifice all the houses along Pinehurst Point if it meant saving the lake. The residents would have to be evacuated and if anything happened to their homes they would be compensated. Even if the whole area slid into the lake, it would be better than not sealing the unstable aquifer.

What they decided was that they could set the charges anywhere within about one hundred feet of the end of the point at the lake's edge. It should work regardless of whether they were a little short of the actual end of the point. What they couldn't do was end up too far out from the point underwater where any slide might not be large enough to bury the opened aquifer. It was settled. They would use the map overlay, which had been very accurate so far, to calculate how far in feet they would need to be from the opening at the Cavern to set the charges. They would calculate a point that they believed was eighty feet from the existing water's edge of the point and that would be ground zero for causing a landslide.

Thayer and Guy were satisfied that the next step of the plan made sense and was something they could do as quickly as they could locate the explosives needed to bring down part of a mountain side.

Guy saw the truck from ALS Technologies drive up to the main dock with all the supplies Jenny had asked for and saw Jenny walking over to meet the truck. He also saw Jerry was walking toward their waiting speed boat.

"Hey guys, I just found out what's happening out there and somehow I've gotten myself into helping. Give me a hand with this gear." Jerry had brought all the equipment down the dock in a two-wheeled hand cart. He started handing the gear down to Guy and Thayer.

"Jenny must have talked you into this. I'm glad. I hated the thought of her trying to do the job alone down there." Guy was genuinely glad to see Jerry was going to help. He knew Jerry was a qualified diver and that he even ran a dive shop and diving class from the dock store but he didn't know that Jerry would volunteer to handle dangerous chemicals and dive to the depths that they were dealing with.

Guy hopped out of the boat and borrowed Jerry's cart to take over to where Jenny was talking to the guy driving the ALS truck. His timing was perfect, she was ready to start unloading gear from the back of the truck. There were eight metal ammo boxes strapped in the bed of the pickup truck. They were clearly marked as explosives. The driver explained that each of the first six ammo boxes contained two thermite canisters so there was twelve for her to use. The remaining two boxes contained the underwater timers. He explained that the mix in each canister had been boosted with additional components to ensure the compounds were capable of sustaining an ignition underwater that would burn through four inches of plate steel. He assured them that they would have no trouble with limestone rock up to six feet thick. Jenny was pleased and reassured Guy that the ledge rock they were dealing with was only about two feet thick at the area that needed to be cut.

Jenny and Guy unloaded the ammo boxes from the cart and handed them to Thayer and Jerry one at a time. They placed the boxes under the consoles in front of the boat seat where Guy would sit for the ride back to the houseboat. Jenny jumped in the boat and hollered for Guy to get in so they could get going. She said she was "ready to kick that whirlpool's ass" and that was enough to make everyone start laughing, breaking the tension that had been building.

As soon as Thayer pulled the boat away from the dock they heard the now unmistakable sound of the steam exploding out of the strangely alien geyser in the middle of the otherwise sleepy little town. They all looked back toward town to see the plume that had become newest landmark for miles around.

Chapter 36

The ride back to the houseboat was quiet and calm. The water was smooth except for the occasional ripple from a slight breeze. The air was warm and the sky was flawlessly clear now. Everyone seemed to be caught up in their own thoughts while enjoying the breezes created as the boat hurried back out to the main channel.

Once they tied up next the houseboat it only took a couple of minutes to unload all the gear. Jenny and Jerry were on the back deck checking the equipment for the next dive. This would be a critical dive and they would probably only get one really good opportunity to make the plan work. If they failed to cut the rock correctly and the ledge missed its intended mark, they wouldn't have any good options to seal the hole.

Jenny sat the thermite canisters out in a line on the deck and started attaching timers to each canister. She set the digital clock on each timer for the same time and then set the start time for ignition at exactly four o'clock on each unit. She had enough time to finish getting the gear checked out and to get a late lunch before making the dive. Jenny explained the basics of how the canisters and timers would work to the rest of the group. Guy, Thayer and the others had slowly gathered on the top deck and had been watching her and Jerry for several minutes.

"We've got sandwich stuff and drinks up here for lunch when you two finish. We also need to talk about your underwater trip and our next step." Guy was holding a cold bottle of water in one hand and sandwich in the other as he spoke. He knew Jenny was nearly finished so he went back to his table and sat down to eat. He also had the planning map spread out on the table for all to study.

"The Corps of Engineers has a fairly good underground geo-positioning system that we use for tunneling projects. I've got someone bringing the unit over from the Memphis area. They should be here around six thirty this evening and will be ready to meet us at the cavern. They will also bring a small crew to drill and set TNT in the roof of the aquifer. These guys are pro's. All we need to do is show them where we want the charges set and how much earth we need them to move and they'll do the rest." Thayer had been on the phone almost continuously since getting back to the houseboat. He was pleased that things were starting to come together with support from his District boss. Whether he ever knew the Governor had anything to do with it or not would remain Guy's secret for now.

"All we really need to do is agree on a location to set the charges and how much of a landslide we want to create. Thayer and I believe that we need to set the charges at a point about eighty feet back from the edge of the point where it meets the lake. We think this will give us our best chance of getting a landslide that will solidly fill the aquifer at that location and stop the water from leaking back into the cavern. If it seals up like it should, then the rest of the aquifer will fill with water and equalize the pressures so that we don't keep having collapses." Guy was marking the map with a pencil showing the estimated location for the charges. He could see that everyone was agreeing and there was no discussion about the location.

"I hope our engineering friends can calculate the amount of explosives needed to get the landslide going." Dr. Owens had nothing further to add at this point and was looking back at Thayer for an answer.

"As a matter of fact, our tunneling experts that are providing the explosives and positioning equipment are busy calculating the loads as we speak. They promised me precise answers by the time our equipment arrives. Of course they will make some final calculations after they see the site. So far the site is an unknown. We don't know yet if we can even walk in like we're hoping." Thayer was ready to get his part of the plan in motion. He was clearly anxious to get his life and the lake back to normal.

"We still need to get the hole plugged before we start patting ourselves on the back." Jenny was just coming up to the top deck and ready for a little break and something to eat before she and Jerry headed out into the mouth of the whirlpool.

"No doubt. Glad you could join us. How about going over your plan with us so we'll know what you two will be doing down there." Guy handed out cold bottled waters and plates with stacked deli style sandwiches ready for the two divers.

As Jenny sat down with her water and sandwich she began to explain. "We will both be making one dive together. We need to get to the bottom quickly and stay on station no longer than eight minutes to avoid decompressing. Each of us will carry half of the thermite canisters. The canisters are already set to go off at four o'clock, so we're going to have to get in the water by three thirty. We will each be tethered like before except that once we reach bottom I'm removing the tethers and securing them to rocks to use to hold our gear while we place the thermite. You will have to keep the tethers tight after we get them tied off. Once we have everything in place we'll cut the tether lines and return to the surface." Jenny had thought this through with great detail. She knew that moving around the whirlpool would be treacherous and the rope tethers would probably get in the way as they tried to set the canisters in specific locations on the big ledge rock.

"So by the time you and Jerry are back on board the whirlpool should have stopped if the thermite and the ledge rock did their job."

Guy was looking at his watch and already beginning to wonder about the timing for the next step in the plan.

"The thermite is pretty quick. I'm guessing that it will take about four minutes for the rock to liquefy and flow allowing the big part of the ledge to tip over and into the hole. If the thermite continues to burn it will melt more rock, almost like lava, and it should flow around the cracks sealing the hole even tighter if we're lucky. Hopefully the aquifer will be dry enough to walk in when we get ready to set the underground charges later." Jenny's statement clearly made sure everyone knew that she included herself in the next phase of the plan. She was still the self-appointed risk manager.

"All it has to do is keep the aquifer from flooding for about four hours. We'll be going in as soon as we can get back to shore to mark the location for the charges and then, with any luck, the drilling crew will be there on time to do their work. All I need to do now is call the Sheriff to get the residents evacuated from Pinehurst Point and to seal off the roads leading to the point. They'll have until six o'clock to clear the area and then will have to keep it secured until we give the all clear." With that, Guy picked up his cell phone and called the Sheriff's office. He made short work of explaining the plan and getting the Sheriff's cooperation. After all, the Sheriff was as ready as anyone to get this problem solved. The Sheriff explained that there were a couple of long time residents at the end of the point that might not be willing to leave immediately, but he was ready to do his best to get them to a safe area.

Several other calls were made during the lunch break. Dr. Owens checked in with the hospital to see how his grad student was doing and then called his office for messages. Kristi was starting to get restless. She had resolved to stay with the group for the experience, even though she had almost nothing to do except the seemingly endless note taking to document the events as they were unfolding. She expected that the material would fit nicely into a dissertation at some point in the future and she was okay with that for now. Guy called the Governor's public relations team to fill them in on the current plan and some of the timing details. He wanted them to be sure to liaison with the Sheriff's office concerning the evacuation of Pinehurst Point. Thayer made a call to his enforcement officers to make sure they had an area around the expected landslide cordoned off by not later than six o'clock that evening.

Jenny finished her light lunch quickly and was on the back deck triple checking her gear and the thermite canisters. Jerry was standing at the railing of the top deck watching the bizarre whirlpool. He thought he had seen everything this lake had to offer, until now that is. There was always the joke during high water periods that someone needed to pull the cork to let some water out. He imagined this is what it might have looked like if that actually were possible. As he watched the water he mumbled to himself, "Somebody needs to put a cork in it and somehow I got myself lassoed into this."

"Having second thoughts about going down there?" Guy had gotten up and was just stepping to the rail to watch the whirlpool with Jerry when he overheard the faint mumbling.

"No, no second thoughts. Jenny needs help and I'm qualified. I just can't believe what's been happening to our lake. We've seen tornadoes, hail, snow, ice storms, floods, straight line winds. Now we have a hole the size of a Buick in the bottom of the lake that goes to hell and back. Not to mention a geyser in the middle our little town. This is crazy." This was the first time that Guy realized that Jerry was nearly exhausted. He figured that Jerry had been up too many hours and at odd times of the day and night since the first night everything started happening.

"You sure you're okay with this dive? It sounds like it will be a bit tricky." Guy was giving him an easy out. Jerry didn't take it.

"I'm good. The sooner this thing gets capped and we stop losing water, the better off we'll all be and the sooner I can start making money again. Tourists have been far and few between this summer with all the high water. I'm just ready for things to get back to something resembling normal." Jerry felt like he could do the job and was somewhat reassuring with his words.

"Hey! If you boys are done yapping up there I could use a little help. We need to get going if we're going to meet our current deadlines. Besides, I don't feel like resetting a bunch of timers. Let's get moving." Jenny was all business. Her focus was on getting the job done quickly and efficiently. She would stay on schedule and hit her target. That's the way she was trained and she wasn't about to start giving up her routine now.

Jerry, Guy and Kristi hustled down the back stairs. Guy was helping Jenny get into her buoyancy compensator vest and tank, Kristi was helping Jerry. Jenny already had the thermite canisters securely placed in two separate mesh bags. As soon as Jenny and Jerry were finished suiting up, Guy secured the tether lines to the boat and to each of the divers' vests. With everything in place Jenny and Jerry stepped off the back of the houseboat and disappeared into the dark clear water leaving only a trail of bubbles as they descended to the bottom.

Chapter 37

Guy hated not knowing what was happening and felt helpless as the two divers descended out of his sight. He trusted Jenny to get the job done, but that didn't calm him very much. He set the timer on his watch and recounted the events in his mind of the last two dives Jenny made. He realized that in both situations unexpected things happened. Jenny could have been hurt both times. Suddenly, his sandwich wasn't setting in his stomach very well. He watched the tether and focused on waiting for the telltale sign that Jenny and Jerry were on the bottom and tying off the ropes. It only took a few minutes before the tugs on the tether made it clear that they were being tied off. Kristi and Guy tightened the lines and held them as they had been instructed. They felt every move the divers made as they removed the mesh bags holding the thermite canisters and the work lights which had been secured to the tethers.

Jerry had set the lights up on the bottom near the ledge rock as Jenny had instructed and as he moved the light in position to shine on the ledge he was mesmerized by the underwater waterfall. He couldn't believe what he was seeing. It was like watching a waterfall from behind the water. Jerry felt a poke as Jenny got him focused back on task. They had very little time and lots to do before they would need to head back to the surface.

Jenny was placing canisters along the top surface of the ledge rock a couple of feet behind where the opening beneath it appeared to be letting the water drain. Cutting the rock too small wouldn't help, cutting it a little big would be okay. Every canister needed to be held in place and that was Jerry's job. He would find rocks and place them securely around each canister. Jenny checked her dive watch and realized they had been on the bottom six and half minutes. They had only one canister left to set and secure and she knew they had enough time before they would have to leave. Jenny grabbed the last canister and set it in place and waited for Jerry to start setting rocks. As she looked around to see where Jerry was she was horrified when she saw the eerie silhouette of his body literally disappear like a ghost into the waterfall. He had somehow moved close enough to the rushing water to get sucked into the vortex. She was shocked that he didn't have time to grab hold of the rock to fight the current or even find a chance to swim free. He was gone, just gone.

Jenny's training took over almost immediately. She turned, found three rocks and secured the last canister. She moved to the tethers and cut them and then spent the remaining minute looking around the ledge for any sign of Jerry before she left him for lost. As she began her ascent she felt herself choking back tears and sobbing into her regulator. Something she wouldn't have done just a few years ago. Losses were expected in combat, that's the way she had trained. But this wasn't combat.

Jenny checked her watch, it was nearly four. The thermite would start about the time she surfaced. All the way up she wondered to herself what she could have done differently.

Jerry knew the risk. She had been explicitly clear about the vortex and showed him the video. She made him watch it twice. They went over every detail of the dive step by step before they got in the water. They discussed what she believed was the safe zone around the vortex. She just couldn't see how this could happen.

Jenny surfaced about eighty feet from the houseboat. As she started swimming on the surface there was a sudden gush of bubbles and smoke on the water around the area of the whirlpool. Everyone seemed to be watching the smoke as Jenny reached the back deck. Guy started grabbing her equipment to bring it on deck. Jenny ripped off her dive mask and respirator and it was very obvious to Guy that she was crying.

"Jerry is gone… just sucked into the hole… gone." Jenny was sobbing.

Guy helped Jenny get on deck as the others were beginning to realize Jerry hadn't surfaced yet. Kristi was the first to say something.

270

"Where's Jerry?" Kristi had heard Jenny say that he disappeared down into the aquifer and couldn't believe it. She started shaking and sobbing. This was another life lost and she was losing her desire to cope. She was near hysteria.

Dr. Owens didn't say anything. He held Kristi and moved her into the cabin to find a chair for her to sit in and to try and console her. Thayer was in shock. His mouth was hanging open and he couldn't make the words come out. Jerry was a long time friend and his best advocate for keeping the lake as pristine as possible.

Guy continued to help Jenny get out of her dive gear. As he did, he realized that she was blaming herself for Jerry's disappearance. Guy knew he couldn't say anything now that would make her feel better and that she would have to work it out for herself. He just let her sob and held her without asking any questions. There would be time for that later.

Dr. Owens took a deep breath and started gathering the rest of Jenny's gear up and stowing it. As he did he quietly reminded everyone that there wasn't much time and that they needed to get moving to be in position for phase two. The team still needed to get to the cavern and make some basic preparations before the explosives team arrived. As he was putting up the last of the equipment his attention was drawn once again to the smoke and bubbles on the water. The whirlpool had stopped. The first step in their plan was working.

"Come on, let's go. The whirlpool has stopped. There's nothing we can do here. Jerry is gone. We only have a couple of hours to get the next part of this plan working or his sacrifice will have meant nothing." Dr. Owens' age was showing. He was calm, loss was something that was easier for him than the others and it was his turn to provide reassurance to others in the face of tragedy.

"Your right Ben, let's get this tub moving. We've still got a lot to do." Guy was back on his feet and Jenny was getting up wiping her face and eyes. They were ready to refocus and get on with the rest of the plan. There would be time for remorse later.

Jenny moved to the helm and started the big motor on the houseboat and got it underway for the short trip back to the marina. The smoke and bubbles had receded and the whirlpool was gone. There was no visible sign that there had ever been a whirlpool. It was hard for anyone to believe that it could happen again. Thayer, Guy and Dr. Owens stood on the back deck and watched the water as they moved away. They knew the fragile aquifer was real and that it could collapse again without warning. They had to get to Pinehurst Point and seal the aquifer if there was going to be any hope of saving the lake.

The group moved back inside where Kristi was sitting. Dr. Owens sat with Kristi while both Thayer and Guy started making calls on their cell phones. Thayer was confirming that the explosives were still scheduled to arrive and that the drilling team would be at the cavern as planned. Guy was calling the public relations team to brief them on their success with stopping the whirlpool and the sacrifice that Jerry made. Guy knew that the loss of Jerry would be a huge shock to the town and entire region.

Guy finished his calls and then sent a short text message to the Governor. He made sure to let him know about Jerry. The Governor had been close friends with Jerry's father, Old Man Don. Don had served on the Arkansas Game and Fish Commission at the same time as the Governor. Losing Jerry wasn't something the Governor needed to hear from anyone else.

Jenny was lost in thought as she piloted the houseboat away from where the whirlpool had been. As she looked up at the hills outlining the town of Bull Shoals she saw one more explosion of steam as the geyser erupted with what she hoped was its last breath. Surely they could stop this craziness. Jerry was still on her mind. She was having more trouble shaking this than she would have only as short couple of years before.

Chapter 38

Thayer Davis went directly from the marina to the Dam Operations Center to check in with his people. He wasted no time chatting with anyone waiting on the docks and ignored questions about what happened out on the lake.

Dr. Owens and Kristi headed up the hill to their Expedition to make a quick run to their cabins for caving gear, heavier clothes and better shoes to explore the aquifer. Kristi was holding her emotions in check with a little help and reassurance from Dr. Owens. She knew that what she was doing was extremely rare and that her experiences, field notes, videos and pictures would be chronicled in her thesis work or a book sometime later in her young life. It would never be worth the loss of life, but she could make her work a tribute to those who had perished or suffered because of the geological events.

Guy and Jenny stayed on the dock for a while after everyone else left. Guy was able to meet with the public relations team to detail what they knew about the whirlpool, the plan for the aquifer and the little they knew about Jerry's demise. He also asked to meet Jerry's brother as soon as possible to explain what happened out on the lake and to express his personal condolences and then the heartfelt sympathy of the Governor as well. Talking to Jerry's brother was extremely difficult. There was nothing he could say that would make the loss any easier to understand or deal with.

As soon as Guy was able to break away from people on the dock he headed up the hill to Jenny's waiting Jeep. Buck was happy to be on dry land again and he didn't waste any time finding a suitable place to take care of his business. Jenny had already loaded clothes and climbing gear into the Jeep and was waiting patiently as Guy walked up.

"You okay?" Jenny was somber as she reached out for Guy's hand.

"Yeah I guess. You?" Guy took Jenny's hand and then wrapped his arms around her for a moment before he whispered, "I'm so sorry I got you into this. Shit just keeps happening to good people. I'm ready for it to be over."

"I feel horrible for Jerry's family and all the rest who have been killed or hurt by this thing. I'm not sorry I'm here. I wish I could have done more to help. Just promise me we'll get this fixed before anyone else gets hurt." Jenny was looking into Guy's eyes. She saw a determination in his face that made her feel better somehow.

Guy released Jenny from his hug and climbed into the passenger seat of the Jeep and watched as Buck leapt up through the driver's seat and into the back seat where he usually rode. Jenny slid in and got the old Jeep going up the hill toward the cavern.

Thayer's tunneling team and explosives experts arrived earlier than he expected. They were already at the Operations Center when he pulled into the parking area. The group made quick work of introductions and decided to get right to the cavern to start preparing for the drilling and blasting. Thayer rode over to the cavern with this new team and explained as much as he could during the short ten minute ride over.

As they neared the cavern area they were checked by one of the town police officers before being cleared to move into the evacuation area. The group was eerily silent as they neared the cavern parking lot. They were staring at the surrounding scenery which was completely alien to any of them.

The trees and bushes for hundreds of feet in all directions looked like limp broccoli just pulled from a steamer. Everything was green but the limbs were sagging and drooping almost as if weighted down by tons of ice and the leaves looked more like dark green boiled spinach. They were hanging in clumps and seemed to be dripping and gooey as they bowed toward the ground. The 1890's Mountain Village entrance gate and fence was falling over toward the parking area away from the geyser blast area and there was debris strewn in all directions. Paint on the remaining parts of buildings that were still standing was peeling off in sheets or melted and running down the walls like colored wax from a spent holiday candle. The place smelled like sulfur and the ground seemed soft all around them. The pavement was soft and their truck left tracks as they rolled to a stop.

The team arrived to find Guy, Jenny, Dr. Owens and Kristi already waiting. They were huddled around the area which had once been the entry gate to the village and were talking with the Sheriff.

Thayer walked up with his team and made the usual introductions. They quickly went around once with names, Thayer asked Guy to brief the team on the plan and to show them the now infamous planning map. Thayer had managed to find topographic and hydrographic survey maps for the northwestern section of the town of Bull Shoals and the lake shore. It gave very clear measurements showing the volume of earth to be moved by the planned explosion. They made quick work of transcribing the planned slide area location to their topo map. All they needed was a quick depth sounding from the shore line at Pinehurst Point to the top of the aquifer below that location to finalize the calculations for how much explosive to haul into the aquifer.

After they were all satisfied with the maps as currently marked, the explosives team decided who would go to Pinehurst Point to get the ground penetrating radar depth readings and who would start the setup in the cavern. With that, everyone was ready to start final preparations to get in the aquifer and find the blast site.

Jenny was out front as they entered the destroyed part of the building that had been the visitor's entrance to the cavern. The group was carrying all their gear, including two extra long extension ladders and rope ladders which would make getting in and out of the cavern's lower pool area and in to the aquifer opening much easier than it had been the first time Jenny and Guy had explored the opening.

As they entered the opening to the cavern they were each struck by the heat and humidity that was coming up from the tunnels below. Everyone shared the same hope and fear about the geyser and the aquifer. Everyone knew the risk once they entered the cavern. There were no guarantees about making it out alive. The aquifer could collapse and bury them, or the water could return and drown them, or a geyser could form and boil them. The odds were definitely on the very risky side. Even so, each person entered cautiously optimistic.

Head lights and hand held flood lights were turned on as each person made his or her way into the now dark abysmal chamber that had been the main corridor leading down to the main level of the cavern. The group moved slowly and carefully along the slippery rocks and made relatively quick passage into the lower pool area. Once there, the team would stage most of their gear and take only what was needed to start drilling and blasting after the site selection and inspections were done.

Thayer would remain at the lower pool with Dr. Owens and three of the guys from the explosives team and wait until the landslide site was selected and to hear back about the measurements from the ground penetrating radar before getting the explosives ready to move into the aquifer. Kristi wanted to be part of the aquifer exploration team and would go with Guy, Jenny and the explosives engineer. She had decided to get as much firsthand knowledge of the aquifer as she could. Kristi could carry gear and still get dozens of photos and some video of an area never seen before.

Thayer had hand held radios for almost everyone. He left one at the cavern entrance with the Sheriff who would relay info from the radar team to the crew below ground. Guy and the explosives expert each had radios and would stay in touch with Thayer as they made their way through the unknown tunnels below.

Jenny and Guy led the group down the ladder and into the aquifer. Once in the aquifer, they agreed to stay close together and to proceed as quickly as possible depending on the terrain. They started moving quickly and quietly away from the area below the lower pool and into the strange dark tunnel that had once been filled with flowing cold water.

As they moved farther into the tunnel they were mesmerized at the structure of the aquifer. The tunnel was approximately twenty feet wide at the widest and about twelve feet from bottom to top. The floor of the aquifer and the sides up to almost the ceiling were silky smooth like they had been carved by a master sculptor from fine marble. The upper parts of the walls and ceiling were rough, gouged looking structures where giant flakes of rock had cast off in the rushing water leaving only a scarred concave dome like ceiling and pock marked upper walls. The aquifer was mostly level with occasional surprise dips and steps up to keep them constantly mindful of their footing. The aquifer was very serpentine and every corner appeared as a dark hole until their lights could shine around each new twist or turn. They were making surprisingly fast progress moving through the aquifer and would be at the general area of Pinehurst Point within thirty minutes if all continued well.

Thayer was pleased to hear about the progress in the aquifer. It sounded like they would not have any real problems moving explosives later. If everything went well he expected to hear the results of the ground penetrating radar about the same time the other team reached the area under Pinehurst Point.

The explosives team was starting their preparation. Each unit of explosives was set out and inspected. Each blasting cap was laid out, inspected, counted and placed back in their protective casings. Detonation cord was inspected. Extra spools of the cord had been brought into the cavern to ensure they would have enough feet of the material to reach from the explosive site at Pinehurst Point and then back to the cavern parking area where they would set off the charges. No one would remain in the cavern or aquifer when the explosives would be detonated. Everyone would remain well clear because of the unknowns in the density and stability of the remaining aquifer.

Thayer's radio chirped and the engineer with the ground penetrating radar was ready to give him and the other engineers the measurements they were waiting for. Then, as if cued, the radio chirped again. It was Guy, they were at the site and reporting that it was not a difficult trip and they could start bringing explosives as soon as the other team was ready. Thayer radioed back that they were finishing the soil volume calculations. Everything was starting to fall in place.

Thayer's radio chirped again. It was Guy. Thayer waited what seemed like minutes before the silence was finally broken. "You're not going to believe this," were the only words that came across and then silence...

Chapter 39

Guy and the others had reached the area in the aquifer that they believed was very close to ground zero as it was being called by the explosives experts. If the underground geolocating equipment was working correctly then they were only a meter or two from being exactly where Thayer and Guy had agreed to create the landslide. The trip through the aquifer hadn't been too difficult, except for the extreme heat and humidity. Guy called Thayer on his radio to report their progress.

"Thayer, this is Guy. We've made good progress. The aquifer is fairly easy to move through. Very few obstacles. We're in position to start marking the explosives location." Guy let off of the talk button and waited to see if Thayer would reply.

"Glad to hear it. We're still waiting for the ground measurements. Will let you know something as soon as it comes in. Be careful in there." Thayer was pleased to hear that their progress through the aquifer had been uneventful. It shouldn't be too hard to move explosives and detonating cord next.

Kristi had captured most of the trip on digital video. She was checking her equipment and reviewing her video as the others started marking the ceiling of the aquifer with spray paint to indicate where the explosives would be located. The explosives expert knew what grid pattern would be required for drilling and setting charges. All they would need before proceeding is a good calculation about how much explosive would be needed.

Guy was holding the small aluminum step ladder for the man making the drilling marks on the ceiling and watching as he laid out what appeared to him as a diamond grid resembling the individual corners of each opening in a chain link fence. Jenny was constantly looking around and shining her spot light up and down the aquifer. She was edgy. Guy could see it, "very edgy", he thought.

As the engineer was finishing his last set of marks, Guy's radio chirped indicating a call coming in. It was Thayer.

"Guy, we've got the measurements back from the ground penetrating radar and we're making the calculations for the explosives load. We'll have it done in about five minutes and then I'm sending the rest of the explosives guys to your location." Thayer's news was welcomed by Guy and the others in the tunnel.

Jenny was still scanning the area, watching and listening for any sign of danger. She was very worried about the aquifer. It had been unpredictable so far and killed several folks without warning. Jerry was its latest victim and Jenny wouldn't be happy until this killer was finally stopped.

"Guy, we need to get moving. Every minute we're here is a minute closer to the next disaster. This tunnel doesn't have feelings and it certainly doesn't give any fair warning when it's about to do something bad." Jenny's feelings about things were usually right.

"We're not going to be here long. The explosives team is probably on the way. We can start some of the drilling now if you can help." Guy knew that the work of setting up the explosives would be a good diversion for Jenny. She was emotionally trapped in the moment and Guy wanted her to snap out of it, so he handed her a battery powered drill with a two foot auger to start drilling.

There were two drills. The explosives expert and Jenny started drilling on the marks that had been painted in the ceiling. The noise of the drills was eerie as the bits penetrated the soft limestone. They sounded like high pitched squeals and squeaks as they cut into the rock. Each hole took only a couple of minutes and they made fairly quick progress on the grid.

The work was a good distraction for the group and before they knew it they could see lights coming up the aquifer. The rest of the explosives team was nearly at their location. As Jenny was taking a break from drilling to watch for the rest of the team to appear she looked around from her perch on the ladder and was suddenly shocked to see a faint light coming from the other direction in the aquifer. The light startled Jenny and she jumped from the ladder, dropping the drill in her hand.

She grabbed her spot light and hollered for Guy. "Guy, there's another light coming from the other way!" Jenny started running in the direction of the other light. There was only one reason for another light to be down there and she was sure she knew what it was.

Guy ran to join Jenny and ran down the tunnel with her. As they reached the next turn in the tunnel they could see the beam of light coming at them. They shined their lights into the darkness toward the other light. When they did, the other light went out and they could see the figure of a man. A man wearing a wet suit and still carrying the spot light he had been using while diving to find rocks to help Jenny set the thermite canisters. It was Jerry!

Guy stood motionless and grabbed his radio to call Thayer and tell him the news. Jenny ran toward Jerry.

"You're alive! I can't believe it, you're alive!" Jenny's honest joy at seeing Jerry alive was very apparent.

"I guess I got to close to that stupid whirlpool. It sucked me in like lint through a Hoover and I went head over heels into the darkness. I got dumped out into this waist deep underground river flowing this way." Jerry was pointing in the direction that he was walking. "Next thing I knew the water was disappearing and then there was a loud roar and a blast of steam headed toward me. I ducked down underwater and stayed there until I realized I was laying on rock with no water around me. So, I guess our little rock cutting experiment worked?" Jerry was smiling and obviously glad to see Jenny and Guy.

"It worked and we're getting close to blowing this place to hell. It's a good thing you showed up when you did or you would have been buried alive. Come on, let's get out here. We can celebrate later." Guy was very happy to see Jerry. He needed to relay a message to the Governor as soon as possible and to let the PR team know. This would be a headline story for sure.

"Come on, let's go. Everyone will be excited to see you." Jenny handed Jerry the water bottle she had hanging on her belt and pointed her spotlight back up the tunnel to where they needed to go.

Kristi was the first to see Guy, Jenny and Jerry coming into the blast area. She started sobbing again. This time, because she was happy to see Jerry still alive. Her emotional roller coaster ride wasn't over quite yet. In fact, she would need a lot of time to get over everything she had been through on this field trip.

The explosives expert had heard about Jerry and when he saw him walk into the work lights with Guy and Jenny he gave a quick cheer and shook Jerry's hand congratulating him on beating the odds. Kristi volunteered to walk Jerry out of the aquifer while the explosives were being set. Jerry was glad to have company on the last mile of the walk and was looking forward to see daylight and getting some fresh air. Kristi was ecstatic to see a life saved rather than lost and was anxious to hear more about how Jerry survived being sucked into the whirlpool. She wanted to capture all of the details and write them into her notes for later publication.

Jerry threw his tank and buoyancy compensator onto the hand cart the team had used to haul in their equipment. He thanked the group for taking his equipment and then he patted Kristi's shoulder and said, "Where's the elevator? Next stop, men's wear. This wet suit is killing me." Kristi just laughed and pointed and then started a quick step toward the exit. Jerry was filled with a new energy and hurried to her side.

Jenny was absolutely reenergized after having seen Jerry. It renewed her spirit. She had really taken the loss hard, much harder than she believed her previous training should have allowed. Life had really changed for Jenny since she had left the Navy. She was more emotional than she had been in years and in many ways she felt more in touch with nature and herself than she had in a long, long time. Her feelings for Guy weren't just a spur of the moment chemical reaction.

She had actually felt a connection with him and then let chemistry take its course. And now, Jerry was alive. He had beaten the odds. Jenny realized she wasn't responsible for his loss or his rescue. She realized that sometimes good things and bad things just happen no matter how much you plan and prepare. Somehow, this was a life affirming moment for Jenny and she found herself shivering and covered with goose bumps as she realized how she was feeling.

Guy was looking at Jenny as she was watching Jerry and Kristi walk away from the blast area and thought he saw a tear forming in her eye. He moved over next to her and could see the goose bumps and was suddenly surprised when she turned and hugged him. She buried her face in his wet shirt and sobbed for just a breath or two before turning her head and then looking up at him. Guy stared at her and could see softness in her face that he hadn't noticed before. Jenny had obviously been hardened by the loss of life in her past and something about seeing Jerry coming up through the dark aquifer alive had been emotionally rejuvenating for her. Guy believed he needed to explore his feelings for Jenny much more as soon as they got out of this deadly place.

Chapter 40

Kristi and Jerry passed the explosives team half way back to the cavern. The team was rolling out detonation cord and cautioned the two of them to be careful as they walked out and to not step on the cord. The three explosives experts gave Jerry hearty handshakes as they each passed. Everyone knew by now that the stories of Jerry's earlier disaster had been greatly exaggerated. In fact, Jerry commented during the hand shaking, "I'm not as dead as they must have reported." Everyone had a little chuckle at his comment and wished him well before they continued their separate ways.

It only took about twenty more minutes for the explosives team to lay out the rest of the cord while making their way to the blast site. With nearly a mile of detonation cord in place, the team went to work laying out the explosives to be placed in the holes that had already been drilled. Jenny and Guy moved away from the work area while the explosives were being laid out and assembled.

Jenny probably knew as much about the explosives that were being used for this job as anyone, but she was just as happy not having to do the work. She watched the team and could tell right away that they had worked on many jobs before. There was no hesitation as each member went about his particular part of the job. Explosives were measured, placed in the holes, primers were set and the detonation cord was attached with no lost energy and no repeated steps. Each attachment was watched and checked by someone not making the connections. They were clearly using the two-man rule method of doing this intricate work to make sure that one person didn't miss any step in the process.

The team made short work of getting the grid of explosives in place. They had just started double checking their work when everyone heard a low rumble and faint sounds that they couldn't quite make out. Jenny and Guy feared the worst. Guy immediately thought that it must be another collapse somewhere in the aquifer, probably under the lake at some distant spot.

"This is bad you guys, we've got to move now!" Jenny hollered to the explosives team as they were finishing their final connections and checks.

Guy started relaying information via radio to Thayer and the rest of the group in the cavern. "Thayer, we've got another collapse somewhere under the lake. All the charges are set and everything is connected and ready for detonation. We're evacuating now. We probably have very little time before we have another geyser. Get everyone out of the cavern. We're going to leave everything we don't need and start running back to your location. All of the evacuations have to be done and we need to be ready to detonate as soon as we clear the aquifer." Guy made sure that Thayer knew there was no time for delay now. He expected that they would get Pinehurst Point evacuated immediately and that the rest of the blast zone needed to be cleared.

Everyone at the detonation site appeared to be fit and able to make the run back out of the aquifer without any problem, assuming that the water didn't rise too rapidly. The floor of the aquifer was already getting wetter under their feet and the extra wetness seemed to increase everyone's stride and speed. Jenny was leading and setting a good pace that everyone could follow. They were covering the distance quickly and should be able to get clear of the aquifer within ten minutes if everyone stayed on pace.

Two minutes into the evacuation and the water had risen to the point that it splashed above the soles of their shoes and it didn't look like it was going to let up. The group stayed focused and continued to run trying not to think about the incoming water. They knew that if the water kept coming it would eventually flood the aquifer enough that a super heated geyser would erupt and most likely kill them all. That was the kind of incentive to make a person run faster and farther than they normally thought they could. This group was moving as quickly as Jenny could lead.

Five more minutes passed and the group was starting to come out of the aquifer, up the rope ladder and into the lower pool of the cavern. The water had already begun filling the aquifer and wouldn't take long before it spilled violently into the opening going to the magma vent. It had been less than a mile of dark and twisted trail but everyone managed to run the entire distance without problems and made it out safely.

When Guy reached the lower pool he immediately climbed the ladder up to the cavern floor and called Thayer on the radio. He was out of breath when he started talking. "Thayer, this is Guy. We're coming out. I'm giving the order to blow this place in three minutes. Do we have an all clear signal from the Sheriff?"

"Guy, we're ready when you are. The Sheriff cleared the point and the safety zone is set up around the point out on the water." Thayer was anxious to see this end and wouldn't allow himself to be part of any delay.

Guy watched as the rest of the group cleared out of the lower pool. With everyone safely back in the cavern he gave the order to start a countdown. They would detonate the explosives in exactly three minutes. While the team was finalizing continuity checks and connections to the detonator Guy got back on the radio with Thayer.

"Thayer, look at your watch and count down three minutes from right now." Guy watched the explosives team and the leader looked up and gave him a nod indicating that they wouldn't have any trouble with the deadline. "I just got the green light on the explosives, we're ready down here."

Thayer started the countdown.

Jenny was watching the water while it was filling the aquifer and could tell that it was beginning to crest at the opening leading to the magma vent. She was mesmerized by the hissing and steam. It wouldn't be long before the water reached a large enough volume so that it wouldn't just hiss and disappear safely as a little steam. It would flood the void and begin to boil and boil under the mounting pressure of more and more water building above the magma. Superheating the water and making high pressure steam that would hold below the opening until the whole column and chamber would flash boil and explode into the destructive geyser they had seen so many times already.

One minute left in the countdown and the water was now running into the magma vent without difficulty. The hissing of the water was now muffled below the cascading water. It would continue flooding into the chasm until it reached a critical point where the pressure from above would be greatly and surprisingly overtaken from below.

Guy was listening to Thayer's countdown on the radio and his thoughts drifted as he recalled something he had read about years before. He remembered reading that Lake Nyos, in Cameroon Africa, literally exploded in August of 1986 and released a dense cloud of carbon dioxide which killed over a thousand people and even more cattle. The lake sits above an active volcano which was venting into the lake, superheating the water falling into the vent and saturating the water with deadly amounts of poisonous gasses. When the pressure was great enough that the lake couldn't hold it back any longer, the water and gas exploded violently. The gas enveloped the surrounding villages and the inhabitants all died of suffocation from the invisible poison that quickly engulfed them. In many ways, Bull Shoals was very fortunate that the magma vent opened below the cavern. If the vent had opened below the weakened aquifer somewhere out in the middle of the lake, the residents may not have known anything was wrong until it was too late. Guy's attention clicked back to reality as he heard the final part of the countdown.

"...Five, Four, Three, Two, One!" As Thayer shouted the last number everyone within range of the radio or his voice quietly tensed anticipating the explosion.

The leader of the explosives team pushed the button on the battery pack to set off the explosion and quietly waited as he and his team watched and listened while standing at the edge of the lower pool where they could see the area leading to the opening of the aquifer. Everyone expected an immediate huge explosion. People waiting with Thayer out in the parking area were holding their hands over their ears and watching some undefined point in the distance that was generally in the direction of Pinehurst Point. Even the boat operators out on the lake keeping the area around the point clear were holding their ears.

Surprisingly, to everyone except the explosives team, the explosion was little more than a muffled thud in the cavern and was barely discernable above ground. The long aquifer acted like a silencer on a pistol and the surrounding rock where the explosives had been planted absorbed the largest part of the noise and shock wave. The explosives team gave each other small high-fives without being too obvious. They knew from the sound of the explosion that it was probably doing its job. Too much noise would have meant that a huge amount of energy from the explosion had been lost and that there would be a chance the explosives wouldn't do the job they intended. This muffled sound was a very good sign.

It seemed like an eternity before radios started chirping again. Thayer's radio was getting the first messages back from the Sheriff as he relayed what his team was watching from around the Pinehurst Point area. The Sheriff, who was usually very stoic even in the face of disaster, was unexpectedly excited by what he saw and heard.

"Thayer, me and my Deputies are watching a HUGE landslide! It started with just a few rocks and a lot of water bubbling and then the whole point started moving. It's still flowing! Trees and rocks are falling into the water. My people in the boats out there are riding out three and four foot waves." The Sheriff's radio cutoff for just a few seconds and then he was back. "The slide is bigger than we were hoping. We're losing part of the old Driftwood Resort at the end of the Point. There it goes." The Sheriff paused again. "It looks like the slide has stopped. The back half of the buildings at the resort are crumbling and falling, but it looks like the rest of the area is okay."

"Guy, I guess you heard that. Looks like we had one helluva landslide." Thayer was anxious to hear how things looked down below.

"We heard, that's great! We've got a bunch of rock dust, smoke and steam down here. It may take a while before we can confirm how good this worked." Guy was staring down into the lower pool where the rest of the team was watching. The work lights were shining into the large pool, however, the view of the pool's floor was obscured by the steam and rock dust.

As the dust began to settle, the group could see that the floor of the lower pool was almost dry. The water flow had apparently stopped. The last wisps of steam were wafting up from the area near the opening of the magma vent and the noticeable hissing of water falling into the vent had stopped. The group could now see that it must have worked, the landslide seems to have stopped the water flow. Guy wondered if it was enough to hold back the enormous pressures that would build behind the slide area. As he stared at the pool he whispered to himself, "God, please let this be enough."

Chapter 41

Jerry was getting no end of teasing back at the marina. He had been driven back by Dr. Owens and Kristi and was given a hero's welcome by his entire crew. Jerry was still wondering who called to tip them off that he was on the way back.

The marina crew had lined up on both sides of the main walkway leading across the water to the floating store and office. They were each holding a can of Coke, purposely and vigorously shaken. As Jerry walked through the crew the cans were opened two at a time and allowed to spew toward their new hero. It was like a twenty-one gun salute, only wetter and stickier. Everyone was having a great laugh and Jerry was feeling very glad to be back. He walked around to the back of the store and found the water hose and washed himself off before finally peeling off the rest of his wet suit. He was wet, tired and hungry.

Dr. Owens and Kristi watched the ceremony from the safety of their Expedition before turning and heading up the hill and back to their rooms at the resort. They had decided to collect their personal gear and depart before the day ended. The University equipment trailer, seismic monitoring devices and computers would remain where they were until Dr. Owens could send a couple of people back to collect them. They were both anxious to get back. Dr. Owens needed to get back to his office and Kristi was ready to see her apartment and boyfriend. This field trip had been emotionally exhausting for her and she wanted and needed to decompress.

Thayer Davis was at the Dam Operations Center within an hour of the latest landslide. He was checking in with the rest of the engineers and contacting his district office before the day ended to let them know about their apparent success. The Corps of Engineers explosives crew had packed up all their gear and headed back to Tennessee where they had been working prior to this emergency. No ceremony, no publicity, they were packed up and gone before almost anyone knew.

Jenny's Jeep was parked in the shade at the far end of Mountain Village parking lot. There was a slight breeze from the north and it felt very cool to Guy and Jenny after having been in the aquifer for the last several hours. Jenny was drinking water while Guy talked on his cell phone to the Governor. Guy's conversation was upbeat as he described their success. When he finished telling the Governor about the explosion and new landscape at Pinehurst Point he went on to remind the Governor that he still intended to get in a short vacation while he was away from Little Rock. It appeared to Jenny that the Governor must have given his okay for Guy to take his much deserved vacation. There was a faint smile on Guy's face as he said his goodbye and was disconnecting from his call.

Jenny waited a second for Guy to put his phone in its holster before she smiled and said, "So, still trying to get that vacation done. Haven't you had enough fun yet?"

"I guess I could just go back to Little Rock." Guy paused just long enough to watch Jenny's reaction. "Although, I was thinking about spending a few days out on that houseboat that Jerry said I could use."

"Really? That's a big boat for a city slicker. Do you think you can handle it all by yourself?" Jenny was sitting in the driver's seat and had her left foot propped up on the side of the steering wheel where she was flicking mud from the bottom of her boot. She had dirt, mud and perspiration all over her and knew her image was less than glamorous to say the least. She was playing, and it was working.

"I bet I could drive that boat as good as anyone. Besides, look at yourself. Who would want that kind of mess hanging around?" Guy had propped his right foot up against the grab rail on the dash of the Jeep and was flicking mud from his boots and was using his dirty finger to scratch his nose. They were both filthy.

"Who you callin' a mess?" Jenny flicked a chunk of mud toward Guy and then started the Jeep. She winked at Guy, put the Jeep in first gear and popped the clutch to throw gravel as she spun the tires weaving the Jeep out of the parking lot and nearly tagging a black pickup truck in the process. Guy smiled and politely saluted to the pickup truck and noticed the logo on their door as he and Jenny sped away.

The Sheriff had just returned from Pinehurst Point to check in with his Deputies. He was shaking his head as he watched Jenny take off and then waved and hollered, "Thanks! Call me later; I need some statements from you two for my reports."

The Sheriff walked around the area talking to his Deputies and shaking hands with residents who were thanking him and his teams for taking care of the problem. The local residents were gathering around to listen as the Sheriff described what was done at Pinehurst Point and what it accomplished. Everyone was amazed that such a bizarre event could have occurred in their little town.

As the Sheriff continued his explanation, the black pickup truck pulled into a debris covered parking space and two men got out. The truck was plain except for a logo painted on the doors. The logo simply said, "GEOTHERM".

The two men walked over and introduced themselves to the Sheriff and explained that they had heard about the magma vent on the

National news and that they wanted to talk to the owner of the cavern property. The Sheriff explained that the owner had died in the first geyser explosion. The men went on to explain that they were interested in using the area to create a geo-thermal energy plant which could benefit the area and the local economy. The Sheriff told them who to contact to find out about the heirs to the property and then introduced them to the Mayor who had just driven up.

The Mayor was speechless as he listened to the new visitors. These guys were offering to put in a geo-thermal plant to generate electricity and capture Hydrogen for fuel cell technology. They also believed they would be creating about two hundred jobs and could pipe hot water throughout town so that every residence would have the option to upgrade their home heating systems to a very inexpensive closed loop heat pump and virtually free hot water forever. As a final carrot, the two also said their company would build a geo-thermal spa for the city to have as its own to operate which would include a heated pool, steam rooms and saunas.

Jenny and Guy didn't waste any time getting back to the marina. They were anxious to get cleaned up and out on the water away from everything. The big motor on the houseboat started up and one of the guys working at the dock untied the mooring lines. Guy was at the helm backing out of the slip while Jenny stood at his side pretending to give him directions about handling the big boat.

For the moment, Guy pondered GEOTHERM. As Director of the ADEQ it certainly sounded much healthier for his environment than pumping chemically altered water into rocks to fracture them and force out natural gas in a highly pressurized manner. For now, releasing pressure seemed much better than creating pressure. He would keep a close eye on the processes at GEOTHERM anyway, just in case…

Guy had slipped his arm around Jenny's waist as he slowly piloted the boat out of the marina. They were both focused on watching the water ahead of them and looking out for other boats as they passed the outlying docks and then cleared the final marker buoys of the marina area. Guy pressed the throttle down and pointed the houseboat on a course that would take the couple up the main lake to what would be a quiet and secluded cove somewhere several miles from where they were. They passed Pinehurst Point on their right and were amazed at the sight of fresh dirt, jagged rock and fallen trees that had plunged into the water. They could each imagine what it looked like below the water in an area where only a few people had ever seen. Jenny shuttered a bit as she looked at the landslide and then tightened her embrace against Guy.

Afterword

All of the businesses and locations in this novel are real. All of the characters, except any historical references or specifically Jim Gaston and Forrest Wood, are fictitious and any similarity to any person living or dead is purely coincidental, though some may be inspired by real people or events. There is absolutely no malice or intention to defame or impugn or otherwise hurt someone's reputation or character and any interpretations as such should be quickly dismissed. If the interpretation happens to improve the character of someone real or makes them better than real life and that's the way they want to feel, then they should enjoy the moment and have fun.

Each of the businesses mentioned by this author are wonderful places to visit and are, in their own way, the best of the best and great representatives of the Bull Shoals Lake area. Destination Yachts are produced by Destination Yachts, Incorporated and are singularly superb for spending time on the lake. Ranger Boats are absolutely great and this author owns one. The Bull Shoals Lake Boat Dock is owned and operated by the Eastwold family and is a great place to "rent fun" as they say. The 1890's Mountain Village and Cavern is a wonderful place to visit and very, very safe. Generations of families have enjoyed the unique and majestic underground Cavern. Lake water in Howard's Creek near the town of Lakeview is, at last report, very safe for swimmers as is all the water in Bull Shoals Lake.

No actual caves, caverns, lakes, people, animals, fish, plants or bugs were harmed in the writing of this book. A few trees may have perished in the printing, sorry.

Made in the USA
Middletown, DE
02 November 2014